R.L. RINNE

# St. Patrick's Scroll of Miracles

## Miracles
(2<sup>nd</sup> book in the Scroll's Journey Series)

## R.L. Rinne

# DEDICATION

Dedicated to CathyJo

# Preface

I was asked, "Why do many Christians today stop believing, or stop going to church?" I think it is because of a lack of Truth displayed throughout the world today. Many Christians live with the fire of Christ inside but are mentally constrained by the concepts of a mortal Jesus – instead of his spiritual reality.

People have not only become content with this material word, but some spend their time producing avatars, games, and even digital worlds with the purpose of living vicariously in them. People try desperately to amuse themselves with drama, fear, excitement. Material concepts are replacing spirituality in our daily lives at an exponential rate. Modern medicine continues to expand, adding new hospitals, clinics, and pharmaceutical companies (along with many new illnesses). Drugs are advertised as solutions to all our ills (while manufacturers provide an expansive list of detrimental effects of the drugs on our health). A dedicated effort to understand God is easily set aside for an ever-growing pursuit of information about material bodies, medicine, climate, geography, history, etc., even though studies of physics show through examinations of the smallest particles of matter, that material structures are not solid – as they appear to our mortal senses.

We are constantly fed false information about Life,

because of mankind's limited perception of what life is. Look beyond this world. Social media, news, healthcare and entertainment all work to create excitement and information about our material conditions – but what did Jesus, his disciples, and other dedicated followers of God do? Always, they did the opposite. Looking away from material images toward Divine reality for guidance, understanding, and for providing both mental and physical healing of all discordant situations. Material issues and challenges were suddenly changed, because of their understanding of Spirit, God.

Born Maewyn Succat, our protagonist was the son of a local decurion while his mother was a cousin of Saint Martin of Tours. He was well educated and poised to follow his father into politics when he was kidnapped and enslaved on Hibernia (Ireland) at the age of sixteen. Stranded in horrible conditions, very few slaves, if any (other than Maewyn) ever returned home. His experience was different because of prayer. The terrible conditions of slavery forced him to turn to God, praying day and night to draw closer to a strong spiritual understanding. During years of starvation, freezing temperatures, and threats from wild animals, he persevered in keeping a herd of sheep safe for his owner, Milcho. Then through Divine guidance, he escaped the island, eventually reunited with his family, became Bishop Patrick, and returned to Hibernia to bless and provide prayers that healed the sick and raised the dead among the people that had enslaved him.

There are many aspects and stories about Saint Patrick's life that are either lost in the sands of time or are complete fabrications. This is a fanciful adventure story that draws loosely from Patrick's own Confession document, along with experiences recorded by Jocelyn of Furness (a Cistercian hagiographer). It contains a small number of the multitude of healing and resurrection works attributed to Patrick, as well as the author's conjectures on his thoughts as related to those healings. Regardless of the precise historical record, Saint Patrick's life is a wonderful example of spiritual growth, forgiveness and primal Christian healing for the world to emulate.

## Prologue

**Date: July 16th, 402 A.D.**
**Place: Hibernian Sea**

Maewyn strained against the rough hemp ropes that bound his arms behind his back. He felt the bow lift and knew another wave of frigid water would soon wash through the bowels of the boat, as it pitched and rolled in rough seas. The boy struggled to roll onto his knees so he could lift his head above the impending flow of putrid liquid. Suddenly a foot stomped down on his neck and pressed his face into slimy deck boards. A wall of seawater flooded over him, filling his mouth and nose as he choked and retched. Above the sound of gurgling water, he heard his captors yelling and laughing in their barbaric language and wished he could understand them.

— • ● • —

"Don't drown him, Kip! He's worth nothing dead," an old man's voice yelled against the wind.

"He ain't worth much alive," a younger man chided, and laughed as he stepped away.

--------•●•--------

*God, please, help us.* Maewyn thought as he raised his head and sucked in a deep breath between coughs. *This is a nightmare,* as he remembered how the swarm of vicious raiders had appeared in the night almost a week ago. They had killed the older men and women in town, then looted and set fire to the buildings as they rounded up any children old enough to be valuable. Thank goodness his mother and father were gone from the village at a political meeting in another town. He and his sister Darerca had tried to outrun the hoard of barbarians, but they had been captured when his sister stumbled on a rock and fell, dragging him to the ground with her. All of the survivors of the raid had been tied together with loops of rough ropes around their necks into a long line and forced to walk for several days. At every misstep or hesitation, the prisoners were whipped with a stout willow limb by one of the savages. It felt like the branch was slicing through his thin shirt, deep into his skin each time. His body was covered in welts and insect bites. The smell of unwashed bodies was unbearable. Once they reached the coast, they were forced aboard one of a group of filthy scows that didn't look seaworthy.

*They are going to sell us as slaves.* He shivered in his soaked clothes, noticing that the sun had begun its slow rise out of the sea behind them. He could see his sister cowering close to the stern as the younger ruffian began to torment her with overt hugs and kisses. "Leave her be," he managed to shout.

The boy looked at him with a twisted grin and grabbed the girl by the hair, pulling her toward him. Just before the craft fell into a trough between the waves, the older man handling the rudder shouted at the ruffian as he strained against the tiller in the heavy seas. With a look of disgust, the boy released Darerca and sneered as he marched pass

Maewyn toward the bow.

"Thank you, God," Maewyn stammered quietly. He saw his sister staring at him in desperation and managed to give her a reassuring smile.

Maewyn rolled onto his knees before the next swell of bilgewater hit him. It washed him into some bundles of animal skins, and he was finally able to lean hard against them and stand up. Looking forward he was able to see what looked like a thin dark strip lying beneath a dense mist.

Another sailor shouted as he pointed at the horizon, and a cheer came up from the savages.

*Why had this happened? Why had God forsaken them? Was it because he had ignored the Lord for most of his young life? Maybe if he prayed harder, he and Darerca could jump overboard and walk on the sea like Jesus did.* **"And in the fourth watch of the night Jesus went unto them, walking on the sea. And when the disciples saw him walking on the sea, they were troubled, saying, 'It is a spirit;' and they cried out for fear. But straightway Jesus spake unto them, saying, 'Be of good cheer; it is I; be not afraid.'"** (1) *Ridiculous.* He shook his head to clear his thoughts. "Please God, help us survive this trial," was his short request as Maewyn found the strength to stagger back and kneel beside his sister. "Don't worry, we'll get through this," he whispered in her ear, not really believing his own words.

**Date: November 18ᵗʰ, 408 A.D.**
**Place: Hiberian Sea**

## Chapter 1
Reunion

The oars squeaked monotonously as Sypher rowed in the slight swells. He kept the bow headed north. Fatigue had drained his strength, but he continued moving mechanically with a dogged sense of responsibility. A sliver of the coast was visible off to his left, as he searched continuously for a safe place to disembark for the night. Stony bluffs, cut and sharpened by eons of wave action had rimmed the seashore ever since they left the fishing village where Magnus almost died at the hands of the cruel bishop. Sypher saw no hospitable landing areas the rest of the day, so he rowed on.

Cynde had reluctantly collapsed into the bottom of the boat after tending to Magnus's shoulder wound. The blood had finally dried on his bandages, and he was sound asleep beside her. Lost in her dreams, Sypher was too gallant to intrude. After a few hours she finally began to stir. "Where are we?" she asked as she rubbed her reddened eyes.

"North of where we were, but that's all I know," Sypher replied weakly, as he strained against the ocean.

———•●•———

"Here, let me take over," she said, realizing that he had reached his physical limits.

Sypher didn't argue but slid painfully forward and sat down upon the rough decking as Cynde stepped carefully around him.

"Why didn't you wake me? I'm sorry I passed out," she added, grabbing both oars.

"I wouldn't impose," he mumbled as he gingerly rolled back and forth and stretched various muscles with low moans. He was too tired to sleep and leaned on the weathered gunwale staring toward the shoreline in the fading twilight as Cynde rowed on. "There," he suddenly shouted stabbing a finger toward a long, low sliver of foam, framed by billows of froth on either side. "That must be a beach." Cynde immediately pulled hard on the outside oar and turned the small craft toward land.

A few fishermen's huts stood across the rocky expanse where she beached the skiff, and Sypher hurried to help Magnus out of the boat, so Cynde and he could pull it onto the shore. The young man groggily stumbled onto the rocky beach and promptly sat down in a heap. "He is still in too much pain and exhaustion to help us." Cynde cried as she held onto the bow, and Sypher tried to drag it forward. Then she noticed a small group of men advancing towards them. "Whatever is going to happen, is going to happen," she muttered under her breath, but the men seemed friendly enough, as they quickly grabbed the vessel's gunwales, and walked the craft up beyond the tideline.

"What you be doing in the sea this late?" one of the men asked awkwardly.

"We are travelling to see a friend of ours, Calpurnius of Kilpatrick." Sypher announced.

"You be a long way from Kilpatrick." One of the other

men replied, "Five days rowing, two days walking," as he looked at their boat.

"I suppose we should walk then. Can you trade us some provisions and blankets in exchange for our boat?" Cynde asked.

The group of men hastily agreed among themselves, and several of them walked off quickly to gather items.

She grabbed Magnus's good arm and helped him stumble across the rocky beach to the nearest hut, as the other men beckoned them forward. When they reached the shack, the boy pulled away from her and sat down heavily against one of the supporting timbers.

"Here, he need a drink," one man said as he thrust a flask toward Magnus.

Magnus grinned weakly and drank it gratefully. "Thank you, sir, I did need that," he wheezed.

Another man showed up with a loaf of rough grain bread and a jug, offering both shyly to Cynde. She quickly shared them with Magnus and Sypher, and soon they all felt a bit better.

In a little while she and both boys were bedded down for the night, next to a bundle of food and a water jug for their trip. Sypher went to sleep in a few minutes while Cynde fidgeted, tossed, and turned. "I don't know if I can sleep tonight," she whispered to Magnus as Sypher began to snore loudly.

"How did you think of offering the torc to the bishop?" Magnus asked as a wide yawn escaped.

"I really don't know. It was like a little voice told me to. I just obeyed," she confessed as she stifled her own yawn.

"I thank God that you did," Magnus said as he gave her a one-armed hug, and she snuggled closer. In a few more minutes they both fell sound asleep.

In the morning, the group bid farewell to the fishermen, and carefully scaled a narrow path to the cliff top. *Great, more walking,* Cynde thought with reluctance. *At least no one is shooting arrows at us.*

They set off across the grassy countryside. Still weak from their exhausting dash to freedom, they travelled mostly in silence,. Waning twilight revealed a silhouetted village of Kilpatrick on the second day, and they continued striding onward through the gathering darkness until they reached Calpurnius's home. Magnus repeatedly knocked on the door until a sleepy voice answered from inside. Calpurnius finally opened the door and immediately embraced them all, as a feeling of relief flooded over Cynde and into her eyes.

"You are part of our family now. I pray you will stay with us," Conchessa offered.

Cynde continued to cry softly as Magnus gently wrapped his good arm around her.

"Do you need anything to eat or drink?" Conchessa asked. When no one answered, she immediately led the exhausted group to bedrooms where they collapsed for the night.

# Chapter 2

**November 21, 408**
**A New Life**

Harsh morning sunlight assaulted Magnus, until he decided that he couldn't sleep any longer. He rolled out of the bed with a loud groan and noticed that he was still wearing filthy clothes. *Must have been too tired to undress,* as he yawned, strapped on his sandals and padded toward the kitchen. "Morning, madam."

Conchessa, turned toward him with tired eyes and seemed to force a smile. "Sit down, I have a lot of food prepared, but you are the first one up."

*Something was wrong.* "What's the matter?" he asked.

Turning away, she wrung her hands. "I'm sorry, I should be satisfied that you three returned here safely, but all night I couldn't sleep, thinking of Patrick and his sister Darerca. I don't even know if they are still alive." Her shoulders shuddered as a quiet wail escaped.

"I trust God that they are," Magnus said awkwardly.

"I know, I prayed all night for them, but it has been so long now, almost six years."

"How old is Maewyn now? I remember meeting him years ago with Bishop Martin. He told me that he had a vison of Maewyn becoming a saint."

"Really? A saint?" Conchessa dabbed at her eyes and

managed a smile. "Martin was a great man of God. Maybe my boy is still alive then if he is to be a saint."

"Bishop Martin was great, a man of God, and definitely not a liar," Magnus encouraged.

"My boy Maewyn was sixteen when he was abducted, so that would make him twenty-two now. I don't know where the years have gone."

"You didn't wake me," Cynde accused loudly as she and Sypher strode into the room.

"I didn't want to ruin your first peaceful dream since I walked into your life," he grinned.

"Oh, I've had a few other good nights since then, but you are right, I slept wonderfully. No nightmares last night. What are you two discussing?"

Conchessa's eyes clouded and darted back to her cooking, as Magnus jumped in. "We were talking about how Bishop Martin told me that Maewyn would become a saint."

"What is a saint?" Cynde asked as she wandered over to the table and grabbed a biscuit and an apple.

"A virtuous person," Conchessa said as she motioned for them to sit down. "Someone we can pray to, so they can provide intercession with our problems. My Maewyn will make a wonderful saint. Did I ever tell you a miracle happened at his baptism?" Magnus watched the woman continue with a lighter heart. "A man named Gormus had a dream that my baby could cure his blindness. He insisted on holding my son's hand as he drew a cross on the ground. Water bubbled up through the ground, and when the man washed his eyes with it, he was healed."

"Goodness. How is that even possible?" Sypher asked, momentarily forgetting the apple he was about to bite.

"What can't God do?" spouted Magnus as he remembered what Jesus did in Bethsaida, **"And he took the blind man by the hand, and led him out of the town; and when he had spit on his eyes, and put his hands upon him, he asked him if he saw ought. And he looked up, and said,**

**I see men as trees, walking. After that he put *his* hands again upon his eyes, and made him look up: and he was restored, and saw every man clearly."** (2) "I'm sure that man prayed to God for a solution, and your innocent son was part of it."

"I was shocked." Conchessa replied. "I could not believe my eyes when it happened, but the man saw clearly after that."

"So, was your son always a perfect child?" Cynde asked.

"Oh my, no." Conchessa laughed. "He was all boy and about the furthest thing from an angel there could be."

"Maybe his adventure in Hibernia are strengthening him in the Lord." Magnus said thinking, *my life's trials sure have.*

Cynde wrapped her arm around Conchessa, "Magnus is right, he was almost beheaded," she said pointing at Magnus, "but God saved him."

"With your help," Magnus winked, "God is my protection as it is written; **'The God of my rock; in him will I trust: *he is* my shield, and the horn of my salvation, my high tower, and my refuge, my saviour; thou savest me from violence.'** (3) I'm sure Maewyn and his sister are being shielded from danger, just as I was."

"Thank you for those kind words. Now, everyone come sit down and let's eat." Conchessa said as Calpurnius entered, and she began carrying the food to the table.

The three struggled through a detailed recounting of the events during their escape over breakfast. Calpurnius was devastated by the news of their betrayal by his "friend" Pontius and swore that he would avenge their honor with a menacing growl, as Conchessa gripped his arm. He also announced that he had assembled a local militia group, in case the bishop and his mercenaries ever dared to return to Kilpatrick.

They were all engrossed in Magnus's explanation of his

pain after being shot by an arrow when a knock at the door interrupted him.

"Who could that be?" Calpurnius arose with an irritated look and shaking his finger, "Don't say anymore, my boy, I want to hear the whole story," as he walked to the door.

Magnus heard the man open the door and say loudly, "We don't feed beggars here, go down to the church in the village." The shabby young man began to murmur quietly. After a long moment of hesitation, Calpurnius screamed, "It cannot be you!"

"My goodness, what is happening out there?" Conchessa said as she jumped up out of her chair and hurried toward the door. Opening her arms, she suddenly ran forward crying "Maewyn!" and wrapped them around the grubby figure in the doorway.

Calpurnius gently pushed them both inside and closed the door. "Looks like we have another tale of adventure to listen to," he announced proudly. "This is my son Maewyn, who was stolen when our village was attacked, I think six years ago. His mother and I have never ceased praying for his return," Calpurnius said with a red face as he clearly struggled with his emotions.

"Your sister, Darerca," his mother interrupted with an anxious voice.

"I have heard that she is well and living on the island of Valentia."

"Married?" his mother asked as tears flooded her eyes.

"I don't know, but I heard she was betrothed to a Conis Meriadoc."

"I pray he is good to her," she said quietly as she wrung her hands.

"When I go back, rest assured that I will search for her and let you know."

"Go back?" his parents questioned in unison.

"You've only just returned to us, and you are leaving? Why are you returning to those heathens?" his mother hissed.

"I have had to grow and trust God to lead me throughout my ordeal, the God I ignored while I grew up. The only thing that sustained me through those trials was constant prayer. I prayed throughout the days and nights for enough strength and courage to go on. Rain or snow, heat or cold, I prayed through six long years for my purpose in life to be shown to me. One day I actually heard a voice say, 'Go home to Briton, your boat is waiting.' I was well inland, but I followed that instruction and evaded capture, during twelve days of travel through a rough countryside."

Magnus suddenly thought of Elijah being called back by the Lord from hiding in the cave, ***"And, behold, there came a voice unto him, and said, What doest thou here, Elijah?"*** (4)

"When I reached the sea, I noticed a ship preparing to sail for Gaul, but the sailors refused to take me. I prayed for another full day until finally, God persuaded the crew to take me along. When we reached the shores of Gaul, the landscape was desolate. The captain asked me to pray for food, and I turned to the group of sailors and told them to trust God from the bottom of their hearts, because nothing was impossible to Him. In a short time, a herd of pigs wandered over to us, and we all were well fed.

"After that, greed overtook the captain. He sold me into captivity for a fistful of coins. I remember on the first night of my incarceration, the word of God came to me that I would be held for two months. That time came, and I was delivered out of their hands. I sought another voyage across the channel, and after weeks and weeks of walking, here I am. Exhausted, but driven to spread the word of the Lord throughout Hibernia, I know what God is calling me to do."

"How do you know?" Conchessa exclaimed.

"I had a vision."

Speechless, his parents just stared at him.

"Can I tell you about it tomorrow? I'm tired, and I

assure you I'm not going back into that land of pagans for some time yet, I need to travel to Gaul and study to be a priest, hopefully under St. Germain in Auxerre."

"That will take years." Magnus announced from the table as he looked at the young man. He was emaciated, just skin and bones, but his eyes burned with a hidden strength.

Maewyn looked surprised at being interrupted but continued. "You are right my friend, but it is a right idea that I must pursue. By the way, I don't remember you."

"Let me introduce myself, Magnus of Rau, and this is my fiancé Cynde of Hastell Cenllys, and our friend Sypher of Kilpatrick."

"They are our new extended family who have had many trials of their own," Conchessa said and gently pulled Maewyn to a seat at the table.

"Magnus was just telling us about the excruciating pain he felt, after being shot by an arrow," his father said.

Maewyn sat quietly and ate while Magnus finished his tale of escape from the bishop and his eternal gratitude for Cynde trading her golden torc for his life. "I only hope that I can someday be worth her investment."

"Stop saying that, you're priceless to me," Cynde stated shyly before changing the subject. "Maewyn, if you feel up to it, tell us about your adventures."

"Can I tell you in the morning, I may fall asleep before I could finish."

"Of course, follow me and I'll get you tucked in," Conchessa interjected quickly, and led the boy away.

# Chapter 3
Maewyn's Story

In the morning the group gathered early for breakfast. Maewyn entered after most of them had already begun to eat and took an empty chair at the end of the table. Immediately the others shoved containers of food toward him, and he ate with enthusiasm. Finally, he pushed back from the table with a satisfied smile.

Calpurnius asked, "Son, can you tell us what happened to you now?"

Maewyn took a few moments to finish chewing and cleared his throat. "Well friends, it is a long and sordid tale of daily misery and pain, until I finally humbled myself and gave my life to God. Mother, you know how much self-pride I had growing up. I don't know how you could stand me."

"Oh, it was difficult at times, but I knew you had a good soul, somewhere," his mother added and laughed as her eyes glistened.

"I know that it took me much too long to find it," he added. "After we were taken from the village, they tied us together with ropes by our necks. We were forced to stumble through woods and rocky trails for three days until we finally reached the coast."

"We searched for all of you as soon as we returned," Calpurnius interjected, "we followed your trail to the coast, but we were too late."

"They made us walk day and night. Then they loaded Darerca and me onto one of six small ships. The voyage was terrible as the boat pitched and rolled for four days until we finally glimpsed the coast of Hibernia. We were herded off like cattle and walked for another day to a large inland village. There they auctioned us all off as slaves to the highest bidder. Darerca was sold before me to an older couple that needed domestic help. A few years into my captivity, I finally began to understand the language of the barbarians. My owner, Milcho, told me that they had travelled from the island of Valentia in the southwest and that she was to be married, but I had no way to contact her."

"At least she is alive," Calpurnius said with a reassuring hug to his wife.

"I was sold to that man to keep his sheep on Slemish mountain in the north part of that island," Maewyn continued. "For six years I tended that herd every day and into the nights. I struggled through blazing heat, snow, freezing sleet, mud and rain. I only had rags to wear. I fought off hungry wolves even as I was starving myself. I continually searched for strays and newborn lambs in the rough and rocky hills. At some point God either found me, or I finally listened to Him, and my heart began to soften. I started to pray continually, every waking moment to express God's grace. I was gradually able to forgive the marauders who attacked us, and even to find gratitude for my owner for giving me small amounts of food, rags for clothes, and shelter. Most of all I felt the Love of God encompassing me as I persevered through a myriad of daily struggles, until the morning when I heard that heavenly voice."

Magnus recalled an evening when he was staying with his grandfather and heard a voice call out his name. *"Did you call me?"* he asked. *"No,"* was the reply. Twice more it happened with the same result. Finally, he drifted off to sleep, and years later, learned the story of the Lord calling Samuel four times. How he now wished his grandfather had told him what Eli told Samuel, and he could have answered, **"Speak; for thy servant heareth."** (5)

"Immediately I struck out across the countryside, fording rivers, climbing mountains and hills. I traveled mainly in darkness, careful to avoid any human contact. I ate grass, berries, even insects as I travelled ever eastward, until I finally reached the coast and saw a ship being loaded with a cargo of dogs."

"Dogs?" Cynde exclaimed.

"Yes, they were Hibernian hounds that they were going to sell. We set sail for Gaul, and they had me take care of the dogs during the voyage. When we anchored and went ashore though, the land was desolate. You know the rest of the story except for one night on my trip through Briton."

"On your way home." Magnus clarified.

"Yes, about halfway through my journey I had a vivid dream where I stood above a restless sea and salt spray swirled around me in the twilight. I could see a small boat beached below, and a well-dressed man struggled to climb the slippery rocks up to me with a large sack upon his back. I remember his name was Victoricus. He smiled and opened the bag which contained letters from all the unborn children of Hibernia. Suddenly, I heard their little voices crying unto me to save them. The man said, 'You can't let them suffer in pagan misery. You can't ignore your holy duty.' I reached out to clasp his hand, and I woke up."

Magnus shivered, recalling his dream of the ruined garden infested with snakes.

Maewyn continued. "They too need to feel the Love of the Lord. They need direction, and guidance away from the false gods of this world.

Magnus noticed the distressed looks of Maewyn's mother and father but said: "Your ministry is going to be a great quest for you, and a blessing for all the people on that island."

Maewyn looked at his parents. "As Jesus, when he was

moved with compassion and saw the people: **'because they were as sheep not having a shepherd: and he began to teach them many things.'** (6) That is what I am compelled by God to do, even though I hate the thought of leaving both of you. I promise to return here after I become a priest, and before I begin my quest in Hibernia," as he stood and embraced his mother and father.

Magnus headed outside as he heard Calpurnius pronounce in a voice filled with distress; "I'm proud of you son."

# Chapter 4
Voyage

The weeks passed quickly as Maewyn prepared for his journey to Gaul. He had just finished packing a large bag when Magnus walked up behind him.

"Where will you begin your studies?"

"Auxerre. That is where Bishop Germanus is. The local priest told me that he is not a supporter of Pelagianism." Maewyn raised his index finger and continued. "Pelagius taught that people are created in the image of God, like it says in Genesis; **'So God created man in his *own* image, in the image of God created he him; male and female created he them.'** (7) Mother tells me that Martin also taught that people were created in the image of perfection, not in matter, but in spiritual unlimited divinity. Mankind has the capacity to express that perfection, and it is truly a gift of God."

"Those ideas are bequeathed to us by Martin in his scroll."

"What scroll?"

"The scroll that Martin gave to your parents. He gave me a copy too. It has some of his thoughts on healing the world. You haven't seen it?"

Magnus watched the confused look on Patrick's face. "I never knew anything about a scroll. I wonder if it burned up in the raid?"

"Ask your parents about it. He must have given a copy to them when they visited Gaul with you. I think you were eight years old. Father Martin gave me a lot of ideas to work with. He also taught me to look at the difference between the first two chapters of Genesis. **'But there went up a mist from the earth, and watered the whole face of the ground.'** (8) The first chapter's vision of a spiritual, omniscient God is replaced by a God who expresses human emotions in a material world after the mist obscures mankind's true vision and understanding in the second chapter, Martin thought that the fog or mist obscured Truth and allowed mankind to imagine God as a limited, anthropomorphic image or entity." Magnus beamed.

"Rather than seeing man as created in a spiritual, infinite image. Of course. I wish I could have been taught by him. However, without the challenges I have faced, I probably would have been a terrible student. I would like to read Martin's thoughts in that scroll though."

"He was a remarkable man. He healed many people and even raised the dead back to life more than once."

"He actually resurrected dead people? Does it say how? I would love to be able to do that too. Imagine if we could do the works of Jesus."

"I'm sure if you read his scroll, it will give you some good instruction. I actually had a kitten return to life one time, so I know it can work."

"Really? Did you learn how to do that from the scroll?"

"I'd say yes because it taught me to see the world as spiritual rather than material. It taught me to see things from God's point of view, rather than the world's limited point of view."

"I definitely want to read it. It sounds like it may explain how miracles occur in this limited world."

"A scroll of miracles that helps reveal God's kingdom of perfection on earth." Magnus said, "Well, if you ever want to review or copy it, my scroll is hidden in a safe place."

"Let it remain secure and safe until after I finish my studies. By then, maybe I'll be able to understand it fully. My schooling should be an interesting experience, if I can..."

Magnus watched a look of despair cross the boy's face. "Can what?"

Wringing his hands, Maewyn replied in a depressed tone. "No, I can't even tell you of my offence. It is my secret until I can find a trustworthy priest to confess my sin to."

Magnus laid his hand on his friend's shoulder. "God forgives, he doesn't punish for past sins. As for understanding Martin's scroll, from the trials you have endured, I think you could understand it now. The thoughts it contains are the only reason I have survived this life so far. By the way, where are you departing Briton from?"

"Conchessa told me of your trials and adventures, and I have decided to make passage from a place you know well, Seaford Downs."

"Stay far away from the bishop. If he thinks you know me, he will kill you." Magnus watched as a smirk began to form on the man's lips and abruptly stopped.

"You're serious, aren't you."

"Deadly," Magnus replied, instinctively touching his ear as he remembered how the knife bit through his earlobe.

Maewyn looked shaken as he replied, "I will keep a very low profile, and I have never heard of Magnus of Rau."

"Or Cynde, Conchessa or Calpurnius?" Magnus felt one eyebrow raise.

"Who are they?" Maewyn smiled as he swung his bundle onto his back and walked out.

"Be safe my son," Conchessa begged, as she thrust a bag of vittles into his arms.

"I will mother, take care of father." Maewyn started to grin at Calpurnius who maintained his stoic composure.

"Are you sure you don't want company on your walk to the sea?" Magnus asked.

"No, I need time to think and pray. *'I must be about my*

***Father's business?'*** (9) I appreciate your offer though."

Cynde was the first one to rush forward and envelope him in a hug. "We will miss you, be safe," she whined. "Remember to stop by Hastell Cenllys and let my father and brother know that we are fine." Magnus watched her face cloud over as she continued. "Ask about the Bishop of Seaford Downs too, but only ask my father, and only if you are alone with him. We want you to be safe. Find out if he is still searching for us, but don't get yourself in trouble."

"I will be careful," Patrick assured her, as the others crowded in around him. The others hugged and shook hands with him amid a flurry of goodbyes and well wishes.

After a few moments, he backed away from the group, "Don't worry, I'll be back as soon as I can call myself a priest." Pausing as he turned away, he solemnly added, "For a while anyway, before my return to Hibernia."

It was a beautiful spring day as Magnus watched young Maewyn trek southward down a well-worn path. *I hope his religious education doesn't take too long.*

# Chapter 5
Hastell Cenllys

The third week into his journey Maewyn finally glimpsed smoke wisping up from dying cooking fires at the small village of Hastell Cenllys. It took him another hour to reach the rotting wooden ramparts encircling the village. He headed toward the largest conical hovel and slowly pushed the door open.

"What do you want?" a skinny boy demanded as he looked up from the central fire pit where red coals peeked from a mound of black ashes.

Maewyn smiled. "Is your name Dwig perchance?"

"How did you know that?"

"I know your sister; she and her young man wanted me to let you know that they are happy and living well north of here."

The boy's mouth sagged open and then twisted into a wide smile. "Father, come here!" he yelled.

Maewyn watched as a stout man quickly emerged through a curtain of hanging deer skins at the rear of the room. "What do you want?" Cynicism showed in the man's face.

"Hello Bynelld, I'm here to give you a message from your daughter."

The man swallowed hard as he reached toward a bench to steady himself. "Cynde? You know Cynde? Where is she?" Stray tears ran down his face, and he swiped at them with his free hand.

"I know her, and she is fine. Before I tell you where she is, what news do you have of the local bishop and his mercenaries?"

"Dead, he was killed by his own hired assassins along with most of the other monks at the abbey. Those butchers murdered almost all of them, and even chopped the bishop into tiny pieces. Something he did must have made them furious. Then those mercenaries stole a boat docked at the Seaford Downs wharf. We haven't heard of them since."

Maewyn hadn't known what to expect but realized that Magnus and Cynde were possibly forgotten now. "Would anyone at the abbey still be chasing your daughter or Magnus?"

"I think not, since that cruel bishop lies beneath sod and only six or seven monks remain there to maintain the property. It was his insane pursuit of Magnus that drove them both to flee from here. Tell me, where is my daughter? Why are you here?"

Maewyn watched the man's brow tighten into a look of distrust. "First, she and Magnus are safe in Kilpatrick, a village about three weeks of walking north of here. They are living with my family." Maewyn watched as joy suddenly soothed the man's face. "As for me, I am traveling to Gaul to hopefully become a priest."

"Thank the gods, or I mean the one true God. You don't know what happiness you have brought to our dwelling. No one would tell us what happened to Cynde when the bishop and his men returned, and the next night the killings and destruction," he raised both hands and held them tightly to his face as he took a deep breath. "I'm sorry, I've just been so worried," he blurted.

"Magnus and Cynde both told me that God took care of them through some extremely dangerous situations."

"Magnus saved my life by praying, right before they

left. I was sick and almost died. Did he tell you about that?"

"No, but I think I know most of the rest of their adventures."

"I'm just glad you brought me the news that they are safe now. By the way, are they married yet?"

"Not yet. It's only been about a month since they arrived in Kilpatrick. I think they are still trying to relax after their strenuous pursuit by the bishop. They are very much in love though, so I don't think it will be very long. Probably next month."

"Sit down, I want to hear all about their escape. Dwig, bring our guest some refreshments."

Dwig kept Macwyn well fed as he recounted the numerous risky escapades his friends had while eluding the bishop, finally telling them about Cynde trading the golden torc in return for Magnus's life.

"My girl, she is a brave one, and unselfish," Bynelld added with tears in his eyes. "I can't believe my sister schemed with that treacherous bishop before her death, and that rascal Anut betrayed Magnus. He did have a lot of extra money when he came back here, and I didn't know why. I should kill him myself," the man growled.

"Please don't, leave things as they are. Let sleeping dogs lie. He will be punished by his own beliefs, until he changes course and is humble toward the Lord, in this life or the next."

"I guess that is true, but it would make me feel better to bash my worthless brother-in-law's head in," Bynelld grumbled.

"It really wouldn't, and then you would be as guilty as he is of believing that physical gratification or punishment of any kind can replace spiritual gifts. Let it go, forgive him. He will be judged."

"As you wish, but I will tell him off the next time he comes here. He won't be welcome at our inn from now on."

"Speaking of that, do you have somewhere that I can

sleep?" as Maewyn tried to stifle a yawn.

"Certainly, and you are welcome to stay as long as you like."

"Thank you, but I must be on my way in the morning. I want to hurry and finish my studies so that I can begin my ministry in Hibernia."

"Will you be in contact with my daughter. Can you tell her and Magnus that they are welcome to visit at any time?"

"Certainly, I will send them a message as soon as I can." Maewyn replied.

"Also, tell her that I love her." Bynelld croaked.

# Chapter 6
Seaford Downs

Patrick walked down the pathway to Seaford Downs and stared up at the cluster of burnt rocky shells of buildings, still standing as sentinels over the little town. *What a waste.* He saw a small ribbon of smoke rising behind one of the outside walls and realized that the remaining monks must be preparing their evening meal. *I wonder if they would accept a guest?* He turned and began walking up the hill.

"Hello, is anyone there?" he questioned before a portal in the wall. The wooden gates had been burned, but the heavy iron hinges still hung on both sides."

"Who is asking?"

"I am Maewyn, a pilgrim undertaking a journey to seek learning in in Auxerre from Bishop Germanus."

"Enter pilgrim, you are welcome to share our meager meal with us. Come and dine."

"I apologize for my intrusion, I thought you might take your meals in silence, but thank you," Maewyn said as he entered and bowed to the six monks. "Are there only six of you?"

"Yes, Gaelwin passed from us last week, so we six remain," one of the monks answered. "We used to take our meals in silence, when we had a monastery, but those rules haven't seemed as important since we were raided. Have a seat anywhere."

"Do you have shelter here?"

"We have a large underground root cellar that wasn't damaged in the bloody massacre that destroyed everything else. We stay there when the weather is bad. Soon we'll have gathered enough timber to rebuild a roof on one of the dormitories. Why are you going to Auxerre to learn?"

"I need to start somewhere, and I thought…"

"You don't want to go there, not for your initial studies. Go to Lérins Abbey, that's where I started."

"Where is that?"

"It is a small island off the coast of Gaul, a beautiful place. I can write you a letter of introduction to the bishop there. I'm sure he is still in charge."

"Thank you, but I don't want to impose."

"No problem at all. It is a much better atmosphere for your initial studies. Then finish your advanced work in Auxerre."

"Aright, sounds good to me." Maewyn smiled.

"We keep all the books that survived the fires in the cellar. I'll find a page that I can use for your letter."

"What's your name?"

"Brother Sardis," the monk answered as he lit a torch from the fire and disappeared into the ground.

Maewyn ate with the other monks while he waited for Sardis to return and asked them about the barbarians' attack, but none of them wanted to talk about it. "Still painful," one of them finally uttered and he quit asking questions.

Sardis reappeared, "It is written, let it dry tonight, and you can take it with you tomorrow morning."

"Who should I see about a ship leaving for Gaul?"

"You are in luck my friend; a ship is leaving in the morning, and I know the owner. I will tell him to take you along to Gaul."

"How much?" Maewyn asked.

"He brings us our supplies from Rome. No charge for you, my brother." Sardis smiled. "Get some sleep. I'll see you in the morning."

In the morning, Maewyn awoke to a gentle nudge. "Time to head down to the boat, young man. We can't dawdle, the boat has to leave at the beginning of ebb tide, otherwise it has to wait another day."

As they walked toward the harbor, Maewyn broached the subject of the raid. "I asked the others about the attack, but they wouldn't tell me about it."

"We all want to forget it, but I'll tell you so you can carry the message to Lérins. Maybe they will send us the help we need. I was sleeping in one of the barns when I awoke to screams and the smell of smoke. I ran to the doorway and saw the dormitories were on fire. Monks were running out of the doorways, but the mercenaries that the bishop had hired were standing outside laughing and butchering them as they fled the flames. It was a military action; obviously they had planned how to kill as many of us as possible." He paused to wipe at his eyes. "I was terrified, I ran out the back of the barn and through the rear gate of the compound. There is a small creek there, and I rolled down the bank and laid still. I prayed desperately until the sun rose, Finally, I dared to lift my head. Smoke still billowed all across the complex, but the horrible screams had stopped. Only seven of us were able to flee or hide. We survived by God's grace. We buried fifty-two of our brothers in the next few days," a wretched sob escaped his lips as the tears flowed.

"I'm sorry I asked you…"

"No, the story needs to be told. We found what was left of the bishop in his palace. Tiny chunks of flesh and bone, they even chopped up his head. I'm sorry to say I never really trusted him. He had one of my good friends in the order executed for just sharing some revolutionary thoughts on God. Bishop Corizone must have cheated those barbarians and made them furious," he said as he shook his head sadly. "They ransacked the buildings and took anything of value.

Then they stole one of the ships in the harbor and sailed away."

"I promise to convey your tragedy to all who will listen."

"No, don't tell it as a tale to anyone. Only tell people in authority who might help us or be able to prevent similar situations. I don't want us to become idle gossip."

"Yes sir, I understand."

When they reached the waterfront, Brother Sardis hailed a man on the dock. "Master Olin. Let me introduce Maewyn Succat to you. He is traveling to become a priest. Can you give him passage to Gaul?"

"For free?" the smile was evident, although hidden beneath the man's facial hair.

"Please? As a favor to the brothers?"

"Get aboard young man. Cast off lines."

Maewyn hurried and jumped onto the deck as the sailors scrambled to their tasks around him, "Thank you Sardis."

"You're welcome, be sure to come back and visit us sometime."

# Chapter 7
**October 23, 418**
Home Again

On a blustery day in the highlands, Magnus was tending a herd of sheep in the tall green grass sprouting between large rocks scattered across the hillside. Shielding his eyes from the late afternoon sun, he noticed a person approaching the home of Calpurnius from the town far below. There was something in the man's gait that he recognized, and he immediately began to sprint down the hill.

When he reached the house, he could hear the celebration inside before he opened the door.

"Look whose here. My boy has returned as a bishop! His name isn't Maewyn now, it's Patrick," Calpurnius smiled as he hobbled forward and thrust a tankard of ale into Magnus's hand.

Magnus took the mug and stared at the group. Watching as the tiny white-haired Conchessa wrapped her skinny arms around her boy's neck and kissed him.

Bishop Patrick looked at him sheepishly from the center of the group. The holy man was being bombarded with a series of questions from the others. "What was Gaul like? What food was your favorite. What cities did you visit?" He finally raised both hands in submission. "Please give me a moment to sit down, and I'll tell you."

Magnus settled on a bench near a window as Cynde

hurried over and sat next to him with a young girl clinging to her.

"Hold on! Who might this little waif be?" Patrick hurried over as the girl tried to hide her face behind Cynde.

Magnus responded, "You have been away quite a while and missed many things. Meet Bertrona, our first born," he said as he pried the little one off of her mother.

She squealed and reached out to Cynde, who shook her head and said, "He is a nice man; it's ok, honey." Bertrona dared a brief glance at the new face and buried her head in her father's chest.

Patrick looked like he was going to cry. His shoulders sagged. "I have missed much, but it hasn't been my will. It is God's."

Conchessa suddenly cut in while wagging a boney finger, "We all know that you loved and missed us. Now tell us about your adventures and schooling."

"Ok my children." He began as if preaching a sermon. "I first traveled to Lérins Abbey off the south coast of Gaul for my postulancy and novitiate or initial studies. The monastery is built next to the water, the weather and sea views were beautiful there. The monks called the sea Mare Nostrum, Latin for 'Our Sea'. In Hebrew writings it was called, 'Great Sea'. After two years of basic studies, I was approved for my Juniorate phase of education with Father Germanus. Auxerre in Gaul was much like it is here, but a bit warmer, a little more sun, less rain and cold. The food was simple, pretty much the same as ours in the countryside. I stayed away from the larger cities because crime was more prevalent there. After I landed on the coast, I made my way to Auxerre where I met Father Germanus who was glad to have me as an eager pupil."

"What is he like?" Conchessa and Cynde asked simultaneously and grinned at each other.

"He was a wonderful teacher for the daily responsibilities, sacraments, rituals and rites including baptism. A very patient and kind man, although stubborn in some areas. I had many differences of opinions on theology with him, but of course, I never let him know that. He was an admirer of Saint Augustine who wrote, 'Miracles are not contrary to nature, but only contrary to what we know about nature.' That is something we both agreed on."

Magnus watched a contemplative smile spread across the man's face as he continued; "Oh, and I forgot to tell you, I happened to meet Father Pelagius that your local priest told me about one day at Lérins Abbey. I believe he was headed to Carthage in North Africa after Alaric sacked Rome in my second year of studies. I'm glad I was safe on the island during those raids. Anyway, he told me that all people have free will and can choose to be good and sinless, and that infants are born blameless. He solidified what you told me about Martin's theories and mankind's ability to be sinless. That gave me hope for humanity, but then he also said that Augustine and Germanus believed in original sin and were working against him in the politics of the church."

"So, dissention is still rampant in religion?" Magnus asked. "I know I had plenty of challengers trying to bury or re-write Martin's beliefs."

"I'm afraid so my friend, but Martin's ideas continue to spark healing thoughts in you. That is the true test of Christianity. I trekked to Auxerre with a fellow acolyte that I met at Lérins. We were walking along a narrow cart path when an ancient oxcart loaded with lumber approached from behind us. I was walking ahead of my friend when I heard him cry out. I turned to see him lying in the dirt. I hurried back and saw the dirty track the cartwheel had made across the top of his legs, and also one of his feet. Apparently, he stepped on a stone, twisted his ankle and fell under the wheel as it rolled by."

"Oh my, was he alive?" Conchessa wondered aloud.

"He was alive, but obviously hurt. No bones seemed to be broken, so I helped him up and we walked slowly down the road until late in the afternoon, when we found an inn to stay at. I had to lift him into bed because he was in too much pain to do it himself. Once I had him on the bed, he confessed that he couldn't turn over or move, and that he would not be able walk the next morning. I told him I would pray for him and went to bed myself."

"What happened?" Sypher blurted.

"I tried to ignore the visions of his accident and pain as I laid there. I concentrated on what God knew about him all through the night. First, that he couldn't have fallen because **'For it is written, He shall give his angels charge over thee, to keep thee: And in *their* hands they shall bear thee up, lest at any time thou dash thy foot against a stone.'** (10) Then I knew that he was created in the image of God. **'So God created man in his *own* image,'** (11) God is Spirit, **'God *is* a Spirit: and they that worship him must worship *him* in spirit and in truth.'** (12) so he wasn't mortal and subject to accidents. I held onto those thoughts like Jacob did when he wrestled all night with his fears. **'And he said, Let me go, for the day breaketh. And he said, I will not let thee go, except thou bless me.'** (13) In the morning, he was amazed that he felt no pain. He didn't even have a limp." He paused and smiled at everyone. "He was able to continue walking all the way to Auxerre without any discomfort. I'm sure his bruises might have taken a while to fade though," he laughed.

"So, you're healing like our master now?" Magnus said as he shifted and Bertrona squirmed off his lap and made a short run over to her grandfather.

Calpurnius lifted her onto his lap and gave her a gentle hug. "She is quite the little flirt." He smiled.

Magnus spoke again, "I've had many healings in my life Patrick. It is a really simple process. Stop trying to understand what is wrong with yourself and start understanding why you are well. Like what you said. Spirit cannot be broken, sick or sad. Can you imagine God being infected with any malady identified by man? No, and you are made in his image." The others were quiet around him. "I'm sorry, I need to leave the preaching to our resident holy man."

The others laughed as Patrick spoke up. "We all need to spread God's message to the world. I loved your short sermon, Magnus. Now, if you all will excuse me, I am exhausted from my journey. I bid you all a good night." He grinned and wiggled his fingers at the girl who quickly buried her face in grandpa's chest.

# Chapter 8
Death in 424 A.D.

Patrick sat sobbing at the kitchen table when he suddenly felt Conchessa's hand stroke his back. Gently she asked, "What is the matter?"

"I walked down to the church today to talk with the village priest. He received news today that a Christian named Benjamin the Deacon has been martyred in Persia. He read me the details of his murder...," he began to sob again, unable to speak.

"Men always try to destroy others whose faith they do not understand." Cynde interjected.

"But all he was doing was preaching and the methods they used to torture and kill him... horrible!" As he covered his eyes in agony. "How could a loving God permit such torment?"

"Do you really think that God permitted it? Or was it a misunderstanding of what God is? There are many kinds of torture in this world. Look at what our Lord Jesus experienced on the cross. It is hard for people to understand a Love so powerful, that he could allow himself to be scorned and crucified, just so he could prove to the world that death is not the end of life! Maybe that is the Love that Benjamin the Deacon felt too."

"I know the words; it is the spirit I am lacking. I am still afraid of death. Even after what I experienced in Hibernia, torture, pain or death could end my ministry at any time."

"If you walk with God, your ministry can never end." Conchessa reached across the table and gently held her son's hand. "Cousin Martin once told me of a woman who passed on during childbirth. She told him that she had been in incredible pain and suddenly it was completely gone, and she was immersed in golden-white light. All she felt at that moment was unlimited love, warmth, and a clear sense that she was in her forever home. There were no physical forms to see, but she was surrounded by people she knew instinctually were a part of the same brilliant light - and she perceived and was able to communicate with them consciously. At some point in the communications, she was questioned about the life she had left behind. She knew she had just given birth and felt a twinge of responsibility. Suddenly she was returned to her body and awoke once more to this limited mortal life."

"Really?" was all he could think of saying.

"Truly, and do you know what Martin told me after that?" After a moment of silence passed, she continued, "He said that he understood at that moment how Lord Jesus was able to raise the dead. Knowing that they had not died, but were still alive and unaffected by material elements, he was able to see them as whole and complete. He saw them spiritually and called them back, knowing that their life was untouched and eternal. Death is not a steppingstone, it is unreal. Life continues forever my son."

Patrick wiped at the tears running down his face, "I'm not worthy," he sobbed.

"You are what God made you, and nothing he has ever made was unworthy or flawed. You have everything you need to express his Love in Hibernia, and also his protection," she added. Suddenly she pulled away from him and pulled a large roll of purple fabric down from a peg on the wall. "I started this after you, and your sister were abducted. I needed to do something to feel like I could hasten your return, so I prayed over every single stitch that my hands made. I was able to finally finish it while you completed your studies in Gaul. I didn't know what possessed me to make this, but now I do," she announced proudly, spilling the cloth across the table.

Patrick stood and gazed at the myriad of colored beadwork gracing the banner. "It's the Mother Mary! She's beautiful!" he gasped. "Where did you get the beads?"

"Martin sent them to me after your disappearance. He must have known that I needed something to occupy my thoughts, and still it was almost unbearable at times." She dabbed at her eyes. "Now it has almost come full circle. You were a slave, and soon you'll be returning as a warrior for the Lord."

"Thank you, mother," he said as he gently enveloped her in a hug. "I will do my best to make you proud."

"Patrick, I will always be proud of you."

"I hope so. Even with my education at the monastery, I still feel unprepared, like something is still missing from my life," he confessed.

"I know what it is. You now have studied God's word, but you haven't felt his compassion. You're missing the spiritual Love that Cousin Martin understood and lived so well."

"I wish I could have met him when I was old enough to understand what he was saying," Patrick shook his head.

"If the thieves hadn't burned our village we would have two copies of his sacred scroll, and I could give you ours," his mother said.

"Two copies?"

"Yes, he gave us a copy when we visited him long ago, but then the raiders burned our house, and the scroll was destroyed, the same attack where you and your sister were kidnapped.

"But you say there is another, the one that Magnus told me about?" he questioned.

Patrick watched as his mother's eyes lit up, "You need to read his scroll. It's filled with his ideas and hidden in our church."

"Where?" as his skin tingled.

"It is a secret that has not left this house. You must swear never to disclose it to anyone." She looked sternly at him.

"I promise mother."

"It lies within the baptismal font."

## Chapter 9
Attack

Magnus was repairing fallen stones in the fence that surrounded the orchard behind the house and had just lifted a heavy rock into place, when he saw Patrick approaching.

"I have decided to begin my holy quest to Ireland on the day after tomorrow. Will you be able to assist me in retrieving St. Martin's scroll tonight? I want to make a copy to take with me."

Magnus wiped a sweaty, grimy hand across his face and focused his eyes on his friend. "You know I will help, even though I will miss you brother."

"We'll have to do it while the priest is asleep. That will give me a whole day to copy it before I leave."

"How do you want to recover it?"

"I guess the same way Calpurnius and Cynde did it last time. It worked once, so it should work again."

"Yes, but it should be easier this time. Father Amos is so old, nothing should wake him," Patrick laughed.

"And he is slower now, so he won't be able to catch us if he does wake up," Magnus smiled.

As they talked in the afternoon sun, Magnus suddenly noticed a pillar of smoke rising from the far end of the village. "What is that?" he interrupted.

Patrick squinted in the direction Magnus was pointing, and also noticed several groups of villagers running in their direction. "If a fire is raging, why wouldn't they stay and fight it?" he asked.

"Because it's an attack." Magnus announced as he sprinted down toward the house. He burst through the door and shouted; "Cynde, Conchessa, Calpurnius, Sypher! The town is being attacked; we need to get out of here."

Patrick arrived out of breath, just as everyone came out of the house and stared down the hill at the groups of fleeing villagers and growing plumes of smoke. "They may burn the church! We need to save Martin's scroll," he demanded.

"No!" Conchessa cried. "Look at our village. It's being destroyed. We can't lose you again," she whimpered as Calpurnius put a steadying arm around her.

Magnus looked down the hill and saw that the fires were spreading quickly through the buildings closest to the docks.

"They have to do the right thing, no matter what," he said quietly, motioning for Cynde to join them.

"Sir, is there somewhere close that you can hide the ladies?" Magnus spurted.

"Possibly in the old burial cave behind the house. The entrance is covered with thick bushes. Why?"

"Then can we borrow your chariot?"

Calpurnius broke into a wide smile, "What's mine is yours, be safe boys. Come along, ladies."

"Hide yourselves, we'll handle this," Magnus announced loudly. "Sypher, hitch the horses to the chariot." Cynde looked concerned and puzzled but didn't resist as she hurried up the hill.

In a few more minutes, Sypher had the pair of horses hitched onto the chariot. The animals could smell the smoke too, and their hooves danced back and forth excitedly as the three boys clambered aboard. Sypher took a thick rope from around his neck, tied it on the railing and then around his waist. "This is bound to be a wild ride, and I don't want to fall out." He blushed.

"Good idea," Magnus said. "The plan is that we make a

breakneck dash to the church. Patrick and I will jump out, retrieve the scroll, and escape on foot. Sypher, you continue as fast as you can out of the city. I haven't seen any mounted raiders, so they probably came by ship without horses, I hope," he added.

"It looks like your plan has a lot of luck and plenty of holes to bury luck in," Patrick growled.

"That may be, but it sounds much better than most of his ideas," Sypher laughed as he gathered the reins.

"Heeyaaah." Leather strips slapped across the horses' broad backs. The chariot lurched forward, and Sypher guided it straight down the hillside toward the town. As it picked up speed, it started to swerve and buck in the uneven ground as Sypher strained to keep the horses under control.

*God help us!* Magnus prayed as he grabbed the rail and peered forward toward another adventure.

# Chapter 10
Save the Scroll

Magnus hung on for dear life as Sypher skillfully maneuvered the team down the hill and into the maze of small streets. Heavy smoke was pouring from large sections of the village now. Several times he had to pull hard on the reins to avoid running over villagers trying to escape the carnage. Magnus watched the white froth of sweat built up and flew from the horses where the leather harness rubbed against them as they raced on.

"The next street is the chapel." Sypher yelled as he slowed the team slightly to make the corner. They careened around the corner as the chariot slid on the gravel. Ahead of them was a throng of attackers filling the street, and they were getting close to the church. "Heeyaah," Sypher cried.

"It's going to be close," Magnus yelled to Patrick as he crouched, holding tightly to the rail, watching the horde of savages advance.

"I'll do what I can," Sypher yelled as he applied a whip to the horse's broad backs. "I hope this makes them mad enough to chase me and leave you two alone. Get ready… now, jump!"

Magnus and Patrick dove out of the chariot and rolled over several times before standing up and hurrying to hide bchind a low stone wall next to the church, Sypher yelled louder and drove Calpurnius's chariot at top speed toward the throng of barbarians.

They watched the group of armed men raise swords and spears in a moment of mock defiance just before the chariot hurtled into them. Horrified, the savages suddenly scrambled out of the way. A few stumbled and fell as the raging team of horses ignored their screams and rushed over top of them and on through the town.

Magnus continued to peer cautiously around the wall and saw at a glance that Sypher had lost control, and was desperately trying to stay standing, while the heavy wooden wheels bounced off bodies left in the street. *I'm glad he decided to tie himself in.* He grinned, as he watched most of the enraged interlopers turn and chase the chariot. A few of the older ones stayed and tried to provide aid to their injured comrades.

"We need to hurry," Patrick whispered as he grabbed Magnus's sleeve and pulled him toward the back of the church. They found that a door in a rear transept was unlocked and hurried inside.

"We need to find a lever," Magnus said while looking around the sanctuary.

"There, the cross," Patrick hurried toward the altar.

"We can't, that's sacred." Magnus felt a bead of sweat roll down his face.

"Everything in here is sacred, but we have to protect the scroll," Patrick cried as he struggled to move a heavy wooden lectern beneath the crucified image of Jesus. "Help me."

Magnus battled his reservations as he quickly stooped and helped walk the heavy stand beneath the effigy. Then Patrick clambered up and strained to pull the base of the cross away from the wall. With a loud crack, the wooden dowels that held the cross splintered. Patrick lost his grip and fell into Magnus's arms, as the cross fell across the lectern and dislodged most of the statue of Jesus in a loud crash.

"Hurry, they might have heard that," Magnus said,

dropping his friend to the floor as he picked up one end of the cross. Together they ran to the baptismal fount and shoved the top end beneath the basin. Using the cross beam as the fulcrum, together they lifted the heavy stone font. "Quickly," Magnus groaned, holding the weight, while Patrick dropped prone on the floor and reached up inside to grab the wax covered cylinder.

"Got it," Patrick announced triumphantly as he rolled away.

Magnus tried to release the pressure slowly, but with the added leverage from the long arm of the cross he couldn't hold on, and the basin smashed into the floor. Then he heard a rear door slam against a wall. "Let's go." They ran through the vestibule to the front of the church. "Go, hide, and protect that scroll. I'll try to lure them away. Now, go." Magnus puffed as he sprinted away down the street.

———— • ● • ————

Patrick didn't hesitate and rolled over the low stone fence, crouched, and held his breath as he heard several attackers run out of the church and pursue Magnus. *Lord, please protect my friend.* He laid still for a few moments, and then crawled on all fours behind the fence until he reached the next house, where he hurriedly climbed through an open window. He thought he saw movement next to him, and then he saw nothing.

He awoke face down on a dirt floor. Pain seared through his skull as he tried to roll over. "Move and you die!" A child's voice cried out.

"Please, I mean you no harm. I was just trying to escape the heathens that attacked the city. I'm sorry, I will leave," as he strained not to move.

"You aren't one of them?"

He relaxed slightly. "If I was, I wouldn't be alone. They travel in packs because they are cowards," he spat.

"Alright, you get up slow, or get hit again,"

It took several long moments for him to roll onto his side and into a kneeling position. He touched his head and felt blood. "I'm bleeding."

"I didn't hit you that hard."

"Well, it certainly felt like you did. I don't look it, but I'm very delicate." He laughed as he focused on the youngster brandishing a heavy iron spit. "Your mum won't like it if you bend her spit on my skull."

"Mum's dead and papa too," the boy said as his eyes clouded up.

Patrick slowly looked around the room and noticed the two bodies lying near the front door. "I'm sorry son, let's get away from here."

"I was behind the house when I heard mum scream, I hid in the bushes until they left…"

"Come on son, we can do no more here, give me your hand, please."

The young man hesitated as a single tear rolled off his cheek. Then he laid the spit down and reached forward, just as two savages entered the home and stumbled over the corpses.

# Chapter 11
Reading the Scroll

Patrick suddenly reached out and grabbed the boy's waist with both hands and threw him out the window over his shoulder. Then he snatched the spit up and sprang forward, just as the first man drew back a massive battle axe for a death blow. The sharp end of the split drove through the man's belly. As the man staggered, Patrick wrestled the broad axe from his grasp. The second attacker advanced screaming, intending to spear him with a sword. Patrick parried the blow with the axe handle and rushed past the man, letting the razor-sharp axe slice deep into the barbarian's stomach. His attacker fell to the ground, moaning in pain. Breathing heavily, he dropped the axe, turned abruptly, and dove out the window.

"Boy!" he yelled as he scrambled to his feet. "Where are you, boy?" He saw a small head peek from behind a hedge several houses away, and sprinted toward it, feeling the wax covered cylinder bouncing against him. As he rounded the hedge, he saw the young man crouched a few feet away. "It's alright, they won't follow us now," he said, bending over to catch his breath.

"They didn't kill you," the boy said with a puzzled look.

"Thank the good Lord for my protection," Patrick said as he stood. "We need to keep moving so we don't run into any more of those blue bas..., those savages," he said catching himself. "They came from the west, so let's head south across the Antonine wall, alright?" The boy just nodded and followed close behind as Patrick threaded his way through the labyrinth of narrow side streets. Finally, they reached a grassy incline at the edge of the city and scampered atop the decaying remains of the old earthen fortification where they sat down to rest. Dismayed, Patrick watched as fires raged throughout the city now, although the screams of fighting were silent. He smiled when he saw a familiar chariot in the distance. The horses were at a gentle trot, heading north. *I pray Magnus was as fortunate.*

"What now?" a tired, small voice said.

"We trust God my boy. By the way, what is your name?"

"Bard sir."

"Are you a poet or singer?" Patrick laughed.

"My mum said I made happy noises when I was born, so she named me that."

"Well, that must have been the Lord singing through you. My name is Patrick, Sir Bard. I'm very pleased to meet you."

The boy just nodded.

"We need to find you a family to stay with. Do you have relatives here?"

"No."

Any friends that you can stay with?"

"No."

Patrick felt stress building in his shoulders. "Do you not know anyone here that would take you in?"

"No… Can I stay with you?"

"I'm afraid not. I'm embarking on a very dangerous mission to Hibernia to convert pagans to be Christians, like the ones that attacked us today."

"I can help."

"You are a fearless little chap at that. Let me pray about it, but first, let's get something to eat," he said, as he struggled to his feet and began walking toward the untouched villa perched on the hill above the town.

They reached the house in the early twilight. "Hello, is anyone home?" Patrick asked as he knocked on the heavy door.

In a few moments he heard locking boards being removed, and Calpurnius's wide smile welcomed them both inside. "We were worried about you son, but what is this tagging along behind you?"

"His name is Bard, but don't let his size deceive you. He's a brute. He knocked me out cold, and I woke up with my face in the dirt." His father looked dubious. "Here, feel this lump on my head! It's the size of a hen's egg."

The older man's eyes grew wide as he looked at his son's head, and then roared with laughter until he grew weak.

"What's going on in here?" Conchessa led the rest of the inhabitants into the room.

"This tiny warrior beat up our little Maewyn." Calpurnius pointed at Bard.

"It isn't funny." Patrick felt himself grin. "Don't laugh, Magnus, or you either, Sypher," as he waved a fist at them.

"Like we are afraid of a big strong man that was overpowered by a boy." Magnus chuckled.

"He is strong!" Bard suddenly yelled. "He killed two men who attacked us."

"My word," Conchessa exclaimed. "Stop talking and let's get these two mighty men some food, they must be famished."

"I am somewhat hungry at that." Patrick smiled, put an arm around the boy's shoulders, and walked in together, through a series of hugs and handshakes. "Magnus, Sypher, you must tell me how you evaded those thugs, and I'll tell you how this lad defeated me."

"I for one can't wait for that story," Cynde said as she pulled chairs out from around the table.

"Them first." Patrick said quickly. "I'm ready to sit and rest a bit."

Sypher cleared his throat. "That was an awful chase they gave me from the church. Thankfully, the few arrows and spears they chucked at me and the team missed us, but I almost lost control and rolled the chariot on several sharp corners. Somehow, it stayed upright, and as we rushed further into the city, that mob couldn't keep up. After a few more blocks, I turned North and just trotted out of town. I waited in the hills for several more hours, then I drove the team home."

"I had to run, and you know how I hate that." Magnus confessed with a smile. "Those two brutes chased me halfway through the town. I was ahead of them and rounded a corner where freshly washed clothes were hung across the street on a rope. There was a big puddle of mud right behind them where the wash women had dumped their tubs of water. I cut the rope and squatted down behind a barrel. As they ran and rounded the corner, I pulled the rope up enough to snag their ankles. They fell down like two sacks of grain and spilled into that sloppy puddle face-first. I didn't wait to watch them try to stand up. I didn't see them after that, but I was very careful coming back, so I wouldn't run into any more of those raiders. They did terrible things to the villagers that weren't able to escape."

"They murdered my parents!" Bard suddenly spouted as tears appeared on his cheeks.

Patrick quickly wrapped a steadying arm around the boy's shoulders. He felt the spasms as sobs racked the young man. "And yet this young man had the fortitude to stay and defend his house from more of those cowardly intruders. He hid next to a window and knocked me cold with an iron spit. I am so proud of him, even though my head still hurts," he announced drawing his arm back to gingerly rub the knot on his head.

The ladies crowded in quickly, hugging and kissing the

small boy.

"Do you still have it?" Magnus questioned loudly.

"Yes, my friend, we are victorious," Patrick said as he drew the leather cylinder out of his tunic. "Why don't we celebrate by reading Martin's precious words?" As murmurs of encouragement spilled around him, Patrick broke the wax sealing the tube and pulled the old scroll out. Everyone was silent as he spread it out on the table, cleared his throat, and began to read:

*"I, Martin, humble servant of the one Lord, do hereby set my hand to this document with humble prayers for all of mankind. I have been blessed with a lifetime of service to others. I have healed many suffering mental and physical ills, including the great nemesis of death. These were not miracles. They were the result of my conscientious and continuous communion with God. For prayer to work, you must look at the spiritual evidence hidden beneath layers of human thought and emotion and strive to understand God's perspective. Every one of my life's questions has been answered through a broadened spiritual understanding.*

*What separates us from the eternal and everlasting spiritual reality that is God? What holds this conglomeration of material experience together for all people and creatures? I believe that it is a false sense of history, for in the sage words of the apostle Paul,* **'For I am persuaded, that neither death, nor life, nor angels, nor principalities, nor powers, nor things present, nor things to come. Nor height, nor depth, nor any other creature, shall be able to separate us from the love of God, which is in Christ Jesus our Lord.'** (14)

*The Lord is infinite, and the only history in an eternity is now. No before, no after, just now. In my own experiences, if a man truly realizes for a moment that he is not separate from the Kingdom of God, false historical images pass away, and he is healed.*

*If mankind would strive after this knowledge, perfection would become increasingly evident in all of our lives. With God realized as each individual's only father/mother, mortals would see God as their one true relative, the only creator. If you perceive everything and everyone as spiritual ideas, discrimination disappears. There is no gender, age, race, or human history to hate, all becomes Love.*

*When material history is seen to be a lie – all anger, resentment, fear must pass into the nothingness that spawned them. Reality then appears as harmony, health, and purity untouched by the lie of an existence separate from God.*

*Remove this keystone of material history, and the façade of a limited life crumbles, replaced by limitless unfoldment. I can best illustrate this with a parable of two young boys:*

*Cain was raised with a belief in a material mother and father. He is continually exposed to fear, sickness, and death. He believes he is entirely separate from God and cannot fathom infinity. He sees mental and physical violence from his father, witnesses its marks left on his mother and siblings, and listens to stories of past violations heaped on his family by others. He becomes a bigot and spews hatred towards others of different faiths, skin color, and social status. Cain believes in a world driven by both good and evil, including people possessed by evil. Challenges to health, prosperity, intelligence, and joy have been handed down to him through generations of ancestors. It is that inheritance that he passes to his own offspring.*

*On the other hand, Abel was raised with an understanding that God was his father/mother. Speaking to God directly, with unselfish motives, he receives God's perfect ideas. He experiences growth in Love, Wisdom, and Harmony. Perceiving the spiritual reality that is obscured by the mist of mortal existence, he sees evil, the devil, as unreal because, as Jesus announced, it is a lie when he said, '**Why do ye not understand my speech? even because ye cannot hear my word. Ye are of your father the devil, and the lusts*** *of your father ye will do. He was a murderer from the beginning, and abode not in the truth, because there is no truth in him. When he speaketh a lie, he speaketh of his own: for he is a liar, and the father of it. And because I tell you the truth, ye believe me not.'* (15)

*Abel is victorious as our master, his disciples, and myself have been at healing disease, fear, and even death, through an understanding of God's allness and the universe as spiritual – not material. God could not be omnipresent if evil lurks in any part of the universe. Otherwise, he would be a house divided against himself, as it is recorded, '**And Jesus knew their thoughts, and said unto them, Every kingdom divided against itself is brought to desolation; and every city or house divided against itself shall not stand: And if Satan cast out Satan, he is divided against himself; how shall then his kingdom stand? And if I by Beelzebub cast out devils, by whom do your children cast them out? therefore they shall be your judges. But if I cast out devils by the Spirit of God, then the kingdom of God is come unto you.'*** (16)

*Abel's inheritance is peace, perfection, and an infinite supply of spiritual ideas that he can demonstrate in his own life. He understands that God is All, and as a reflection of God, he is himself unlimited by any material laws or restrictions. Remember how our master walked on water? '**And when even was now come, his disciples went down to the sea. And entered into a ship and went over the sea toward Capernaum. And it was now dark, and Jesus was not come to them. And the sea arose by reason of a great wind that blew. So, when they had rowed about five and twenty or thirty furlongs, they see Jesus walking on the sea, and drawing nigh unto the ship: and they were afraid. But he saith unto them, It is I; be not afraid. Then they willingly received him into the ship: and immediately the ship was at the land whither they went.'*** (17)

*Their two lives are opposites. Which one will prove to*

*be true? Cain holds the tatters of ruined, limited lives and beliefs around him as he walks through a dismal existence with fleeting promises of happiness. Abel is free of mortal encumbrances and shares the unlimited joys of the universe with others. Which experience do you aspire to?*

*The latter legacy I intend to leave with my flock. It is the heritage of salvation for this world, as it is the Kingdom of God discerned by mankind. I have no material roots! I wish only to bless this world as an expression of the Love of God. **'And thou, child, shalt be called the prophet of the Highest: for thou shalt go before the face of the Lord to prepare his ways; To give knowledge of salvation unto his people by the remission of their sins, Through the tender mercy of our God; whereby the dayspring from on high hath visited us. To give light to them that sit in darkness and in the shadow of death, to guide our feet in the way of peace.'** (18)*

*This verity pertains to all races, creeds, and creatures upon this earth. As people struggle to free themselves from the lures and anchors of mortal reasoning, realization occurs. As beliefs in sin and materiality wash away, they find 'at one ment' with all the ideas of creation in the Mind of God. Mankind must see itself as not removed from God. With no material history to bind them, man and woman become free to discover their true origins. Earthly yearnings subside as they discover that they themselves are the perfect images and likenesses of God. Strive to perceive materiality through the lens of Spirit. Discern the Heavenly qualities expressed in corporeal ideas. Learn the opposite of what the world is teaching you. Study the Laws of God, which protect and guide. Heal yourself and others on this earthly plain. Be Deity reflected.*

*I humbly petition God daily to be a better example for others of freedom from material limits. A vocation that sorely needs to be nurtured in this coarse world. I am leaving copies of this document with a few of the receptive minds that I have encountered on my life journey. This knowledge is my most valuable possession, and I bequeath it to all generations that must follow. With people, there is always dissension. The only balm for this irritation is spiritual concepts. Mankind must understand that they have never fallen from God's grace, for God, being infinite, knows nothing opposed to himself. This is the only solution for harmony and healing in this world!*

*Awaken my children to the latent joy and power of Christianity. You are not mortals. You are spiritual creatures! Beauty lies beyond the Adam dream.*

*Humble servant of the one Lord,*
*Martin of Tours*

*Magnus,*
*One copy of this treatise resides with my relatives, Conchessa of Kilpatrick, and her husband Calphurnius. They have promised to help protect and nurture these ideas with others. If you need assistance, contact them.*
*Go with God's Love and protection, my son.*
*Martin"*

Everyone was silent as Patrick dabbed at his eyes in an effort to clear his vision. "Thank you, God, for your precious gift of Father Martin to this cruel world. As John the Baptist said of Jesus, I vow to Martin: **'whose shoe's latchet I am not worthy to unloose.'** (19) I dedicate my life to follow in your footsteps. I solemnly promise to spread the word of God to pagans dwelling in darkness across the land of Hibernia.

Magnus clasped Patrick's hand and shook it firmly with a wide smile. "We don't know if those barbarians will attack us again or not. You're not going to have time to copy the scroll anymore tonight, so take it away with you tomorrow and see that it returns to us when your efforts and ministry are victorious."

"Thank you for trusting me with it." As Patrick swiped at his tears again.

Cynde wiped her own tears and wrapped her arms around him, "A beautiful reading Bishop Patrick. I pray your crusade will provide the healing words those people need." As the others crowded closer with well wishes.

Patrick heard a small voice in the clamor of sounds, "I'm going with him."

# Chapter 12
Big Decision

"My goodness, you are up early son," Conchessa exclaimed as she entered the kitchen just before dawn.

Patrick just grunted, "Morning."

She turned abruptly and confronted him. "What is your problem?" She let the words hang and peered at him until he responded.

"I couldn't sleep last night. I don't know what to do about Bard."

"Is that all? I thought you were a man of the cloth. You're supposed to let the Lord make the decisions."

"It's not that simple, he wants to go with me, and I…"

"Don't want the responsibility?" she added.

"If anything happens to him, I couldn't forgive myself."

"Again, that is not your job. Only one can truly forgive a man's mistakes." She winked and waggled a finger at him.

"It would be safer to leave him here with you. I don't know what dangers I'll encounter. He might interfere with my mission."

"Or he might bless it with the pure insights of a child's innocence. Remember, he may not be protected here if those heathens attack again."

"I know, I know."

"I've watched him. He is a few years younger than you when you were stolen, but he is as full of fight and spirit as any boy I've seen. He has bonded with you. If you leave him here, it will break his heart, and maybe his spirit too." She smiled lovingly and began the process of cooking breakfast.

"Can I help?" Patrick questioned.

"No, I have my duties, you tend to yours."

With a loud sigh he pushed away from the table and walked out the door into the crisp morning air. The sun was just topping the trees in the distance as he stood and watched its brilliant rays strike low clouds. *Father, what should I do?*

"Are you leaving?" a small, accusing voice behind him asked.

"No, Bard, I'm watching beauty painted in the sky. It reminds me that God is everywhere, always."

"Are you leaving soon?"

"No, my son." He closed his eyes and after a long pause he announced, "We are leaving soon." Turning, he gathered the laughing boy into his arms.

"We leave to battle the world's Goliath of mortal sense with the sling of righteousness and the stones of Truth. As David did with the Philistine. **'Then said David to the Philistine, Thou comest to me with a sword, and with a spear, and with a shield: but I come to thee in the name of the LORD of hosts, the God of the armies of Israel, whom thou hast defied.'** (20) and then he ran toward the giant." Patrick smiled as he looked at the child's tousled hair.

"What happened then?" the boy asked.

**"David put his hand in his bag, and took thence a stone, and slang *it*, and smote the Philistine in his forehead, that the stone sunk into his forehead; and he fell upon his face to the earth. So David prevailed over the Philistine with a sling and with a stone, and smote the Philistine, and slew him; but *there was* no sword in the hand of David."** (21)

"Wow, we go forward to do battle with bad people." He lifted a tiny fist.

"Ha, ha, almost, young Bard. We battle to turn their bad

thoughts into Godlike thoughts, to give peace and hope to the lost sheep in this world. You don't want people to grow up with the same fears and terror we both have faced in our lives, do you?"

Patrick watched as the boy morphed into a serious expression and finally shook his head slowly for a few moments. "No, never."

"Then we leave to do battle with the armor of God," he announced thinking of (22) ***"For the weapons of our warfare are not carnal, but mighty through God to the pulling down of strong holds;"***

"What armor?"

"We must be armed with the grace of God. As it says in the good book; **'Wherefore take unto you the whole armour of God, that ye may be able to withstand in the evil day, and having done all, to stand. Stand therefore, having your loins girt about with truth, and having on the breastplate of righteousness; And your feet shod with the preparation of the gospel of peace; Above all, taking the shield of faith, wherewith ye shall be able to quench all the fiery darts of the wicked. And take the helmet of salvation, and the sword of the Spirit, which is the word of God:'** (23) Our weapons are supplied by the Lord."

"Not real swords?" The boy pouted.

Patrick smiled as he put his hand on the boy's shoulder and guided him back toward the house. "No son, our weapon is Love for the world and all those in it. Now we must pack, say our fond goodbyes, and begin our quest for victory among the inhabitants of Hibernia!"

# Chapter 13
Sailing to Hibernia

A few days later, Patrick and Bard were both seasick, as they held desperately onto the gunwale of the shabby ship as it plied through choppy waters. Patrick hated seeing Bard in misery, but there was no other way to travel to the island. "Hang on my boy, it will get better with time."

Bard looked wilted as he clung to the rail, shivering in wet clothes. Hanging on with one hand, Patrick removed his cloak and draped it over the boy, and knelt, wrapping his free arm around him. "There, that should warm you in a bit."

Bard managed a weak smile. "How did Jesus walk on the sea?"

"I wish I knew," Patrick laughed. "You know this isn't my first voyage, and I wish I could have stepped off of that slave ship. I see now that it was a step toward my destiny to help the people on the island. As far as Jesus, I suppose he prayed, understanding that God, Spirit is the real fabric of the universe, and just strode atop the waves toward his disciple's ship, because it was his destination."

Bard's thoughtful face stared up at him.

"Wait until you see this land we are headed to; it is beautiful, green, and rugged."

"First time you been on a ship?" a stout sailor asked with a laugh.

"For him it is." Patrick answered, "and I can't say that I

missed it much."

"Oh, it's beautiful in fair winds, but this is a bit rough. We're making good headway though. We'll be on the island in a couple days. Can I get you gents something for your tummies, Pickled pig's feet maybe?" He laughed loudly as they both turned and retched over the rail again.

*This is wrong,* Patrick thought as he wiped his beard. *I am a man of God, I can pray. How did the disciples feel in the tempest on the ship when Jesus slept?* **"And he was in the hinder part of the ship, asleep on a pillow: and they awake him, and say unto him, Master, carest thou not that we perish? And he arose, and rebuked the wind, and said unto the sea, Peace, be still. And the wind ceased, and there was a great calm. And he said unto them, Why are ye so fearful? how is it that ye have no faith?"** (24) *I do have faith, the Lord has sustained me through worse torments than this.* He wrapped his arm tighter around the boy and prayed until their stomachs calmed.

As twilight fell, so did the ocean swells, and the ship glided smoothly through the water. Bard sat quietly as he watched a clear sky full of stars. "I'm sorry for before, I couldn't resist," a gruff voice apologized.

Patrick turned and recognized the sailor. "You're forgiven. We feel better now."

"Do you know what the stars show us lad?" The man continued as Bard shook his head. "That's how we know where we are. There look at those stars." He pointed off the starboard side. "That group of stars there, that's 'Taurus the Bull', see those two bright stars off to the left? Those are the tips of his horns." He pointed to another group of nine stars. "That's 'Leo the Lion" over there. See that bright star there?" Bard nodded with wide eyes and a slight smile that Patrick noticed. "That, young man is 'Stella Polaris' the North star. We see that, we know our course is correct."

"What about storm clouds?"

"Good question, my boy. In a storm we concentrate and

drive the boat against the swells, so we don't swamp or overturn. When the seas calm, we search the sky for stars, the sun, or if it is still cloudy but calm enough, the captain has a magnetic needle that he puts on a cork in a bowl of water to find the North. You gentlemen have a good night; I've got to get back to my tasks."

"Thank you, what is your name?" Patrick asked.

"Amice sir." He walked aft.

"Father, why was he nice now?" Bard asked.

"I think we just saw Amice, the real man, the sailor we saw before was a false image that mortals put on in order to entertain themselves."

"I liked the real man better."

"Yes, Bard, I like the real man too."

When Patrick awoke the following morning, it saw full sunshine and a felt a strong, steady wind. Sailors scurried around, adjusting the large square sail, as they tacked back and forth into the wind.

Bard watched them with fascination. *He is a marvelous boy. Thank you, God, for providing him to me. Please protect us on our quest to give your Word to the hungry hearts in Hibernia.* As waves gently rocked the boat, he quietly fell asleep again.

A storm overtook them late in the afternoon, and Patrick comforted Bard by sitting him on his knee and wrapping his cloak tightly around them both. Thunder rolled as lightning bolts licked the seas around them. One group of sailors hurriedly deployed a sea anchor to hold the ship into the wind, while others climbed up to the yard to reef the huge sail. Patrick sat and recited the Lord's prayer in a comforting voice to the boy until they both fell asleep.

A huge bolt of lightning hit the sea just off the port side in a blaze of light. Patrick awoke immediately as a mixture of strange words were palpable, almost like they were hanging in the air.

*Who is speaking?* Patrick wondered. He heard verbal

speech in an authoritative voice and struggled to understand the strange words. At the end of the oration, he perceived the final words; *"The one who gave his life for you, he it is who speaks to you."*

He was immediately full of joy as Bard shook and held tightly to him. Patrick hugged him tightly. "Don't worry, Bard, Jesus is going with us on our mission to heal and educate the people of Hibernia."

Late the next afternoon, Patrick heard a sailor shout out "Land dead ahead."

"What land is that? We should be at Antrim!" the captain yelled.

"I think, yes, it looks like Antrim over there to the south, but we are headed north. It must be the currents," another sailor answered.

"All hands, I can't hold her on course. We will try to put her in through Strangford Lough."

Patrick began praying that the ship wouldn't pile up on the rocky shore, and then remembered with humility, that Jesus was with him. He grabbed Bard's hand and his bag and walked forward to the bow. He stood there, calmly watching as the coast drew nearer.

The sailors cheered as the boat slipped through the narrow channel, and soon he and Bard disembarked in County Down. After thanking the sailors for their skill, he and Bard walked away from the stoney shore, toward a field of emerald, green grass to find shelter for the night.

"Wait," a cry came from behind. Amice ran up holding a bag. "Here, can you take this food to my parents? They live in Saul, a village over the hill next to that rock." He pointed at a large boulder set on a crest in the distance. "I need to stay and help unload the ship tonight. Tell them that I sent you and that you should stay with them.

"Thank you, Amice. We will." Patrick smiled when Bard didn't hesitate but grunted as he lifted the bundle to his small shoulder.

# Chapter 14
Hibernian welcome

Patrick and Bard finally entered the small village at twilight. A few people stared at them from around dying fires.

A man cried, "Attack Lobo," and a large dog sprang toward them with its jaws snapping violently but suddenly stopped and stood quietly a few feet away.

"Can you tell us where the parents of Amice live?" Patrick announced.

"Who's asking?" Other residents scattered as a giant of a man stepped out from behind one of the hovels.

"My name is Bishop Patrick, and this is my friend Bard. Amice told us to seek out his parents."

"Drop your sacks and I might let you live, or maybe not." He leered at them as he drew out a large sword.

Bard took a quick step backward. Unfazed, Patrick stepped forward and watched the man's eyes open in surprise. "I take it you consider yourself to be the bully of this village."

"I am the strongest..." As confusion painted his face when he tried to raise his sword but could not.

"What is your name sir?"

"Dichu, they call me the Savage. King of this region." As he grasped the hilt of the sword with both hands and struggled to raise it.

"Strength lies with the one and only God, and I have

arrived to proclaim his Word across this island. Will you join me?"

Dichu stared and swallowed hard. "What have you done to me?" he stammered as sweat streamed from his brow.

"I have done nothing, but you have threatened a servant of the one true God." Patrick stood erect, with a loving smile.

Dichu dropped to his knees and bowed his head. "I don't understand. I feel…"

"Reborn? You are my son, evil has been driven from you, and you are free to express the grace and love of a loving God."

Tears flooded the big man's face as a crowd of curious villagers crowded around him.

"Please, do any of you know the parents of Amice?" Patrick repeated.

Dichu struggled to his feet. "I do, let me guide you. Please." The man's sudden humility was apparent.

"Thank you, sir. Lead on." Bard looked at him with undisguised curiosity and whispered, "What did you do?"

"I did nothing other than view Dichu in the image of Spirit."

Bard looked unconvinced as Dichu gazed at his sword lying in the dirt, turned and walked through the village toward an ancient hut. "Cathal, Aine, I have visitors for you to welcome." An elderly couple crept through the doorway. "Amice sent these two visitors to you."

"He brought back these gifts for you," Bard said as he handed over the bag to the man.

"Come in, welcome." They both smiled and beckoned them inside.

As Dichu walked off, Patrick called after him, "Don't forget your sword. You don't want to leave that laying around for someone else to use."

"Yes sir, but how…"

"I'll explain it later, walk with Love, my son." He entered the hovel.

The older couple were sitting cross-legged on the ground sorting and storing the dried meat, fruit, small bags of grain and some vegetables into baskets. "Thank you for bringing this. Will Amice visit tomorrow?" Aine asked.

"I think so, he had to help unload the ship first. He thought you might allow us to spend the night with you."

"Yes, and we will have a grand meal first." Cathal grinned as he brushed dirt off of a large turnip. "Can you boys bring in a few bundles of flax to burn?"

"Certainly." Patrick answered.

"How did you do that? That huge brute was going to kill us!" Bard demanded when they were outside.

Patrick paused and looked deeply into the boy's eyes. "I am learning to see the real individual that God made, not the vindictive monsters that humans see. I try to perceive the qualities of God in people, instead of their limitations, threatenings, or outward appearance. Love, Compassion, Intelligence, Life and Spirit, those thoughts can heal both disease and sin. Dichu has a good heart, but he was hiding it to appear fearless. Looking at the man, I suddenly remembered what Ezekial said; **'All hands shall be feeble, and all knees shall be weak *as* water.'** (25) and the devilish thoughts left him."

"Did you do that for Amice too. Is that why he changed?"

"You don't understand, he didn't change, but my thinking did." Patrick winked as he watched confusion shake the boy's head.

The next morning Patrick heard Dichu calling to him. He stepped outside into the fog covered village. "Sir, I am a changed man, my family is here. They know I have changed, but we don't know how or why. Please tell us."

Tears welled in Patrick's eyes as he embraced the man. "Brother Dichu, yesterday you entered the Kingdom of God. **'Therefore if any man *be* in Christ, *he is* a new creature: old things are passed away; behold, all things are become**

**new.'** (26) I want to baptize you and your family as Christians, as followers of Jesus. Will you accept this gift?"

The big man struggled to utter the word, "Yes," as his tears flowed.

"Is there a stream near here and maybe some flax for a warm fire?" Patrick continued.

After the fog burned away, the day was sunny and unseasonably warm. Patrick took that as a good sign and waded into a stream with Dichu following, as his family waited onshore for their turn to be baptized.

When they were drying off and sitting around the fire warming themselves. Dichu said, "Can I tell you why I attacked you?"

"If you want to my son."

"Chief King Leogaire told us of a prophecy by soothsayers of a man who would come to this island and in their words, 'destroy our gods, and overturn their altars, and he shall subdue unto himself the kings that resist him, or put them unto death, and his doctrine shall reign for ever and ever.' (27) Leogaire decreed that we should expel that man from our country as soon as he arrived on our shores." After a long pause, he asked. "Are you him?"

"Yes, I believe I am."

# Chapter 15
The First Church

News spread quickly that fearsome "Dichu the Savage King" had changed his persona completely after meeting a traveler from Briton. People began to arrive from many regions of the island to hear the stranger's preaching.

Dichu watched as the groups of people grew in number day by day. After one rainy evening, he confronted Patrick. "How do you expect to give your message to these pilgrims when bad weather threatens like yesterday?"

"God will provide."

"We will provide, my friend. I want you to build one of these churches you told me about. There, atop the hill Slieve, where all may see it." He pointed toward a lush green plain nearby where a couple of men were unloading large rocks and logs from an oxcart. "You see? We are beginning to build it already. You need to tell them what you want it to look like."

Patrick's eyes filled with tears as he managed to say, "Bless you."

"You already have." Dichu said with a wide grin. "Now go over there and tell them where you want the corners set for Sabhail Church."

Patrick called to Bard and together they trotted over to the building site. Patrick first checked the sun to get his bearings. "Stand here by this rock," he said, as he paced fifteen steps south. "Bring three smaller rocks here."

Patrick watched as Bard searched and found a few chunks of stone that had broken off when the stones had fallen atop one another off the cart. Bard began running toward him. "Slow down, don't trip, boy. Here give them to me." Breathlessly, the youngster handed them over.

"Thank you, we'll drop one here, and then maybe eight steps to the west," as he counted them off. "Now, to place the final stone," as he headed north. "Let's make sure it's square now," and they spent the next hour pacing and re-pacing diagonally between two opposing corners and around the perimeter, carefully adjusting the stones to form a perfect rectangle.

The oxcart was returning just as they were finished. Patrick explained the design to the men, as he placed a few more small stones for the doors and windows, before returning to the village.

They found the king in his house. "Dichu, could Bard and I borrow some loys for Sabhail?"

"Certainly, and a few men to wield them I wager." The big man laughed. "Give me a bit of time and I'll send some over."

"What's a loy, and what is Sabhail?" Bard asked quietly as they walked toward the hill again.

"A loy is a digging tool. We'll dig trenches to set the walls and dig up the grass inside to set a stone floor. 'Sabhail' means barn in their language, but I think we'll call it Saul Church. Just think Bard, our first church in Hibernia will soon be a reality. Then next, we will build a monastery. A place of learning and reflection for the faithful. We will spread the glory of God across this island. As it is written, **'...I *am* the LORD your God, and none else: and my people shall never be ashamed. And it shall come to pass afterward, *that* I will pour out my spirit upon all flesh; and your sons and your daughters shall prophesy, your old men shall dream dreams, your young men shall see**

**visions:'** (28) This is the beginning of an epic transformation of all the willing souls on this island."

"Bishop?"

Patrick turned to see the question came from a beautiful red-haired girl of about seventeen. "I have been to several of your sermons and then you baptized me. Might I be able to join your ministry?"

"My dear, what prompted you to ask?"

The girl blushed as she hung her head. "I had a message from an angel I suppose. After your stories. I heard a voice in the night. It told me that I should be a virgin of Christ and live to grow closer to the true God."

"What is your name?" Bard abruptly asked as Patrick noticed his eyes light up.

"I am Fiadh. Daughter of Fintan."

"I apologize for my outspoken friend here. Bless you, my child. I am humbled and grateful for your request. You are the very first female to ask to join us." He closed his eyes as he began to pray and make the sign of the cross.

Suddenly, an older man in a rage ran up, violently grabbed the girl spun her around and threw her to the ground. "Get yourself home. You'll not be running away and leaving your mother and me without help."

Patrick leaped forward and confronted the man. "Do you know who I am?" he shouted.

The man answered unsteadily. "You're the stranger who defeated and changed Dichu."

"How did I do that?"

"Bewitched?" the man stammered.

"No, I prayed to the one and only God for his salvation. Do you want me to pray for you now?" As he smiled.

"No, stay away. Keep away from my daughter." As he pointed at the girl.

"My friend, she is no longer your daughter. An angel spoke to her. She knows that she is God's child from now on. Go home and tell your wife that she is fulfilling her purpose here. She will be learning about the Christ to help and heal all the people in this region."

The man hesitated as his eyes glistened.

"I promise that she will be safe with us, and you can visit anytime, now go." He commanded.

The man's shoulders slumped as he finally turned and walked away.

The girl was crying quietly as Patrick stretched out a caring hand and lifted her up. "Don't worry, my dear. I know it hurts for the moment, but I promise you will bless your parents' lives in ways they cannot imagine. Now to begin our labor of Love." He gripped Bard's hand, and the three of them walked toward the site for the new church.

Later, as the shadows became long, Patrick sent Fiadh back to the village to get something to eat. Then he walked over to Bard who was idly shoveling scoops of grass away from the floor area, while staring at the girl walking away. "Bard, you need to constrain your thoughts as long as you are my helper."

The boy's red face swung around. "How did you know I was…"

"Men are always boys inside, and we know what boys think." He winked. "She is the Lord's child now, don't allow yourself to be drawn toward sin. You need to temper your thoughts to obey only God's direction now. One day I will release you from your vow to me and you will be free to marry, but until that day." He raised a finger as the boy grudgingly nodded his head. "Even distracted, you did a fine job today. Now let's see if Fiadh left us anything to eat."

Patrick was glad to see the building rise quickly in the next few months. Dichu stayed true to his word supplying a steady stream of materials and workers, and even helped build portions of it himself. On the twelfth Sunday after he had first stepped a loy into the soft sod, it was finished enough to consecrate in a celebration. As visitors filled the tiny village, he led a procession to the new church and stood before the door.

"I want to thank God for leading me to this village to begin my ministry, and express my gratitude to all of you, especially King Dichu, for providing this refuge for prayer for the faithful. These people will no longer serve idols and unclean things but will be washed in the Spirit. Among you shall rise monks and virgins of Christ to minister unto the heathen and lift them into an understanding of Christ Jesus's parables. To lift them above their pain and sorrows into health and everlasting life. This edifice is the first seed of a crop that shall spread across this land to feed the hungry hearts. Thank you and bless you all." Patrick stepped aside to shake hands as a line of people formed to enter the church.

"Nice speech, what comes next?" Bard said.

"First, we build a monastery with more shelters for the brothers and sisters that will join us. Then I will appoint a promising abbot out of the group to manage it. After that, I want to visit Milcho, the man who bought me as a slave. I would love to convert him from his wicked ways"

# Chapter 16
Milcho

"How much further?" Bard asked breathlessly as he trudged up a steep hillside between stacks of boulders.

"Maybe a day. I used to herd sheep in the valley behind this hill. I remember when I ran down this hill to escape my slavery."

"A lot easier than climbing it, I bet," the boy said.

"I was a couple years older than you, but I was in better shape than I am now," he puffed. Bard said nothing, but his frown told Patrick everything. "You'll be in better shape than I was in no time. As it says in the good book, **'Even the youths shall faint and be weary, and the young men shall utterly fall: But they that wait upon the LORD shall renew *their* strength; they shall mount up with wings as eagles; they shall run, and not be weary; *and* they shall walk, and not faint.'** (29) I pray those words will provide you with energy when you need it."

Bard grunted but had a more determined look as they continued up the steep hillside, pursued by lengthening shadows.

When they reached the crest of the hill Patrick paused to catch his breath and scan the landscape as the sun sat on the horizon. "There, do you see that large dwelling on the hill over there? That is Milcho's house.

"Who are ye?" a man yelled. Patrick looked down the

hill and saw a group of armed men approaching.

"I am Patrick, Bishop of the church. I am going to visit my friend Milcho."

"Did he grant you an audience?"

"No. I have not seen Milcho for several decades, and I did not take time to say goodbye when I left his employ as his shepherd. Announce me, tell him his former slave Maewyn has returned as a prince of the church."

"Are you the man who defeated Dichu?" another man yelled.

"No, I did not defeat him. I released him from the shackles of ignorance that bound him in misery and anger."

The men talked among themselves for a few moments before replying. "Remain here tonight. We will let Milcho know you are here to visit him."

"Agreed, friends. We shall see you tomorrow then." Patrick waved and sat down. "We need some rest anyway after our travels up and down these hills." As he stifled a yawn.

"Father, there is a man and a boy that we found tonight on the far hilltop."

"Did you kill them?" Milcho replied.

"No, the man calls himself Bishop Patrick, and said he was here to visit you as a friend, He also said that he had been your slave?"

"A slave?" Milcho thundered. "I have only lost one slave, and even he must be dead long ago. He couldn't have been my slave."

"He knows King Dichu. I think he is the man that changed him."

"No, it can't be him!" Milcho spat. "He is coming to destroy me. Are you sure he said that I had enslaved him?"

"Yes, my lord, as your shepherd."

"Oh no. He is coming to change me like he did to poor Dichu. He is no longer the Savage, but a mere man now. I won't listen to the man. I won't allow him to desecrate my home. He was just a scrawny servant boy that I bought to herd my sheep. I never imagined that he could still be alive, or that he would ever amount to anything if he did live. Maewyn is coming to destroy my gods, my idols, my world! Do you hear?"

"Yes, sire."

"Gather all that I own and bring it here. Stack it up however it will fit. It will be a barricade that he cannot cross. Do it now." Milcho saw his sons hesitate. "I said now!" as he lashed out at them in a blind fury.

They scattered at their father's command. He was a hard man and still forceful, although he knew at times he succumbed to uncontrollable, irrational fears. He felt them welling up inside of him now, an irresistible force of terror taking control of his thoughts. He sat next to the central fire pit and fidgeted in a cold sweat as the men toiled and filled his house to overflowing.

"Is that everything?" Milcho asked when the men were silent for a while.

"Yes father, you are surrounded by all your possessions. Do you want us to clear a path to you, so you can get out?"

"No, go away. Go to your homes. My gods have shown me how to escape from that devil Maewyn this night." Laughing, Milcho picked up a burning log and thrust it into a large pile of flax.

———— • ● • ————

"No." Patrick whispered as shrieks of pain and yells in the distance woke him from a deep sleep. "Milcho, I hope you know that I forgave you years ago. I only wanted to bless you with the gift of God's goodness." Tears ran from his eyes as he sat and watched a massive tower of flames rise in the night sky. *Why do people like Micho refuse to know Truth? Maybe because they are more comfortable believing lies?*

Bard stirred in his sleep as Patrick sat and watched the blaze gradually die on the far hill. *We will return to Dichu tomorrow, my young friend. We have many more souls to save, but how many will refuse and perish?*

# Chapter 17
Journey to Tara

They returned to Saul Church with Patrick still feeling immersed in a cloud of defeat. A visibly distraught Dichu met them at the outskirts of the village.

"King Leogaire has kidnapped and imprisoned two of my sons, and also the sons of the other provincial chiefs that haven't captured you. Those of us living on all the lands that border his kingdom."

"Why?" Patrick asked, already knowing the answer.

"He is forcing us all to bow to his wishes, his idols and wizards. He is furious that we listened to you and allowed you to live." Dichu replied with his desperation evident. "He is already refusing to provide food and drink to the captives."

Patrick emitted a long sigh, turned away, and was silent for a number of minutes. When Dichu started to ask a question, Bard held up his hand and shook his head.

"They will have drink to slack their thirst tonight, and they will find themselves free to return to their homes very soon." Patrick announced as he finally turned around to face Dichu. "I guess it is finally time for me to visit this mighty King Leogaire. I will leave immediately."

"I and my men will accompany you," Dichu said as he raised his fists.

"No, I don't think that is wise. Stay here and protect your village. Bard, run to the church and bring me mother's banner."

"You can't go alone. He'll kill you on sight," Dichu argued. "His fortress is ringed with his supporter's lands. They won't let you pass."

"I am never alone; God is with me. Do you remember the story I told you about Elisha? **'And when the servant of the man of God was risen early, and gone forth, behold, an host compassed the city both with horses and chariots. And his servant said unto him, Alas, my master! how shall we do? And he answered, Fear not: for they that *be* with us *are* more than they that *be* with them. And Elisha prayed, and said, LORD, I pray thee, open his eyes, that he may see. And the LORD opened the eyes of the young man; and he saw: and, behold, the mountain *was* full of horses and chariots of fire round about Elisha.'** (30) I will be protected by the omnipotent power of the Lord."

"I can attest to that power. I'll never forget it." Dichu smiled.

"Don't worry, Brother Dichu, just take care of our fledgling flock here. I promise to return your lost sheep to your fold."

"Here it is." Bard announced as he trotted up next to Patrick carrying the large bundle.

"Give it to me, I want you to stay with Dichu while I am gone. I will be back soon. Be a good boy."

"No. I'm going with you."

"But Bard, this is more dangerous than any of the threats I've faced before. I have no idea what I might face."

"Do you think God won't protect me too?"

Feeling exasperated, Patrick replied, **"Out of the mouth of babes and sucklings hast thou ordained strength because of thine enemies, that thou mightest still the enemy and the avenger."** (31) "You are right, and I stand corrected." Turning back to Dichu he said, "Can you have someone fetch us some food for our journey?"

"Yes, immediately." The king said and waved a finger

at one of the women. "Do you want me to supply a guide?"

"Not if you can give me good directions. How do we get to King Leogaire?"

"He lives maybe one or two days southeast of here in in Tara, in the Skryne valley. He is the chief king of the island. Tara is the center of our high kings' banquets and celebrations. Our inauguration stone is there where all our kings are crowned."

Patrick suddenly tipped his head to the side and asked, "Are there any pagan celebrations that Leogaire will be observing soon?"

"Yes, their festival 'Rach', they celebrate as followers of the prince of darkness. On that night every fire will be extinguished in that province until a fire is lit first in Leogaire's palace. It will occur in two days."

"Interesting, that is very helpful, Father. We will follow your direction."

"Father?" Dichu asked as the woman returned with a satchel of food.

"Our Father/Mother God, friend Dichu. It was him who told me to ask about pagan celebrations. We must leave immediately," as Patrick accepted the bag from the woman. "Thank you," he said as he abruptly turned and began trudging away into the growing twilight.

"Don't you want to wait and travel in the daylight?" Dichu cried after him.

"We will be safer on our journey covered by the dark of night. Continue in your prayers for us and your children though."

Patrick and Bard walked along in silence through the gathering darkness until Patrick said, "Thank you, Bard, you are a real soldier of Christ."

"I have a good teacher," the boy replied as he carried the folded banner.

"Thank you but I don't think I…"

"Not you, our Savior. I can hear him too you know?" as

he cackled with laughter.

Patrick tried to keep a straight face but gave up as he felt a smile stretch wide. "I am proud of you, son, keep listening to him, not to me."

As the sun began to rise, they found a dense patch of willows next to a stream and crawled in among them to sleep. As dusk fell, they continued on across the creek and began to climb a steep mountain, studded with rocky outcroppings.

"Careful my boy, this is a treacherous trail."

"I'm alright. **'For he shall give his angels charge over thee, to keep thee in all thy ways. They shall bear thee up in *their* hands, lest thou dash thy foot against a stone.'** (32) That applies to both of us," he added.

Patrick gripped the rough edge of a boulder and wheezed as he drew himself up. "I was much lighter when I was sixteen so I hope the angels can still lift me." He laughed.

"They can do anything." Bard replied seriously.

Patrick wiped sweat from his eyes as he sought another foothold. *Thank you, God, for the lion in a boy's body. Another night of travel and we will be in the devil's lair. Protect us and deliver the innocents safely out of Leogaire's hand.*

## Chapter 18
Paschal Fire

It was late in the afternoon when Patrick crawled forward over a rocky crest and pointed to an expansive hillfort across a wide valley. "There, Bard, do you see that smoke rising in the distance? That's Tara, where the king's palace is."

"I see a hillfort and a lot of earthen structures. It looks massive."

"It should, it is the home of the most powerful king on this island."

"Halt, who be you?" a voice said.

"I am Patrick, Bishop of Hibernia, and you are?"

"You're the one who defeated Dichu?" the large man in leather armor said as his mouth fell open.

Patrick turned to Bard as he clambered up from the ground holding his staff. "Why does everyone say that?"

"You're famous," Bard snickered.

"…and you are?" Patrick repeated to the man.

"Cathal. I am sworn to protect King Leogaire." As he slowly withdrew a sword. "Are you here to kill my king?"

"No, we are here to ask for the return of the princes he has taken prisoner, and to give him the opportunity for eternal life, I swear it to you." Patrick said as he tightened his grip on the heavy oak staff.

"I have heard of you. I have fought alongside King Dichu and have trusted him with my life many times. I don't understand how a man of your weak stature defeated him. I don't understand why he follows you now instead of my king's wizards, but I do not approve the kidnapping of sons of kings." Suddenly the man loudly slapped the blade across his other palm and kneeled to offer up it to Patrick. "If you promise not to kill my king, I will be in your service."

"That I promise. Rise Cathal and here, meet my companion, Bard."

The two shook hands as Patrick asked, "Do you know of any Christian slaves on the surrounding farms?"

"There be slaves, but I know not if they are Cris-ti-anne," the man replied with difficulty as he replaced his sword.

Patrick stepped forward and gazed steadily into the sentry's eyes. "I don't want you to get into any trouble with your master. Don't tell anyone that you have seen us yet. Please continue making your security rounds through the various properties where slaves are housed and ask them to come here tonight under the cover of darkness. For a 'Christian' celebration," he enunciated. "Don't return here though, go and spend the night somewhere else that your master might expect you to be. Understand?"

"Yes, sire, thank you." The man bowed and began walking down the hill.

"Wait a moment Cathal, what do they call this place?"

"Feartfethin," guard called over his shoulder.

"What are we going to do?" Bard's small voice drifted up to his ears.

"Since this is the Sabbath before the Vigil of the Passover, we are going to build the biggest Paschal fire that we possibly can. See that dead tree over there? We'll start by dragging and stacking its fallen branches around its trunk."

As twilight gathered, they had a dense pile of branches and tree limbs that stood higher than Patrick entwined around the massive dead tree. "That should be good enough to start with. I hope we can get some help if we need more wood later."

Bard gave him a quizzical look but stayed silent.

"Where did I put my iron and flint?"

"Here, you told me to keep it for you. It is chilly tonight," he whispered.

"I don't know what I would do without you, my boy. While we still have a bit of light, hide the banner satchel somewhere safe. Then come back here. I'm not going to light this until we have full darkness."

Patrick shivered as he watched the sky darken with dense clouds that quickly obscured all fragments of moonlight. *A perfect night for Leogaire to worship the Prince of Darkness.* Fifteen minutes later when Bard dropped to his knees next him, Patrick began to strike the flint against the iron bar as Bard knelt low and softly blew on the smoking flax. In a few minutes they were rewarded as a tiny flame licked upwards. "Where did you hide the banner?"

"I found a cleft between two boulders below the brow of this hill."

"Let's go sit by our stashed ensign as our blessed beacon grows brighter to herald the approach of Easter morning."

"Wait." Bard grabbed Patrick's arm and pointed into the darkness. "Soldiers are coming."

As he peered into the darkness, he saw a few indistinct shapes moving slowly closer in the darkness. "Those aren't guards. Those are slaves. Look, there's another small group over there. Let us rise and greet our friends."

The flames climbed higher on the dry timber revealing more individuals scaling the hill. "Welcome friends to this holy night. Come closer and hear the words of the one true God!" Patrick walked in a wide circle around the flaming tree loudly cajoling them all to approach the burning signal of hope. "My friends, come close and pray with us. Christians are celebrating the works of Jesus on Hibernia tonight." Suddenly Patrick recalled the last words from St. Martin's scroll and spoke, ***"Awaken my children to the latent joy and power of Christianity. You are not mortals. You are spiritual creatures! Beauty lies beyond the Adam dream."*** *Those words will provide us with victory tonight and thank you God for guiding my sermon to these lost souls.*

# Chapter 19
Duel with a Wizard

"**W**hat is that?" The king fumed as he slammed a beefy fist onto a bench in his darkened palace. "Who is defying my order of darkness? Every flame should be extinguished until I decide to light one."

"My liege," one of his magicians answered. "Unless yonder fire be this night extinguished, he who lighted it will, together with his followers, reign over the whole island."

"That man has to be stopped!" The King roared. "It must be that Patrick fellow. He's trying to destroy our heritage, my power." Cursing the king continued to shout, "Call all my guards. Bring my arms. We ride to destroy those cursed rebels."

One of the guards hurried over. "Here are your weapons my king, the horses are being harnessed to the chariots."

"How many?" Leogaire spat.

"Twenty-seven, sire."

The king felt a wicked smile cross his lips. *A strong show of force to crush this little rebellion.* He yelled, "Those rebels will pay the price of defying my proclamation with pools of their blood. Mount up," as he leaped onto the lead chariot with his sword held high, the driver slapped the reins down on the horses' backs.

———•●•———

The dark clouds dissipated somewhat and bathed the surroundings in a cool white moonlight as the tree burned brightly. Suddenly, slaves were backing away from the towering fire, prepared to run for their lives as they watched the king's chariots approaching in the distance through the darkened valley. "Don't fear anyone but the Lord." Patrick announced in a booming voice and watched calmly as the pack of chariots raced toward him. "Some in chariots and some on horses; but we will invoke the name of the Lord," he said thinking of (33) ***"Some trust in chariots, and some in horses: but we will remember the name of the LORD our God."***

———•●•———

King Leogaire held tightly onto the rail of the chariot as it raced through the darkness toward the tower of flames in the distance. A brisk wind was blowing and caused his eyes to water. He swiped his other hand across his face to clear his vision. *I'll kill all of them, no one defies me and lives.*

A magician suddenly yelled to Leogaire from the chariot next to him. "Sire, it may be more desirous to ignore the group and gathering. This Bishop Patrick might slip away as dark as it is and escape into the night. The damage has been done, the fire is already lit for your subjects to view. We don't want our populous to believe that you are honoring a man with your presence, as with adoration or reverence. I believe you should send messengers unto this Patrick and command that he appear before you as nothing more than your subject. He would be more easily captured, punished or killed at your palace."

Gradually the thought appealed to the king as his driver

drew closer to the fire. *I like that, make him bow before me in my chambers and honor me as the infidel that he is. I will have to make some interesting plans for this 'Patrick,' I think. Like how best to kill him as a memorable example of my power for all my subjects to witness.* He could clearly see the small group gathered in the distance from the light of the burning tree. His chariots were halfway up the hillside when he made his decision. "Turn downhill driver." The king lifted his sword and waved it in a wide circle as all of his chariots churned the soft sod with their heavy wheels and curved away from the flaming tree.

---

"You may have saved our kingdom this night with your wise suggestion." The wizard said with a wide smile as he held tightly to the chariot's rail. "What is your name?"

"Cathal," his driver said.

---

Embers flickered in the massive pile of ashes in the early morning hours as Patrick blessed the final few slaves that had attended the holy fire and sent them away with heartfelt promises to pray for their deliverance. "A good night's work," he yawned to Bard who was already asleep. Hoofbeats woke him a few hours later as the sun began to rise.

"Are you Patrick the Bishop?" demanded the rider.

"Yes sir, and you are?"

"King Leogaire demands your presence at his castle this day. Don't make him wait." As the horseman rode off.

"It will take most of this day to walk to Tara." He yelled. *Pleasant chap, but always in too much of a hurry.* Patrick grinned at the sleepy visage of Bard. "I better take a chunk of dried venison for breakfast. I'll be back after you wake up." He whispered as he patted the exhausted boy's shoulder. Then he scribbled a short note on a large flat stone with a piece of charcoal from the burned tree and began to wander down the hill toward Tara.

———•●•———

"If that is your price, I agree to it, but you must kill him before he enters my palace so all the villagers can witness his death," the king stated flatly.

"I would be happy to destroy this enemy of yours for nothing, but I do have my reputation and pride sire." The wizard's evil grin showed rows of blackened teeth. "I am worth ten times the sum I ask. I will attack as soon as this bishop ventures near. Tell your subjects to come and witness the man's suffering and painful demise at my hands. The devil himself has linked arms with me in this mission. My master shall not allow me to fail," The man's wild eyes bore through King Leogaire for a long moment, and the king began to uncontrollably shiver before the magician turned with an abrupt flourish and marched away. *Lochu was a lunatic, a self-declared god of Satan, and the most powerful dark wizard in his kingdom. Surely, he would be able to destroy this upstart, Patrick.* Leogaire took a deep breath to calm his nerves and smiled as he shivered again. *Lochu had enough magical power to destroy anyone.*

Patrick had just passed a small grove of trees on his walk to Tara in the early afternoon. He saw a small crowd gathered ahead, blocking his way into the village. A skinny man with wild hair, dressed in dark colors stood in front of the group making strange hand movements and chanting rapidly. "Hello, I am Patrick, Bishop of Hibernia. King Leogaire asked that I visit him this morning."

"I am Lochu, lord over all the king's magicians. He asked that I cordially greet you, Patrick, before I exterminate you." He laughed maniacally and twirled in a circle. "My master Beelzebub hates you, your followers, and your impotent God." Leaning backwards with his arms outstretched he screamed. "My Lord, Satan, send out your demons and minions to lift me up on the clouds of your darkness." Then he pointed at the crowd and sneered, "You peasants watch closely as I destroy this interloper who threatens our king and our gods."

Patrick stared as the man twirled faster and gradually lifted off the ground. He was calm as he thought, ***"Thus saith the LORD unto you, Be not afraid nor dismayed by reason of this great multitude; for the battle is not yours, but God's."*** (34) *God will defend me from your legions of demons, wizard.* A collective gasp came from the crowd as many of them knelt in reverence to the exhibition of dark wizardry. The magician wasn't spinning now, but gained height and flew toward him, still making strange hand movements and chanting incessantly, as the air itself seemed electrified.

"Oh, omnipotent God! Destroy this blasphemer of Thine holy name, or let him hinder or hurt those true believers who now return or may hereafter return unto Thee!"

Suddenly, the magician seemed to lose control and violently jerked in midair as his incantations became loud calls of help, "Satan, what is happening? Hold me up. Don't let me fall. Help me," were his last words as he dropped from the sky and fell at the feet of Patrick. The wizard's head hit a large flat stone and made a sound like a ripe melon hitting a rock. His terrible eyes focused on Patrick with a look of confusion as he mouthed, "How?" and quickly passed away. Patrick stood still and watched as the crowd crept forward to view the carcass. "The power of the one true God is omnipotent. **'As the whirlwind passeth, so *is* the wicked no *more*: but the righteous *is* an everlasting foundation.'** (35) Put blasphemy and witchcraft behind you and join us. I see how your king welcomes me, but his gods and idols shall be defeated, just as this wizard was." Looking up, he saw Leogaire running toward him with a large company of men and sensed the murderous thoughts of the people as he shouted, **"Let God arise, let his enemies be scattered: let them also that hate him flee before him."** (36) A lightning bolt suddenly struck next to the group as Patrick continued, **"Yea, he sent out his arrows, and scattered them; and he shot out lightnings, and discomfited them."** (37) As the crowd paused, he said. "King Leogaire, kneel before God. **'Know ye not that the unrighteous shall not inherit the kingdom of God? Be not deceived: neither fornicators, nor idolaters,'** (38) Repent while you still can and lead your subjects from their false gods." More lightning bolts hit the ground in rapid succession, as the king turned and fled back to the village. Discipline lost, the crowd shoved and trampled over each other as they battled their way back to the safety of their homes.

Patrick stood silently in the calm following the maelstrom, urgently praying for harmony, when he saw a lone figure approaching. "Do you wish to join us?"

"I do," said the queen as she knelt before him. "Please bless me and forgive my husband the king. His pride makes him extremely unwise at times. I will tell him to come and pray for forgiveness from your God."

"Bless you my child, God forgives actions sincerely repented. I will be most grateful if you will send him to me." She rose and called to Leogaire who finally crept forward from a darkened doorway. Patrick watched the man's eyes shift from side to side as he approached. "You're a very lucky man. Your queen is a marvelous and intelligent woman. She reminds me of Abigail."

"Who is Abigail?"

"She was the beautiful wife of a stingy rich man named Nabal who was asked by David for some provisions for his troops since they were protecting him, but the man refused to give anything away. So, David decided to kill Nabal and take all of his possessions. Abigail heard what Nabal had done, and do you know what she did?"

"How could I?" the king sneered as he dropped to his knees.

"I will tell you, my son. Abigail left her house and took two hundred loaves, some wine, and five sheep, along with parched *corn,* and raisins, and cakes of figs, and packed it all up on donkeys, and left for David's camp without telling her husband. When Abigail saw David, she jumped off the ass, and fell before David on her face, and bowed herself to the ground. She told him that she had brought all the gifts for the men who followed him. She also told him that God was going to make him ruler over Israel, and that he shouldn't shed blood for worthless vengeance that would make him feel grief. **'And David said to Abigail, Blessed** *be* **the LORD God of Israel, which sent thee this day to meet me:'** (39) Abigail expressed a humility that day which allowed her house, even her brutal, greedy husband to survive. She listened to God for direction and acted immediately on his guidance. Will you be blessed and follow the one true God, forsaking all pagan idols, and witchcraft in your future?"

"I… will," the king replied, but the man's hesitation was evident to Patrick.

"I do not believe that your heart is true. Nevertheless, I will bless you and trust that the Lord will constrain you from the evils you envision."

"Thank you, Patrick, I will do my best."

*To kill me.* "I know you will, son, but you will not succeed, nor your evil magicians." He saw the man's visage turn vicious but remain silent. "In this life, or the next, you will embrace the Truth. Now, go back to your duties, I will see you soon enough." The king arose, grabbed the hilt of his sword, then dropped his gaze and walked off. He stopped a few steps later and said, "Return here tomorrow to baptize my queen and I."

"I go when and where the Lord leads and commands me. I will see you soon though."

# Chapter 20
## Fire and Water

Patrick returned to find Bard in a frenzy standing beside the large pile of ashes that surrounded the blackened, smoking tree trunk.

"Why didn't you wake me? I didn't know when or if you would be back."

"I left you a note on the rock."

"I saw it."

"The king asked that I pay him an urgent visit today. So, I went. Did you sleep well?" he stifled a yawn.

"You should have told me." The boy fretted.

"You were sleeping, it was fine, both the queen and the king actually kneeled for a blessing."

"Really? They didn't attack you? I wish I could have seen the king kneel before you."

"Well, they sent a dark wizard out to attack me first. He was flying toward me, but somehow, he fell down and died."

"Oh please, if you don't want to tell me about it, don't. I'm not going to listen to some fairytale." Bard wrinkled his nose.

"Right, let's forget it for now." Patrick's joints ached as he sat down heavily, leaning back against a large, flat rock. "Let me get some rest for a while my boy. The king asked me to visit him tomorrow. I will ask God. Maybe we will go back tomorrow, but probably the next day."

———•●•———

"I should have killed him myself when he lit that fire!" Leogaire heard himself thunder. "Why did you stop me?" He watched the magician cower before him.

"Sire, we couldn't have shown him any consideration, we can't honor him in any way or if he should escape, he could raise an army against us. We need to discredit him, somehow show everyone that he is powerless against you."

"That is what Lochu tried to do, and the idiot got himself killed. Now all of my subjects are terrified of this bishop."

"Lochu was too flamboyant, he was always on the verge of losing control of his dark powers. I agree he was powerful, but extremely careless. I am much more reserved. This bishop doesn't scare me."

"You are stupid then. He swatted Lochu from the sky like a fly."

"I am wise in the ways of both men and the inhabitants of the spirit world. I will not take foolish chances in our contest."

"Contest? That is a wonderful idea. I will announce a contest where you and the bishop are pitted against each other, and where the winner takes all. You better win Lugaich," he growled as he watched the man swallow and nod his head vigorously. "What events do you propose?"

———•●•———

Patrick and Bard entered the village of Tara around noon on the second day. A bard was strumming and pouring forth a song that praised idols and false gods as they walked past. The man paused his song and ran over to Patrick. "Your eminence, I saw your battle with Lochu. I saw him fall from the sky and die at your feet. Then I watched as the crowd rushed forward to kill you, but you defeated them all with your God's bolts of lightning. Please, will you make me a follower of Him. I promise to only sing songs of praise to Him from now on."

Patrick watched Bard's mouth fall open as he said, "Yes, brother, I will bless you here and now. What songs will fill your heart for our Lord?"

"I need to learn more of him, but I feel he is a God of peace, love, harmony, protection and health. The opposite of the dark idols we were forced to worship by our king."

"Bless you and your desire to know God. You are correct my son. I'll baptize you soon, but I feel I have more pressing issues at the moment." He watched as the smiling king approached with another man swathed completely in black robes.

"Bishop Patrick, my friend. Allow me to introduce you to Lugaish Mael. He has many believers among my subjects. He suggested that you two might have a friendly competition to prove to all of us whose God or gods are more powerful."

"I'm afraid there is no friendship between light and darkness. Light destroys darkness, just as good destroys evil."

"Darkness can veil the light and destroy it." Lugaish uttered quickly from beneath his hood.

"Do you really believe that?"

"I live to extinguish the flames of goodness with the darkness of my lord, the Devil. There is one other thing you should know, unlike Lochu, I have always been successful at it." The magician's sly smile revealed several missing teeth. A large crowd was quickly forming around them.

"Maybe that was the only time Lochu failed?" Patrick shot back. "King Leogaire, **'The thief cometh not, but for to steal, and to kill, and to destroy: I am come that they might have life, and that they might have *it* more abundantly.'** (40) I only came here today to baptize you and your subjects as Christians, not to play games or produce an entertainment spectacle."

"Nevertheless, if you refuse the challenge, you leave me no choice other than to declare the dark wizard Lugaish the winner, and his gods as the champions of this land." The king smiled sadly.

Patrick closed his eyes and prayed for a few moments, *Father, what should I do?* Then his eyes snapped open. "Alright, you leave me no choice other than participation. What will be the first challenge?"

"Bring down signs from the heavens above," the magician's scratchy voice demanded."

"I will not tempt the Lord for your amusement."

"Look at me all of you. This bishop is afraid to perform his magic, but I will show you now what our gods can do." He began chanting in earnest as heavy clouds gathered and snow began to fall. The temperature quickly fell below freezing.

"Stop this cold and snow! Is this your only trick?" Patrick bellowed as he watched the villagers, and Bard, hug their clothing tighter around them.

The wizard sneered and refused to answer.

"Oh, you can work iniquity for Satan, wizard, and can cause evil, but you cannot replace that evil with good. I do not use magic, but only express to you the good of works of a loving God." Dropping his gaze to the ground, he stooped down and grabbed a three-leaf clover. Raising his hand Patrick said, "Do you people all see the three leaves of this clover? Always remember to bless this land with goodness for all of its inhabitants with the following three names: The Father, the Son, and the Holy Ghost." Immediately, a strong warm wind began to blow the clouds away. As the sun returned, the snow melted, and the temperature returned to normal.

"Hogswallow," the magician yelled. But his words were drowned out in loud sounds of gratitude, as all the people thanked Patrick for dispersing the bitter cold. The magician began chanting loudly once more. A dense cloud quickly formed and enveloped their surroundings in darkness.

Patrick closed his eyes; unimpressed as fearful murmurings spread around him. Patrick remembered when *"Moses stretched forth his hand toward heaven; and there was a thick darkness in all the land of Egypt three days:"* (41) Then he announced in a loud voice, "You are a fledgling of the devil, magician. You may be able to create the illusion of his dark power on earth, but it will never be real since Satan, **'he is a liar, and the father of it.'** (42) Dear Lord, remove this false darkness with the light of Truth." Immediately bright rays of sunlight began to pierce the thick fog and disperse it. The crowd began to cheer for Patrick once again.

Lugaich scoffed at the beams of light when they appeared. "My master is lord of this world. His mighty wicked and perverse powers can snuff out your light anytime he wants to. He only toys with you bishop." Turning to the crowd he raised his arms and snarled, "And you peasants, I can destroy you all, right now." As the crowd shrank backward in fear.

"Gentlemen, this is going nowhere. We must know which of you is the most powerful," King Leogaire shouted as he threw a withering glare at the magician. "Don't make my subjects suffer anymore, either one of you. Decide on a contest that is agreeable to both of you. We need to know which of you is more powerful."

"Good versus evil. That is an uneven contest." Patrick smiled.

The king spoke, "Take your sacred books and let them be thrown into water. The writings that survive the liquid, let that man's preaching be believed."

Patrick nodded in agreement.

"No, he wants to baptize you in water, this bishop worships water and he shall bend it to his will," the wizard cried.

The king spoke again, "Then you both shall throw your sacred books into a fire, and the book that survives, let it be the doctrine across this land."

"We cannot, for this bishop also worships fire and will bend it to his will."

Patrick felt a smile cross his lips. "Let it be known that I worship no material element. Not the earth, fire, air or water. I only worship the one true God."

"He lies. I will not assent to such a challenge," The magician fumed.

The king was becoming more distraught as he shouted. "What do you suggest the contest should be, wizard?"

The grubby man rubbed his chin thoughtfully and responded. "This is a contest between good and evil, innocence and sin." He grinned. "Let us have a trial by fire and water, between innocence and sin. Let us build a house that is half green wood and the other half dry and eaten with worms. This innocent bishop shall stand in the dry part, and I in the other while it is set afire. We shall see whose powers are greatest."

"This contest I cannot agree to. Only because I am not innocent, I am only forgiven by God," Patrick replied.

"Then let an innocent take your place." Lugaich grabbed Bard by the shoulders and pulled him into the center of the group. "Sire, you will tie this young man and me back-to-back onto the center wall, let this challenge begin."

"So be it," the king decreed before Patrick could respond. "Hurry all of you and build the house. The survivor shall proclaim his doctrine across my kingdom." A cheer went up as a group of the king's servants left to gather the needed building materials.

Bard wrestled himself free from the magician's grip and ran to embrace Patrick. "Don't worry, my boy. This is God's plan, and Jesus stands with us, remember?" He winked.

In several hours a small hut was constructed with two

small rooms. Bard stood quietly in the dry side and the magician stood with his back against the wall in the green wood section. Stretching out their arms, the king tied their wrists to a heavy crossbeam in the common wall separating them.

"Are you ready?" the king inquired.

"Ready, sire," the magician answered in a self-assured voice.

Patrick watched Bard make a small nod, as he continued to pray for the boy's protection. The story of Shadrach, Meshach, and Abed-nego popped into his thoughts. ***"Then Nebuchadnezzar the king was astonied, and rose up in haste, and spake, and said unto his counsellors, Did not we cast three men bound into the midst of the fire? They answered and said unto the king, True, O king. He answered and said, Lo, I see four men loose, walking in the midst of the fire, and they have no hurt; and the form of the fourth is like the Son of God."*** (43) *Nebuchadnezzar died five- and one-half centuries before Jesus. Maybe that's why Jesus said,* ***"Verily, verily, I say unto you, Before Abraham was, I am."*** (44) *Maybe he was actually walking with those Hebrew boys too?*

The king then touched a torch to the common wall separating Bard and the wizard.

Flames flared as the tinder dry wood ignited, and Patrick's heart sank for a moment as he heard the wizard laugh manically inside. A few seconds later though, the green wood also began to smoke heavily. The fire on the tinder dry wood was quickly snuffed out as a strong wind suddenly blew across the hillside. At the same time a hot blaze erupted across the face of the green wood wall as the steady breeze fed a growing inferno.

"No, master. Reverse the flames. Green wood should not burn. I am your faithful servant, Lugaisch. Defeat this bishop and kill the boy. Protect me!" Patrick listened in anguish as he heard the magician's desperate pleas, coughs, and screams gradually quiet as heavy smoke poured from the green wood end of the building. That half of the building suddenly collapsed in a shower of sparks and Bard raced out of the structure, with smoking ropes still clinging to his wrists.

"You did it," he said excitedly.

Kneeling down, Patrick hurriedly loosened the glowing ropes and threw them on the ground, "No, my son, God is our only protection." As he hugged the boy tightly amid the inhabitants' cheers. Out of the corner of his eye, he saw the king glare at him. *So, the battle is not yet over.* He sighed.

"Tomorrow, the victor, Bishop Patrick will return to us and explain his doctrine of the one true God. I expect you all to attend." The king announced without exuberance, followed by the murmured voices of the crowd the people began to disperse into the gathering twilight.

"It will be two days before our return to this village, and please send a chariot to pick us up, we are tired of walking." Patrick said in a loud voice and bowed graciously to the king before he and Bard turned and walked away.

"How was I protected?" Bard finally asked when they were about a mile away from the village.

"I thought of several things while I prayed for your deliverance. The first was of course the story of the three boys who wouldn't worship King Nebuchadnezzar's golden idol."

"I remember that story. The king heated the furnace seven times hotter than ever before. Then he had his strongest guards bind them and throw them into the furnace!"

"Yes, it was said that those guards were killed by the flames because the fire was so hot. Then the king looked and saw four men walking around in the flames. He called them **'servants of the most high God. And the princes, governors, and captains, and the king's counsellors, being gathered together, saw these men, upon whose**

**bodies the fire had no power, nor was an hair of their head singed, neither were their coats changed, nor the smell of fire had passed on them.'** (45) Only the ropes that bound them burned off."

"Just like the ropes burned off my wrists."

"By the way, did you see Jesus walking around in there while you were tied to the wall?

"No, but I did remember that you said he was traveling with us. Believe me, I prayed that he was with me." Bard clasped his hands together.

"I know that he was and is, son."

# Chapter 21
Lord's Prayer

Patrick and Bard once again retreated to the site of the Paschal fire by walking throughout the night. The horizon was becoming lighter as they finally reached the scorched trunk. Bard found a stick and shoved it through the deep pile of ash until he had a small pile of glowing coals pushed into a pile. Then he gathered other twigs and sticks until he had a nice roaring fire built. He and Patrick sat next to it and shared a meal of stale bread and nuts, along with a few strips of dried venison.

"Did you think about anything else while I was tied to that evil wizard?"

"I prayed on several things. One was the story of John the Divine. He and his brother James were disciples of Jesus and sons of Zebedee the fisherman. When John was ninety years old, Emperor Domitian ordered him to be boiled alive in a large cauldron of oil. The vessel was filled with oil, pitch and resin as a fire burned beneath it. A large crowd watched as the old man was whipped and led toward the cauldron. After John had been dropped into the boiling liquid, the flames obscured the vision of John from the crowd, but they heard a voice singing. More fuel was piled onto the fire and the heat was unbearable around the pot as steam and smoke rose into the air, but the voice continued singing hymns of praise. Finally, when the fire burned out. The crowd ventured up to the cauldron and stared inside. The liquid had boiled away, but the aged man sat quietly in the midst of the vessel, completely unharmed."

"How was that possible?"

Patrick watched doubt reflected in the boy's face. "Your experience with the wizard didn't teach you anything?"

"What else did you pray when I was tied to that wizard?" Bard asked with a touch of irritation.

"I was earnestly praying the prayer our master taught us, the Lord's prayer." Patrick confessed.

"I remember it, but it doesn't say anything about magicians or fire or stupid contests. How did that help?"

"Those things are covered in that prayer, along with all the ills that mankind faces every day. Do you want to know what I think it is really saying?" Bard nodded in silence.

"**'Our Father which art in heaven, Hallowed be thy name.'** What does that mean to you, my boy?" Bard shrugged his shoulders as he stared at Patrick. "It means our God dwells in harmony, in perfect concepts of Love, Life, Abundance, Harmony, Perfection, Bliss. Above our human, limited visions of material life, and his names are to be revered. **'Thy kingdom come. Thy will be done in earth, as *it is* in heaven.'** This is bringing the harmony of God's spiritual kingdom to our experience in this world. Expressing Love, safety, healing and peace in our lives. Also, the protection which you experienced today," he added. **'Give us this day our daily bread.'** Of course, this is providing us with what we need in our lives, food, shelter, but also with the experiences that help us to grow in God's grace and to help others. Meeting new people, sharing the gospel, breaking bread to inform and bless. **'And forgive us our debts, as we forgive our debtors.'** I sinned as a young man, and God has forgiven me, even though I still sometimes struggle to forgive myself. I had to forgive those magicians that wanted to kill me, and the king who directed them to try. Forgiveness frees the soul to think higher thoughts and to touch ideas from heaven. **'And lead us not into temptation, but deliver us from evil:'** Again, we both experienced deliverance from evil thoughts and actions today. This is also a prayer not to be tempted by the idols and lures of this world that pull our attention away from godlike thoughts that make us wallow in selfishness and self-love until the heavy load of pain or shame points our attention toward Spirit again."

"I know, when I think about girls." Bard grumbled.

Patrick just smiled and continued. **"'For thine is the kingdom, and the power, and the glory, for ever.'** God is infinite and omnipotent. He is the substance, force and intelligence of all things, forever. We live in Him, and if we are made in His image, we are spiritual beings, rather than these mortal shells which we all display." (46)

"Too much to remember," Bard said sleepily.

"It is infinite possibilities, but also simple directions," Patrick replied as he gently patted the boys head before nodding off to sleep.

# Chapter 22
The Gift

Patrick awoke to the sounds of horse's hooves approaching on the second morning. "Bard, our transportation will arrive soon. Hurry and grab our bundle that you hid in the rocks. I think we should present it to the king and queen as a gift," Patrick said as he began gathering a few of his belongings. "Do you think you understand the Lord's prayer now?"

Bard rubbed the sleep from his eyes before he ran over to the boulders, shifted a large flat rock to the side, and pulled out the package beneath it. Running back to Patrick, he said, "I understand more, but I can't remember everything clearly. I was pretty tired after yesterday's adventure."

"Proud of you, son. Here I can carry that for you."

"No, I have to help the 'Bishop of Hibernia', that is my task in this life."

"Only for a while my young friend. In a few years, I will release you from my service here and ask that you perform a holy assignment for me in Briton."

"Leave you here?" a quaver was noticeable in Bard's voice.

"We all must do the Lord's work, sometimes that means separating, so we can add more glory to the remnant of Israel and extend His family of worshippers."

"But what can I do?"

"You are going to protect my most valuable artifact and

see that it is safe for future generations. Don't worry about it now though. You and I are going to travel across this island for decades before that happens. I just wanted you to know that at some point you will be free to chase girls," he smiled.

"Is the artifact the scroll?" Bard asked as his face reddened.

"Yes, Saint Martin's scroll, now let us prepare ourselves with prayer for our meeting with the king and the inhabitants of Tara." Patrick said as they waited until the chariot stopped a few feet away, and they climbed aboard.

"Cathal, I didn't expect you to be our driver?"

"I asked to be allowed this task. I have heard the stories of your battles with the wizards, and I wish to be baptized today."

Patrick looked deep into the man's eyes and felt a rush of joy. "It will be my honor to welcome you into the world of Christianity, my son."

A few hours later, Cathal drew back on the reins until the horses stopped at the entrance of the city.

"Hail King Leogaire. Are you ready to join us in worshipping the one true God?"

"I am ready to listen to your doctrine, Patrick, as are my subjects." The king replied without much enthusiasm.

Patrick raised his arms and motioned for the crowd to draw nearer as he began speaking. **"Thus saith the Lord GOD; Repent, and turn *yourselves* from your idols; and turn away your faces from all your abominations."** (47) **"And what agreement hath the temple of God with idols? for ye are the temple of the living God; as God hath said, I will dwell in them, and walk in *them;* and I will be their God, and they shall be my people."** (48) **"God *is* a Spirit: and they that worship him must worship *him* in spirit and in truth."** (49)

Patrick watched the crowd as he spoke and felt an overwhelming sense of Love for all the men and women living in darkness as he continued his sermon. **"The Spirit**

**of the Lord *is* upon me, because he hath anointed me to preach the gospel to the poor; he hath sent me to heal the brokenhearted, to preach deliverance to the captives, and recovering of sight to the blind, to set at liberty them that are bruised,"** (50) **"Beware of false prophets, which come to you in sheep's clothing, but inwardly they are ravening wolves. Wherefore by their fruits ye shall know them."** (51) At the end he offered to bless his audience immediately, followed by baptism in the nearby river of all who sincerely wanted to become Christians. The queen approached first along with the king's brother, and a long line of people quickly formed behind them. After blessing her, she stood off to the side to await the baptism, and most of the people joined her, reverently waiting in silence.

The last man was the king himself, who came forward unsteadily, and knelt before Patrick. The queen hurried over to his side and placed her hand on his shoulder.

"My king, I have not come to destroy you, nor to give your power to any other, but to give you eternal life. You have thwarted and challenged me and tried to kill me before the faces of your people. I can see that you will never abandon your idols, or your beliefs in darkness, and yet I will now bless you, although I cannot baptize you into the church."

"I understand." The king said as he kneeled before Patrick. "I am a good man, I want the best for my subjects, but somehow I can't give up the gods of my fathers, however impotent they appear to be."

"Bless you King Leogaire. Because of your humility and truthfulness, I do want to give you and your subjects one of my most precious gifts. This image is of the blessed mother of Jesus." Patrick motioned to Bard, who began to unfold the fabric as the queen and others rushed over to help him spread it out.

The king gazed transfixed, staring at the beautiful, beaded image. "I promise my people and I will raise you a church to display this treasure," he said quietly, looking quite overcome with emotion. "Who made it?"

"My mother. She began creating it after I was taken into slavery on this island. Display it as a token of love from me and my family to you and your people."

The king shook hands with Patrick. "Agreed, I'll try to remember that beauty is always better than darkness. I'm sorry for…"

"No need to apologize, sire. We all must be open to where Truth leads us." Patrick watched as the joyful queen hurried back to kiss her husband on his cheek.

"Never worship it as an idol though. Only tell your people to worship a spiritual God. The Lord of Truth, Life and Love. Do you promise?"

"Yes Patrick, I so swear." The king answered with a grateful smile as he arose and wrapped a loving arm around his wife.

# Chapter 23
Accusation

"Now we return to Sabhail church?" Bard asked as they walked away from Tara.

"Yes, I will send a couple of my advanced acolytes back to begin a ministry here. Leogaire's subjects shouldn't have any trouble getting a church built with their guidance, and soon, mother's image of Mary will be hanging inside for all to see." Patrick waved to several of the slaves he recognized from the night of the Paschal fire as he passed by.

"Why did you give that beautiful hanging to an unbeliever, do you think he ever will accept Christ?"

"He is the chief king in this land, and his followers and contacts are many. He accepted my gift and is building a church for God's children to gather, thus other kingdoms in this land will more readily accept the word of the Lord. **But now the LORD my God hath given me rest on every side,** *so that there is* **neither adversary nor evil occurrent.'** (52) He may not ever believe in the one true God, but he is helping to advance our ministry."

"Do you hate him?"

"There is nothing to hate. Sure, he tried to have me killed, but I can only pity a man who would rather live surrounded with his fears, than to try and understand reality."

Bard slipped on a loose rock and went down onto one

knee before bouncing back up. "Where will we travel next?"

"I'd like to visit my sister Darercha; she is living on the island of Valentia. I wonder if she is married yet?"

"How old is she?" Bard asked too quickly.

"Too old for you, young man. Be patient, your time will come."

When they reached Saul, they entered the church and kneeled to pray before the altar. Dichu entered the church and ran forward to them. "Bishop, my boys came back just as you said they would. One of King Leogaire's guards smuggled small amounts of water to sustain them, and then dropped a broken piece of pottery into their cell a few days later. They used it to cut the leather cords binding the wooden staves they were held behind. Thank you." He said in a voice choked with emotion.

Patrick wondered if it had been Cathal.

"Also, this letter came for you shortly after you left." Dichu continued.

"From the Church High Council in Briton. I wonder if they are sending more priests to help us expand our ministry?" Patrick hands shook with excitement as he tore open the wax seal and quickly read the message. Suddenly, he crushed the letter and clenched his eyes closed in anger.

"What is it?" Bard and Dichu asked in unison.

For a few long moments he was silent as he calmed himself. "They have commanded me to return to Briton to face a tribunal for my sin." He snorted and tossed the crumpled note behind the altar.

"What sin?" Dichu spurted.

Weakness enveloped him as he answered. "Years ago, before I was taken into slavery, I committed a sin which I confessed to no man. I kept it as my coveted secret until my first years of catechesis, religious training. Then I felt bound to confess my sin to a fellow priest and clear my conscience before continuing my studies. I considered that priest to be a trustworthy friend who would never divulge my transgression to others. Apparently, I was wrong."

"Will you go back?" Bard asked with a worried look.

"I will have to earnestly pray about it. Please leave me alone for now." He said quietly, as he began shuffling toward the west wall of the church. He placed his back against the wall and slid down the rough timbers. Feeling splinters grab at his cloak until he finally sat on the cold stone floor.

He was tired of walking, of preaching, of living. His back rubbed against the rough timbers as he sat still on the floor and folded his hands. Where was the gratitude he should experience? His life was filled with nothing but constant toil and suffering, and a few awful battles with wizards. He forced a laugh. The power was God's, and he lived and moved in that power. "Dear God help me." As he thought, ***"Fear thou not; for I* am *with thee: be not dismayed; for I* am *thy God: I will strengthen thee; yea, I will help thee; yea, I will uphold thee with the right hand of my righteousness. Behold, all they that were incensed against thee shall be ashamed and confounded: they shall be as nothing; and they that strive with thee shall perish. Thou shalt seek them, and shalt not find them,* even *them that contended with thee: they that war against thee shall be as nothing, and as a thing of nought. For I the LORD thy God will hold thy right hand, saying unto thee, Fear not; I will help thee."*** (53) His eyes grew heavy as he wrestled for hours with his thoughts, until he finally drifted off to sleep.

"That's it." he cried aloud as he awoke and struggled to his feet. Rummaging behind the altar he found a quill and some ink. Smoothing the crumpled letter out, he began writing on the back of it:

*Dearest Brothers in Christ,*
*I received your dispatch, requesting my return to the shores of Briton for possible disciplinary action. How I stridently wish myself to be in a position to acquiesce to your*

*request. I hopelessly wish to return to Briton, to visit my beloved home and parents, and even to return to Gaul and see the faces of the saints which I knew. Alas, I cannot because I am given this holy mission among these people who never understood God but have in their ignorance served idols and unclean things.*

*As for the charge of sin against me. It is true. Thirty years ago, before becoming a Deacon, I finally confessed my sin to a dear friend of mine. Knowing that he would never reveal it to any man, but only to God in his prayers for me. I now grieve for my friend, the one person I entrusted my secret to. The close friend who also told me I had been given the rank of bishop. I forgive him because the temptation of man always seems to tear down, rather than build.*

*As I prayed for guidance in this matter, I fell asleep and saw a vision of writing before my face and heard this answer from God. "We have seen with displeasure the face of the one who was chosen deprived of his good name." Did you notice that He said I was chosen for this mission? Thus, it is with a heavy heart that I must ignore your pleas for my return, only to be judged by a panel of mere mortals. I have been adjudicated by Supreme law and forgiven in this matter. I will continue to serve in humility the inhabitants of Hibernia for as long as our Lord wills it.*

*With all sincerity and prayers for your well-being,*
*Patrick, Bishop of Hibernia*

"Bard, are you there?"

"Yes sir." Bard entered abruptly.

"We are staying. I will not abandon my ministry. Find Dichu, I am ready to send my response to the Bishops' Council in Briton."

# Chapter 24
## Two Dead Women

"How far is it to Valentia Island?" Bard asked as they strode out of the village in an early morning fog that shrouded the nearby hills.

"If we minister to the masses along the way, it may be a very long journey. I have a feeling that we will be blessed with many opportunities to help others."

"So, you mean it will be a very long time before we return," Bard said flatly.

"I'm afraid so, why? Is there a young girl on your mind?" Patrick watched as the boy's cheeks flushed red. "I understand what you are feeling, but we must follow His direction. If it is from God, a right idea, it will unfold."

Bard looked unconvinced but dutifully trudged on.

Patrick taught, preached, and performed healings in many villages and groups as they traveled toward the Southwest corner of Ireland for almost a week. On the morning of the seventh day, he and Bard arrived at a place called Fearta. A group of men were just finishing patting dirt atop two fresh graves on the side of a hill, as a small crowd of villagers looked on. Some were crying, while others talked in hushed voices. "Good day to you gentlemen. Can you tell me who has passed on?"

"Who is asking?" came the reply from one of the men.

"He is Patrick, Bishop of Hibernia." Bard shot back.

"I've heard of him." One of the men said in a low voice to the others. "He performs miracles. He defeated two of King Leogaire's wizards."

"Again, I ask who has passed?" Patrick persisted, as he watched the men share questioning looks among themselves.

One of the men finally removed his hat, bowed and stepped forward. "These be the resting places of two of the finest women from our village. They took sick a fortnight ago and died."

Patrick walked forward and commanded. "Please, can you remove the dirt from both of their graves."

"For what purpose?" the man asked aghast, as all of their eyes narrowed in suspicion.

"To show you that life is eternal, right?" Bard said quickly looking at Patrick.

"Please remove the dirt, so I may see both of them. Here, I will pay you for your extra toil as he distributed coins to each of them." Patrick was grateful when the men pocketed the money, picked up their loys, and began scraping the sod away from the bodies. As the last of the dirt was carefully removed, he asked, "Please, can you lift them up onto the ground."

Protests began to rise in their throats, but under the stern stare of Patrick, they knelt down and pulled the carcasses up onto the grass.

Patrick raised his arms as he addressed the crowd. "Thank you, ladies and gentlemen. Some of you have heard of me. My name is Bishop Patrick, and I am a servant of the one true God, and his son Jesus the Christ. In the name of Jesus, as in the miracle of Lazarus where Jesus said **'I am the resurrection and the life: he that believeth in me, though he were dead, yet shall he live: Father, I thank thee that thou hast heard me.'** (54) I want you all to know that Life is eternal, just as God is. Watch as I say unto these ladies, **'Awake thou that sleepest, and arise from the dead, and Christ shall give thee light.'** (55) Awaken!"

For a few moments silence ensued, and then one of the corpses coughed and began to move its arms. A collective gasp came from the group of villagers as the other cadaver suddenly sneezed. The men backed away in fear as Patrick walked forward, knelt and said, "No, loose them and let them go." As he began to gently loosen the fabric wrapped around the first woman's face.

"What is going on?" the woman asked as soon as her mouth was uncovered. Bard ran forward and began to quickly free the other lady.

"You and your friend have been recalled to Life as examples of the power of God." Patrick motioned to the crowd. "Come forward and welcome your sisters who have returned to you."

The crowd moved slowly forward, led by the gravediggers. Once the two women were standing on their feet, the people quickly crowded around, hugging them and crying freely. Patrick was inundated with questions about the sudden resurrections. As the people quieted, he began to teach them about the Christ and its ability to heal and restore people's lives, even after the transformation called death. The two women whom he had raised, supported his claims and proclaimed that what they learned in death was that their gods were devils and their idols impotent. He announced that the idols were false deities, and the gods of their fathers were powerless to create anything but evil. He offered to usher them all into Christ's kingdom, and soon, all the villagers were eagerly baptized and glorified the Lord in a celebration that lasted far into the night.

"How?" was Bard's only comment as they settled down to sleep under a large tree much later.

Patrick knew what his question was. "You and the others saw dead bodies; I saw them as living expressions of Life. Life is a quality of God and needs to be expressed by everyone. You know it says, **'So God created man in his *own* image, in the image of God created he him; male and**

**female created he them.'** (56) God is eternal Life, and people are created in His own image and substance. Created in Spirit, not in matter that can suffer and die. The devils are subject to me because I see them as impotent lies, pretending that there is a separation between God and man. As you and I approached that hillside, I felt those ladies couldn't be dead in Christ. They had to express Life, understand?"

"They sure looked dead when those guys dug them up. How could I understand?" Bard said.

"If God is all and everywhere, we live in his kingdom, and in His kingdom, there is no death. You need to listen to what Spirit is telling you, not what you see and hear in this world. It guides you to heal yourself and others. Can you do that?" he said, thinking of Elisha praying for his servant to see the power of the Lord, **'And Elisha prayed, and said, LORD, I pray thee, open his eyes, that he may see. And the LORD opened the eyes of the young man; and he saw: and, behold, the mountain *was* full of horses and chariots of fire round about Elisha.'** (57)"

"I will try," the boy said with a pronounced yawn, but then added, "Why don't you raise everyone who has died?"

Patrick felt the smile crease his face. "It might get awfully crowded here if I did that. I can only answer by saying that I try to listen to Spirit for all my instructions. It says in the Bible, **'Trust in the LORD with all thine heart; and lean not unto thine own understanding.'** (58) When it feels right, I do everything I can to pray for Life to be expressed, otherwise I wait patiently for His direction.

"Huh," was Bard's only response as he rolled over to sleep.

# Chapter 25
## Dead Woman/Unborn Child

"How long are we going to stay here? I thought you wanted to see your sister." Bard complained after they had spent a couple of weeks in the village, working to help gather supplies for a new church to be built.

"My work here is not done yet. We will move on in due time, but only when I'm done."

"What more work do you have to do? You raised the two ladies from the dead, healed a bunch of sick people and baptized all the villagers. The men have promised to build a church with the materials we gathered, and maybe a monastery later on. You'll send a priest here to guide them. Can't we just come back in a couple months or three when they're finished?"

"No, be patient. I think the time draws near." Patrick winked and waved toward a group of people in the distance, approaching the town.

Several men from the village met the group, and voices rose as they earnestly pointed at Patrick. "I believe my next appointment is here. What could that possibly be that they are carrying? Come along son." Patrick said as he hurried ahead.

One of the strangers ran forward to him and collapsed at his feet. "I seek the blessed Bishop Patrick. I pray the stories that we have heard about him are true. My wife, she was giving birth and died. They tell me he can raise her to live again. Please, please help us," He pleaded.

"I am Patrick, and I will do all I can," Patrick said as he grasped the man's outstretched hands and lifted him up. "Let's go to her."

As Patrick approached, the strangers gently placed the deceased woman on the ground in the shade of an oak tree and stepped away. Patrick watched Bard's wide-eyed stare at the pregnant woman's rigid body with mild amusement. "Do you remember what I told you about Life?"

"Some of it," the boy answered as beads of sweat glistened on his forehead. "Can you help her?"

Patrick ignored the question as he knelt beside the prone form and prayed silently for a few minutes. **"I do nothing of myself; but as my Father hath taught me, I speak these things."** (59) Patrick replied in a reverent voice. **"But if the Spirit of him that raised up Jesus from the dead dwell in you, he that raised up Christ from the dead shall also quicken your mortal bodies by his Spirit that dwelleth in you."** (60) "Let this maid arise alive, along with her child and let their story be a testament to reveal the power of God for all the inhabitants of this island. Thank you, Lord."

The group watched awestruck as the woman's pasty blue complexion began to transform into warmer hues. Her limbs slowly relaxed from their stiffened poses. Suddenly the woman sneezed loudly as her eyelids fluttered open. "I'm having a baby." She croaked.

"Yes, you are my dear, just breathe deep. Everything is going to be fine. Can one of you bring her some water? She has to be thirsty. Bring the midwife and some pelts and blankets too." For a few moments the group stood transfixed as the father kneeled, held and kissed his wife's hand. "Now people," Patrick clapped his hands as the people scattered to bring the needed supplies.

"If you don't close your mouth, you might catch a fly, Bard." The boy suddenly swallowed hard, even though he couldn't stop staring. Patrick grabbed the boy's shoulder and spun him to look directly at his face. "Don't look for signs of life in the body. See eternal Life." Patrick squeezed the boy's shoulder as he pointed at the world around them. "Don't look at what you can see, look only for the true qualities of Spirit. Things like Life, Truth, Joy, Harmony, and most of all Love continually expressed in all things. Watch for the Kingdom of God in all things. Don't be impressed by this world. Do you understand?"

Bard looked thoughtful as he nodded his head slowly but then said, "I don't. but I'm trying. I have so much to un-learn."

"Believe me, even though it contains infinite possibilities and rewards, this Christian life is far simpler than what the rest of the world experiences with their petty dramas and fears."

The midwife arrived and began to take charge of the situation. "Bring the water and towels over here by me. Lift her head and put those pelts under her till she's comfortable. Everything is going to be fine, darlin.'"

"Let's go wait over by that tree." Patrick said and steered Bard away from the activity of birth. As they were walking away, a voice called to him.

"Excuse me your holiness, please accept our families' unbounded gratitude. Will you allow us all to become, I believe the word is Christians? We are poor people, but we can work." Patrick looked at an older man leaning heavily on a stout staff.

"I will be honored to welcome all of you into our fold, sir. Please watch and care for the new mother for now and ask us again in a few days. I'd like to include her in the baptism if she feels up to it."

"Thank you, we will, and no man has ever called me 'sir' before," the old man added as his wrinkled eyes filled with tears.

"It is a term of respect, and you deserve respect, sir.

Now Bard, let's find something to eat. I'm famished."

As they walked away through the village, the boy asked, "How did you know these people were coming?"

"I didn't, I just knew I was supposed to wait here."

"So, in three or four days we will be traveling again?"

"No, my restless friend. Something else is going to happen here, I'm sure of it. Then we will be on our way, but not before."

"Do you know what will occur this time?"

"I have an idea, but I want you to be surprised, so I won't tell you."

Bard looked disgusted as he turned and kicked a stone across the pathway.

# Chapter 26
Another Dead Woman/Unborn Child

Patrick and Bard busied themselves for the next few days as they gathered more materials with the villagers to begin to build the church. On the fourth day, the visitors showed up as a group and asked to be baptized, along with the new mother and her baby boy. Patrick sprinkled water on the new mother and child rather than immerse them in cold water. "It's the same water," he told a dubious Bard. "I wouldn't want them to be chilled." He finished the ceremony, and the people dispersed under the shade of a grove of trees, as an oxcart slowly approached with a large contingent of peasants following. They stopped beside the people gathered under the trees, and Patrick watched as fingers pointed in his direction. Once again, a young man sprinted forward from the group and fell breathlessly at his feet.

"Here we go again," Bard spouted as Patrick silenced him with a glare.

The man sucked in a few deep breaths and wheezed, "Please, my wife died in childbirth, and the same day news of your miracle of raising a mother back to life came to us. Please can you help her?"

Patrick groaned and said, **"Jesus said unto her, I am the resurrection, and the life: he that believeth in me, though he were dead, yet shall he live:"** (61) He watched the man's thin frame shudder as he sobbed beneath him and found himself quoting Jesus again, **"If thou canst believe, all things *are* possible to him that believeth."** (62)

"I will try, sir. If the stories are true, I know you can bring her back."

Patrick saw Bard clasping his hands with his eyes closed and felt a grin cross his lips. "The stories are true. Do you see the woman with the child by that tree over there?" He pointed where a woman sat cradling a baby.

The man brushed tears away from his eyes and stared. "Yes, I see her."

"That is the woman who was resurrected and gave birth. Please take me to your wife."

While they approached the wagon, Patrick whispered, "Tell your friends to leave us and rest under the trees by the stream." The man walked slowly around the wagon and herded the crowd of chattering people toward the creek. By the time he returned, the bishop again quoted Jesus, **"Fear not: believe only, and she shall be made whole."** (63) After a few silent moments of reflection on the qualities of God she should express, he said, "Maiden, awaken from your sleep."

Once again, the pasty complexion of the woman's skin began to slowly change as the frozen limbs began to loosen. The frightened husband let out a loud gasp, but Patrick brought a finger up to silence him. He looked over at Bard and was pleased that the boy had his eyes closed in supplication, blotting out the physical image of the pregnant girl.

Her cheeks began to redden, and her brilliant green eyes flew open. "Where am I?" Tears streamed down the young man's face as he hurriedly grasped her hand and kissed it.

"You are safe here with your husband, young lady, and you are having a baby." Patrick said quietly while motioning for the midwife to come over. "In a few minutes, you will be the mother of a perfect child."

She suddenly gritted her teeth and clamped down on her

husband's hand as the next contraction hit. "Ow, it's alright, dear. I love you," the man said as the local midwife arrived, and shooed Patrick and Bard away.

"Thank you for your prayers." Patrick said as they walked away from the oxcart. "What did you pray about?"

"I tried to see what God knew about the girl. That she was created in his spiritual image, and could only demonstrate eternal life, and her baby too," he added.

"Very good, young man. You have attained the basic ideas to become a healer of minds and bodies. Keep striving to see what God sees. Any human situation can be changed and blessed by understanding what He knows about it. Congratulations."

"Thank you, Father." Bard beamed. "You know, I feel very patient now."

"I'm glad." He said as he patted the lad's head. "Well, we're not going to leave for a while now. Let's go welcome our new visitors."

The crowd watched intently as they approached. **"But thanks *be* to God, which giveth us the victory through our Lord Jesus Christ."** (64) Patrick announced as he smiled, "Your sister is made alive in Christ, and there should be an additional surprise for you shortly." Distrust showed in some of their strained faces until a few moments later when a baby's loud wail pierced the air. Tears filled their eyes as one by one they dropped to their knees to honor Patrick.

"Please, do not honor me. It is God whom you should praise. He alone creates and preserves life. You are all welcome to join us in fellowship and worship the Christ."

"Who are you?" a man's hesitant voice questioned.

Bard stepped forward and shouted, "He is Patrick, holy Bishop of this island. A servant of the one true God, and a destroyer of idols and false beliefs. Arise, join him, and share eternal life in Christ."

As the people moved forward, they addressed Bard with

questions. Patrick watched with pride as he perceived the newfound spiritual strength blossoming in his protégé. He saw the boy's unceasing smile and knew that Bard loved all of this herd of lost sheep. *Thank you, Father, for blessing my life's mission with this young man.*

# Chapter 27
One Child Dead, Another Dying

"Are you happy now?"

Bard smiled back at him. "I am, and I'm glad we stayed as long as we did. How many do you think were baptized in these last months?"

"A thousand or maybe two. Our mission has truly been blessed with all of these new adherents. They will spread the gospel farther than the two of us ever could."

"How far is it to where your sister lives?"

"With our without our stops for holy work?"

"Just travel time, your stops will add decades." Bard's laugh echoed through the emerald-green grass-covered hills.

"It should only take about six weeks of walking. I think we will make it to Dublina, the next kingdom, by this evening. Hopefully, they will be a hospitable and receptive audience."

As they approached the village in the late afternoon there was very little activity in the streets. The few people walking in the streets were morose and depressed. Wails of sorrow came from a few of the houses.

Patrick stopped one of the first peasants he came to, "What is going on here? Why is everyone sad?"

The man's long face developed a prolonged grimace. "Our young prince lies at the point of death, and his sister drowned in the river earlier today. Our king is beside himself with grief. You had best be gone from here; we don't need strangers to share our sorrows."

"Can you take us to your king?"

The man sputtered in astonishment, "Didn't you hear me? He is in anguish. He'll probably have you killed if you disturb his time of mourning."

"Can you tell me where we can find him?" Patrick persisted with a solemn countenance.

Shaking his head in dis-belief the man pointed to the center of the compound. "That way. The largest house in town."

"Of course it would be, thank you sir." He motioned to Bard and both of them trudged away. In a few minutes, they stood outside a very large stone compound and were immediately surrounded by several angry, armed men.

"Good day to you, gentlemen. I am seeking your king to assist him. Can you take me to him?"

Confusion painted the faces of the men. The largest brute stepped forward while drawing out a heavy sword. Opening his mouth only a few teeth showed as he snapped. "Who be you?"

"I am Bishop Patrick, and I have been sent to help your king."

Irritated the man thrust his face forward as spittle flew from his mouth onto Patrick. "Who sent you?"

"God."

"I've heard tales of a bishop what brings people back to life, Macleve. My brother told me. This could be him," one of the other men said quickly.

Macleve turned on the smaller man. "No one come back once dead."

"Why not?" Patrick asked with a determined scowl on his face. "What if death is a lie?"

Veins popped out on the sides of Macleve's head as he spun back to face Patrick and snarled. "I have killed many men; they never walk again."

"Well, I wasn't there to help them, but I am here now. Please escort me to your king."

The muscles in the man's arm tensed as he raised his weapon for a strike.

"Macleve, what is going on?" An older, well-muscled man stepped from a doorway. "Who dares to disturb my time of bereavement?"

"This man wants to see you. Should he die?"

"There has been enough death in my kingdom today. Just send him away."

"But he can heal your son!" Bard shouted. "Please, let him try." The boy looked surprised at his own outburst.

"What did you say?" the king stared with reddened eyes and skepticism painted on his face.

Bard swallowed hard before answering. "He can heal the prince. Have you not heard of Patrick? The bishop who defeated Dichu and Leogaire's wizards? The man who has healed and raised the dead across this island?"

"I have heard stories, but I never allowed myself to believe them," the king admitted.

"The stories are true," Patrick spoke. "My young friend is incorrect on one significant point. **'I do nothing of myself;'** (65) It is God that heals. I would like to try and help you and your children though."

The king continued to look skeptical as he paused for several moments, but finally made a decision, "Bring them inside."

Macleve grumbled curses under his breath as he reluctantly sheathed his sword and pointed toward the entrance.

Patrick and Bard were led through a cavernous great room held up by massive wooden timbers. There was still bark on most of the beams. They followed the king into a smaller side chamber with fitted rock walls. There they saw the prince, laying down, shrouded in pelts and blankets. "The sickness started a week ago. He has only grown worse each day," the king said in a low, despondent tone. "My magicians have been of no help."

"Could you leave us alone with him to pray?" Patrick asked.

With a longing gaze at his son, the king nodded and turned slowly to leave. "Call if you need anything."

Patrick could sense the rage, fear, and selfishness resident in the boy laying before him. "Young man, I know you can hear me. I want to tell you about what life really is. God is Life, which you can never be deprived of. God is Love, which you have never been deprived of. God is the good which always surrounds you. You express good throughout your life. You are loved, you are safe, you are forgiven for any sins that have bound you. You can defeat any discord that holds you, and you are free to express health, happiness and joy."

Patrick kept talking. He also watched Bard listen for a while, but eventually the young man sank into a deep sleep.

In a little while, the prince opened his eyes. "Can I have some water?"

"Certainly, let me call for some," Patrick said as he turned and looked at the wide-eyed face peeking through the deer hides covering the doorway. Quietly he said, "Malcleve, please bring some water for the prince right away."

Malcleve returned with the water, and Patrick saw a smile creep across the big man's lips. "Leave us for a few more minutes."

After some more prayer and conversation, the prince said that he would like to stand up. Patrick held onto his arm and drew back the heavy hide drapes as they both walked into the great room. The king and Malcleve were waiting just outside the doorway.

"My boy!" the king exclaimed, not believing his eyes. He rushed over and buried his son in a bear hug. "How do you feel?"

"A little weak, but fine otherwise. How long have I been sick?"

"A full week, my son. I thought for sure that I would lose you, but then this man showed up today, and now you are well. I don't know how he did it."

"I don't mean to interrupt you, sire, but can you take me to your daughter?" Patrick quietly interjected.

———•●•———

Bard yawned and stretched as he slowly awakened from a lucid dream. Suddenly he realized he was alone.

"Patrick!" he cried and froze for a moment as Macleve rushed into the room. "Stop, Patrick, where are you?" Bard yelled as he scrambled upright and quickly backed against the far wall as he pulled his knife from its sheath.

"It be alright," the big man said with his limited smile as he opened his arms wide. "The prince walks. He be alive."

"Where is Patrick? Take me to him, please," he added, still suspicious.

"Sure, come along. I take you." The menacing manner was gone, replaced by a jovial expression which Bard thought looked completely out of place on the man's monstrous visage. *What had happened?*

———•●•———

The king and his son led Patrick to another, larger side chamber where a group of women loudly wailed in sorrow around the princess's body. Knowing he couldn't possibly concentrate with the howls of bereavement, he said. "Please send them all out of here for now and please tell them to be quiet."

"You heard him." As the king motioned with his arm. The women gasped suddenly when the prince entered, and quickly exited, although their excited banter rose in pitch as a guard escorted them away.

Patrick knelt by the girl's body that had been placed on a rough bench. Her clothes were still soaked and covered in mud and slimy moss. She smelled like stagnant river water. "Again sire, please leave me alone."

"Certainly, anything you wish. You have brought my son back from the verge of death, it is too much for me to hope my daughter could…" The words congealed in the king's throat as his son pulled on the man's shoulders in an effort to turn him toward the doorway.

"In the words of my master, **'Fear not: believe only, and she shall be made whole.'** (66) God is Life, and he is the only power in the universe. Let me pray…" As Bard sprinted around the king and prince and threw his arms around Patrick.

"I didn't know where you went," he said breathlessly.

"You know I only go where God's work is to be done. Sit down quietly, and try to stay awake this time," he said with a wink. "Sorry for this interruption, sire. I will get to work now."

Patrick cleared his thinking and began to pray, letting the concepts of pure spiritual Love flood his mind. Knowing the princess could never have been beyond God's loving control and could never have passed away by drowning in the river, but was still alive in Christ, and should be expressing the qualities of God. Qualities that included: life, energy, goodness, strength, joy, intelligence, and most of all Love!

After a number of minutes, Bard suddenly got up and crept out the door as quietly as he could.

Patrick noticed but said nothing as he continued his mental quest to be at one with God and to see past the limitations of the material world. He didn't know how long he had been praying when the girl's arm slowly slid off her chest. He watched as she lifted her other arm and leg, rolled off the rough wooden bench onto her knees and began to cough and vomit river water. *Thank you, Father!* As tears of joy flooded his eyes.

The wide-eyed girl finally sat back, wiped her mouth and mumbled, "Who are you? What has happened to me? Why am I soaking wet?"

"I am Bishop Patrick, a friend your father has allowed to visit. Nothing has really happened to you. You have never been separated from your perfect image." As he spoke the king rushed through the doorway and fell to his knees to hug and kiss his daughter as the prince stood smiling in the doorway.

"I didn't have a chance to thank you before," the prince said, extending his hand. "Thank you for healing me, sir. How did you do it, but an even bigger question is, how did you bring my dear sister back from the shadows of death?"

"You are most welcome young man, but it was not I but God who healed you and resurrected your sister."

"Wait. What? I was dead?" the girl's eyes widened in terror.

Her father hugged her tighter as he said, "You drowned in the river this morning. You know your brother was already on death's door. My whole world crumbled around me today, until this man, Patrick, returned you two to me." He loosened his grip on his daughter, and began crying. His children hurriedly knelt and embraced him.

The son looked up with watery eyes and said, "I have been taught by the druids and know of many gods. Who is the one who healed me?"

The king collected himself, wiped his eyes and lifted his daughter up gently. He turned to enter the conversation. "He healed my daughter too. What God has the power to do such miracles?"

"Gentlemen and young lady, allow me the pleasure of telling you the greatest story in the history of the world." Patrick saw Bard roll his eyes and frowned at him briefly.

"Years ago, a virgin gave birth to a child in a manger and called his name Jesus."

"Where?" the prince asked.

"In a little village called Bethlehem. It was written, **'Therefore the Lord himself shall give you a sign; Behold, a virgin shall conceive, and bear a son, and shall call his name Immanuel.'** (67) The boy was born in a manger."

"A virgin? How is such a thing possible?" sputtered the king.

"How is resurrection of those who appear to have passed on possible? It is a long story, but very informative and it will explain how your children were returned to you."

"Sir, you have given me back the gift of my children. All I have is yours. I want to hear the whole story of this Jesus and after that, I want to know how I and my subjects can learn to heal others and help your cause prosper in my kingdom and all across our island."

Patrick was filled with compassion as all of them smiled, even Macleve. "Thank you, sire. You will have no regrets."

# Chapter 28
## Nineteen Men Raised

Twelve months later, a church was built, a monastery was almost completed, and a new community of acolytes were learning to express the Christ in all situations. Patrick and Bard said goodbye, along with their promises to return as soon as they could, and finally were able to continue their journey.

As they walked away from the village, Patrick said, "I haven't wanted to ask you before, but now that we are leaving. Why did you leave the chamber as I prayed for the princess on our first day here?"

"I tried to pray but couldn't concentrate. I was distracted. I kept looking at her body for any movement, and I knew if my thinking was there, looking at the body, it wasn't with God and I wasn't helping. So, I left, and tried to pray where I couldn't see her."

"That was a very wise decision you made. I am really proud of you, my boy. We have given a wonderful gift to those people."

"Why can't I heal like you do? I try, but then I get confused about what to think and finally give up."

"Don't try to do anything yourself, it is an understanding of God that heals. Learn who and what he is, and you can't avoid healing yourself and others."

"I've listened and know the words, but I'm missing

something."

"Love, unselfish love. Love overflowing in everything you do. Work to attain compassion for others and always listen to God for what your patient needs to hear. He knows all and provides all."

Bard said nothing, but Patrick was happy to notice a look of determination on his young face. *Clearly, he will be healing soon.*

"Where will we be going next?"

"It is called the kingdom of Momonia; their king lives in a village called Cassel a few days walking to the north."

In a few days they reached the outskirts of the town. Several armed men asked for their names. When Patrick answered grins suddenly creased the faces of the guards, and they were quickly escorted to King Oengus's palace. They were led up to a large hillfort overlooking the region.

"This way gentlemen," another guard beckoned, and they wound around the concentric stone walls until exiting next to the door of a large stone structure, the roof was covered with sod. "Wait here please," as the guard entered and talked to a man at the far end of the dim lit room.

The man looked up and rushed to the doorway with his arms extended. "Greetings Bishop Patrick. I was told by several recent travelers that you might be passing through my kingdom. I have relished the stories told by those strangers of the miracles you've performed. Please sit and tell me more."

"King Oengus, I am only a humble servant of the Lord. I have been blessed with the opportunities to meet and heal many suffering souls."

"I thought you would arrive today, because when I visited my temple this morning, all of my idols were thrown down. I tried to raise several of them, but they would not stand up. I have heard that you say all of man's idols are false gods and preach of a real God beyond our sight."

"I only speak the Truth of God's word, sire. The goal of

my ministry is to bring visions of His kingdom to the inhabitants of this island."

"Can you teach me? Can you usher me into this hidden kingdom?"

"If thou wish to become a Christian, I can. Let me first tell you the story of Jesus the Son of God." Bard walked over beside a rock wall and stretched out on the ground to take a nap.

Patrick saw Bard stir as he was finishing his recounting of Jesus's life and miracles and motioned for him to come over. **"And it came to pass, while he blessed them, he was parted from them, and carried up into heaven."** (68)

"Are there more stories about Jesus and his followers?"

"Yes, sire, but way too many for me to recite tonight.

"I want to hear them all, can I join your Christianity?" he asked eagerly.

"Kneel King Oengus and I will baptize you in the name of the Father, the Son, and the Holy Ghost." Bard handed Patrick a small earthen container. Patrick poured a small amount of holy water into his hand and applied it to the king's forehead. "I now pronounce you baptized as a brother in Christ. Arise in His Spirit." Patrick felt a little overzealous as he held his heavy oak staff up and carelessly slammed it back down. Feeling resistance, he looked down and saw that his sharpened staff had pierced the king's foot. For a moment, despair enveloped him as he stared at the injury, then he immediately turned his heart to prayer. *Accidents never occur in God's kingdom.* He thrust the staff into Bard's hands and noticed the king was still smiling. *He hadn't felt any pain!* Patrick quickly fell to his knees, and as he made the sign of the cross on the man's wounded foot, the wound closed. "How do you feel, sire?"

"Like I have been washed a thousand times in pure rivers. I feel loved."

"And so, you are, my king. Now you need to destroy those pagan idols in your temple and remain in God's Love forever."

"I will, I will, and you must remain with us and teach my people and welcome them into your church with divine thoughts."

"Do you agree to build a church and monastery to promote and perpetuate Christ's doctrine in your kingdom?"

"I do, and I will do everything to support your ministry."

"Hogwash!" the voice came from an open doorway. "You are too trusting my king; he is just another charlatan seeking his fortune from your royal treasury."

"Did you not hear his story about the man, Jesus? I know you've heard the stories about the dead he raised to life across this island."

"That's exactly what they are. Fanciful fairy tales, elaborate myths created to entertain and deceive simple people like you, my husband," the queen said with an icy edge in her voice. "Why don't you ask this vagabond to raise a corpse or two for our entertainment?"

"Be courteous my queen."

"She is quite right, my liege. You both really don't know me or have proof of my God yet. I should be given a challenge to prove my veracity."

"I trust you, Bishop Patrick."

"Well, I don't," the queen said with a sour face. "Make him raise some of your moldy friends. I know, start with old Fotus."

"No dear, he has lain in the grave for ten years now. There can't be much of him left."

Patrick shook his head. "Never mind how long, please take me to Fotus and his friends. Ours is the God of eternal life," he announced as Bard handed Patrick's staff back to him.

"Follow me," the king said sadly, as he, the queen and a few guards led them out of the palace and through town. A few curious villagers followed them to a nearby wooded hillside with a small valley.

"There is Fotus's cist," as he pointed at a heap of stones atop the man's grave. The other cists in this area are his friends.

"How many in all?" Patrick asked.

"There are nineteen souls entombed here." the queen said lyrically. "Can you wake at least one for me?"

"I do nothing for anyone but the one Lord, your majesty. If he wills it, I will raise the dead."

"I'm sure," she scoffed.

"Sire, can you have your soldiers remove the stones from the graves?

"All of them?" the king stuttered in surprise.

"Yes please, and then allow us some privacy in this glade. Remain at the entrance to this valley. We will come to you when we are ready."

After the various graves were uncovered and the others had left, Bard crept forward to peer into the closest grave. "Stop, you can't help raise the dead if you're looking for life in matter." The boy hurried back and sat down at Patrick's side.

"I'm sorry, I forgot again."

"Just sit and pray, knowing that Life is God, and always expressed by his images. **So God created man in his *own* image, in the image of God created he him; male and female created he them.'** (69) Mankind must demonstrate Life because God is Life."

They sat quietly together for a number of minutes until they finally heard faint scraping sounds, then a cough, and a sneeze from another direction. Bard shifted, but Patrick put a finger to his lips to keep him silent. A withered hand emerged from Fotus's grave and grasped at the stones lining the crypt as they pulled the man's body to an upright position. He peeked out of the hole and asked hoarsely, "Can you help me out?"

Patrick stood up and quickly offered his hand to the

man. Others were stirring as Patrick and Bard hurried around the graves, helping the men crawl out and steadied them as they tried to walk upright. "How many is that?" Patrick eventually asked Bard.

"I count eighteen. I don't think anyone came out of the one over there," he said as he pointed to a grave set off to one side.

Patrick hurried over and gazed into the hole. A plaintive voice wailed, "Leave me alone, let me sleep. I beg of you."

"Satan cannot hold you sir; I say you must arise in the name of the Lord. Now!" Patrick commanded, and two hands reluctantly reached up to him. "I'm afraid," the man cried as he was lifted up.

"Nothing will hurt you my son, we are all friends here." As Patrick opened his arms wide and hugged the man dressed in tatters. "Now, let's all go and pay our respects to the queen, follow me." Murmurs followed him, "Did he say the queen?" one shaky voice asked.

As Patrick and Bard approached the open end of the valley, they could see that the crowd had grown into a large number of curious onlookers and had surrounded the king's party at the entrance. A loud collective gasp was heard as the nineteen former corpses came into view, walking behind them. "King Oengus, allow me to present Fotus and his fellow former cadavers to you and your queen."

The queen eyes grew wide with fear, "It is a trick, it is black magic, it cannot be real," she screamed as she reeled and ran a short distance away, pursued by a number of the village women that were too frightened to chatter.

The king ran forward smiling and fell prone at the holy man's feet. "I knew you could do it! My kingdom is forever grateful for this demonstration." Tears flowed from his eyes as he shifted his gaze, "Fotus, come forward and let me shake your hand. Let me shake hands with all of you who have returned." Then he sprang up and ran to Fotus, wrapping his arms around the old man for a long moment. Stepping back, he asked, "What was death like?"

The other men who had been raised crowded around Fotus as he recounted the pains he had suffered, and the other men substantiated each of his reflections. Finally, he told the king and everyone in the community that Patrick had preached the true and living words of God. "Without him, we wouldn't have redemption."

The king and his people were astounded at the stories. As their voices rose in a cacophony of conversations, the king suddenly raised his arms and shouted to quiet them.

"Friends, we are indeed fortunate to have witnessed this unimaginable miracle in our kingdom. Bishop Patrick, great prophet of the unseen God, will you please baptize my queen, my subjects, and myself as soon as possible." Patrick watched as his wife, still staring with her mouth open, hesitated before nodding her assent.

"Us too master Patrick. We want to become servants of the most high." Came the plaintive cries from all nineteen men.

Patrick stayed silent until all the voices finally quieted, "It will be my honor to usher you all into His kingdom. I have many stories and valuable information to share. Will you all be a receptive audience?" he asked, as he glanced at the queen. She was smiling as she added her voice to the cries of affirmation. "Then, first I ask that we feed, bathe and clothe our friends who have slept so long, before subjecting them to one of my long sermons."

The king immediately appointed several of his attendants to see to the details, and the crowd dispersed to the village to welcome the group of newly alive with a celebration.

In another year of Patrick's guidance, the community was a thriving Christian community. Patrick had summoned a few young priests from other established monasteries to guide and serve the pilgrims who traveled from all over the island to hear his sermons. A large monastery was almost finished, and a number of men, including all nineteen of those raised from death, had donned monastic habits and were actively ministering to people throughout the region.

"I think it's time we continue our journey, Bard." Patrick announced one morning.

"Give me a few minutes to gather our belongings." The young man said with a smile. "Are you going to notify the king?"

"Of course I will. I am sorry to leave these people, but we have provided the seed they needed to grow. Now though, we must spread more healing messages across this land. This certainly was a most rewarding stop on our travels though. Are you still keeping a journal of our trials and victories?"

"Yes sir. Every detail I can. I want to remember them all. Look at those clouds gathering, do you think it's going to rain?"

"I am certain of it."

"Should we wait for dry weather before leaving?"

"I wish we could, but I feel a drastic demonstration of God's power coming on. We'll leave now."

As they walked, Bard said, "I didn't want to mention it before, but I saw you heal the king's foot after you speared it."

"I still can't believe I did that; I was feeling so good about his receptivity to our message of good, and I forgot my self-control."

"He didn't seem to notice."

"Yes, at that point his thoughts rose higher than mine did. I thank the Lord he was healed, before he realized he was hurt. Hey, was that a raindrop?"

# Chapter 29
## Locked Up

Shivers ran throughout his body as Patrick waded waist-deep against a strong current in the icy water. At every slogging step he probed the bottom for an area free of stones and drove his staff deep into the river's muddy bottom to anchor himself. The heavy rain soaked through his hood and streamed down his forehead, into his eyes. "Hang onto me, Bard." *Are you sure you called me on this dreadful journey, Lord?*

"I am," came the reply through chattering teeth.

"We are over halfway now," Patrick continued while holding their bundle of belongings atop his head with one hand, as he continued to stumble over slippery rocks hidden beneath the swollen flow of muddy water.

"I wish it would stop raining. My head is as wet as my feet. Why did we cross the river here?" Bard complained.

"There are no bridges close, and this is the shallowest crossing for miles. We'll make a fire as soon as we climb out. It's just a bit farther to…" He stopped talking loudly as he noticed figures moving along the shore. "We have a reception committee son, better start to pray about more than the weather."

"Look lads, invaders to our lands," a gruff voice cried out as an exhausted Patrick and Bard grabbed at clumps of grass in a feeble effort to crawl out of the river.

"They not invaders, they're drowned river rats," another laughed.

"Do we kill them now, or take them to the king?" A third voice questioned.

"If we do away with them here, we'll spend the rest of the night soaked on watch. Let's take them back to the palace as an excuse to get out of this storm." A murmur of affirmation ran through the group, and Patrick and Bard's wrists were bound with rough twine. Then they were marched along narrow paths through dripping wet foliage for an hour before they noticed the faint smell of smoke.

"We be close now. Soon you meet the king," the guard next to Patrick muttered.

"What is he like?"

The guard's face changed abruptly into a sour expression. "Well, I can tell you that he hates thieves that trespass on his lands."

After fifteen more minutes of walking, they came upon the outskirts of a village. The streets were rivers of mud six inches deep. They were prodded by the guards as they slogged and slid in the mud between the rough wooden dwellings. Finally, they were both roughly pushed through a doorway and sprawled together onto a wet floor.

"What is the meaning of this?" a man shouted near a central firepit.

"We found them crossing the river in this downpour, we think they must be criminals trying to escape punishment," one of the guards replied.

"We are not. My name is…"

"Silence, what is in their satchel?" the king demanded, as the guards hurriedly unpacked and inspected their belongings.

"Hey tha.." Bard started to say, but Patrick stopped him with a firm grip on his shoulder and a slight shake of his head.

"Not a lot. Some gold and silver though. Books,

parchment, blankets…"

"Strip search them and throw them into our prison. We will show them how we deal with villains."

As the men pulled Patrick's robes off, one of them reached up to pull the cylinder from around his neck. "No, please, I ask sire that I am allowed to keep this on my person. I have been charged with its protection."

"Well, I'd say that you aren't much of a guardian then," he smirked. "Bring it to me, along with their other belongings," he said laughing loudly.

Stripped of their clothes, Patrick and Bard were roughly herded into a small rocky cave a short distance away. Several other prisoners scrambled out of the way as they were unceremoniously shoved through an iron gate, which was quickly locked behind them. The smell of human waste and body odor was horrible, but they still huddled closely together on the damp ground with the other inmates to survive the night's cold and wet conditions.

Bard wrapped his arms around himself and said as he shivered, "I wish he hadn't taken the scroll."

"The king was correct, I am not much of a guardian, but God is," Patrick replied with a calm demeanor and quickly fell asleep.

In the morning the sun glistened off the damp stone walls at the entrance, as a warm breeze stirred the air in the rocky grotto. Bard was up, furiously rubbing dried mud from his limbs as Patrick opened his eyes.

"How long do you think they will keep us here?" Bard asked in a frenzy.

"Patience young man, the Lord will release us at the perfect time. **'And ye shall know the truth, and the truth shall make you free.'** (70) Those aren't idle words my boy, they can free you from any untoward situation."

"But when?"

"Patience, now." Patrick grumbled as he rolled over in the mud and went back to sleep.

For fourteen nights and days they endured the continuous cursing of the guards and inmates, being fed only a small cup of thin gruel each day. The weather had changed to a continuous dry, warm breeze, which made living in the cave almost bearable. Bard eventually calmed as he prayed along with Patrick to be free to do God's work. On the morning of the fourteenth day, they awoke to the rattle of a key in the lock.

"The king is releasing you," the guard said. "I am to take you to him. I have brought your clothes and belongings."

"All of them? Patrick questioned.

"Yes, sir. All of them."

Patrick didn't miss the fact that the guard had called him "sir," "Can you please direct us to the nearest warm and clean stream where we can bathe first? We are a little gamey after these primitive accommodations." Patrick smiled.

The guard mumbled, "Yes sir, follow me." He led them on a path around the village to a small stream nearby with a shallow pool of clear water, rimmed with rocks and warmed by the sun. After a long dip, they both felt and smelled much better.

As they bent to dress, Patrick first rummaged through the pile of clothing to locate his leather thong necklace. He opened it and checked that the scroll was intact and unharmed before he reverently placed it around his neck.

"I am always amazed at God's power and grace," Bard said as he struggled to pull up his pants over his wet legs.

"Me too," Patrick replied, "I'm glad he loves us."

When they were dressed, they followed the guard to the king's residence. "Sire, here are Bishop Patrick and his companion." He stood to the side as he motioned them to walk forward toward a table filled with food.

"Bishop Patrick, please allow me to apologize for my grievous mistake. I have entertained messengers from King Oengus who told me of your wonderous miracles and triumphs, and that you had left his kingdom to visit your sister on the island of Valentia. Suddenly, I remembered you two, but I couldn't imagine a man of your stature fording a river in such a terrible storm."

**"I can do all things through Christ which strengtheneth me."** (71) "A raging river is but a mild annoyance to us, as is incarceration in a cold and filthy cave." He winked.

"You could have struck me dead, as you did Leogaire's wizards. Why did you allow me to persecute you?"

"Our God is not vengeful, He is forgiving, loving. I imagine that there was no other way to protect me from the magician's evil than to defeat its minions in those situations. With you though, I just had to be patient."

The king was astonished. "How can you be filled with such grace as to forgive me for the undeserved hardships I imposed on you?"

"In Spirit there are no hardships, only harmony. We live in Spirit. We are not infected with the quest for power and riches of material life. We express humility and Love for others as our prime endeavors in life."

"He's better at it than I am, but I'm learning," Bard added brightly.

The king was completely confused, and his face showed it. In a few moments, he said, "Please come and eat your fill and tell me about this Spirit," as the king's eyes inexplicably filled with penitent tears.

Patrick watched as Bard desperately gorged himself with food and drink until he had his fill and curled up for a nap on a soft pile of flax nearby. Patrick slowly picked at his food, while he once again expounded on the concepts of Spirit illustrated throughout the bible and his own healing experiences across the island for hours.

When Patrick paused for a long moment before continuing the story of Saul the persecutor of Christians, becoming Paul the Christian evangelist, the king suddenly knelt before him. "Can I and my subjects be forgiven our ignorance and sins, and be permitted to join your righteous cause?"

"Yes, indeed, sire. **'The people which sat in darkness saw great light; and to them which sat in the region and shadow of death light is sprung up.'** (72) It will be my honor to shine the light of Truth on you and your people and welcome all of you into His kingdom." A large yawn escaped as he asked. "Where should we sleep tonight?" The next morning Patrick awoke with the king seated nearby. "Good morning, bishop, I hope you slept well. I had my guards make their regular rounds about the kingdom last night, but I also had them stop and tell many of my subjects about you and your promise to let them join your church. Many of them walked here during the night and are waiting outside to be baptized already. Can I be first?" the king asked with humility.

Patrick rubbed his eyes. "Yes, sire, you will be first, and I must be about my father's business," he said sleepily. ***"And he said unto them, How is it that ye sought me? wist ye not that I must be about my Father's business?"*** (73) *Morning God, thank you.* "Bard, wake up. We have work to do." He ate a few bites of food and hurried outside as quickly as he could. The king was waiting just outside the door along, with a long line of people that trailed through the village streets. "Follow me to the stream," he said. "Please hold your position in line," as he traipsed out of town as the silent throng followed.

He led them to the pool where he and Bard had bathed. "Please, sire, follow me in," he said as he waded into the water up to his waist. He placed one arm behind the king's back, and a hand on his chest. "Hold your nose closed," he said, and the king pinched his nose shut. **"John did baptize in the wilderness, and preach the baptism of repentance for the remission of sins."** (74) "Do you accept Jesus as your Lord and savior? Do you renounce your past indiscretions and swear to obey the ten commandments?"

The king nodded as he held his nose.

"Then I, Patrick, Bishop of Hibernia, baptize you for admission into the church of the one true God," he waited until the king took a large breath of air and held it. Then he lowered him beneath the surface of the water and raised him up as his subjects cheered.

# Chapter 30
Gone Fishing

"Another kingdom conquered with humility and God's word." Bard said as they walked along the ridge of a high hill one day after they had left the village.

"Yes, I didn't even need to perform many miracles. Once they learned the basics, they healed themselves and each other quickly."

"I healed that criminal's broken arm," Bard pronounced with a wide smile. "I finally cured someone."

"Whoa young man. God is the only healer, but you were able to understand the spiritual reality and thus bring harmony to that man's situation. I am very proud of you. I'm also extremely grateful that another king now trusts the word of God."

"I was surprised that he released all the prisoners once they agreed to follow the ten commandments."

"If they only follow the first commandment, their lives will improve. Do you remember what it is?"

"Sure, **'Thou shalt have no other gods before me.'** (75) If they obey the first, they must obey all the others."

"Right, and do you know the eleventh commandment?"

"Yes sir, the one Jesus added. **'A new commandment I give unto you, That ye love one another; as I have loved you, that ye also love one another.'** (76) The world would be a wonderful place if that rule was followed by all men."

"It gets a little better when any man follows it. I think the king there will obey it from now on," Patrick said, shielding his eyes as he looked at the sun dipping into the horizon.

"How many years are left in our journey to see your sister?"

Patrick ignored the jab. "Not many. Do you smell that?" He watched Bard sniff the air. "That is the ocean, we are very close."

"You said she lived on an island. How do we get to it?"

"I thought we would just wait for low tide and wade across, like we did at the river."

Bard's mouth fell open. "You're kidding, right?"

In another day of walking, they finally reached a bluff that overlooked the coastline and could see Valentia Island in the distance. "Unless you can teach me to walk on water like Jesus, you'd better find us a boat," the young man grinned.

"We will find a way." Patrick sighed as he led the way down a narrow path that clung to the face of a bluff, toward the sea far below.

Patrick reached the bottom of the cliff and pointed at a distant wisp of smoke. "We should find someone to assist us there," he shouted over the sounds of crashing waves. Together they crawled and stumbled over the jagged rocks that covered the shoreline.

"Ow," Bard cried, "I twisted my ankle."

Patrick stopped and looked at the boy in mock amazement. "What do you want me to do? Fix your ankle? Are you material or spiritual? Have you forgotten what you learned?

Bard looked sheepishly at him. "No, just give me a few moments to clear my thinking." *I am on a holy quest as an aid to Patrick in his holy ministry. Spirit rules, and it is perfect. I reflect that perfection because I am made in His image. Nothing can be torn or separated in God's kingdom.*

*Spirit can't be torn.* "Alright, I'm ready to go on now," he finally said as he rotated his ankle, amazed that most of the pain had fled so quickly.

"Marvelous work, Bard. Keep it up and you might walk on water yet."

As they drew closer, they could see a few huts clustered near a small beach that had most of the large rocks cleared away. Several animal skin-covered dingys had been pulled up above the tide line.

"What are those flimsy things?" Bard pointed at the boats.

"They call them currachs. Animal skins stretched over wooden frames. They don't waste any wood to make real boats here."

"There are some men coming."

"Yes, I see them." Patrick waited patiently until the group of haggard fishermen had formed a semi-circle around them. "Greetings, men of the sea. I am Bishop Patrick and my sister lives on yonder island. I have not seen her in many years, but I hear she is married with three sons. Can you take us there?" Patrick listened to the strange words spilling from the men. He had heard many accents across the island, but these fishermen conversed in a dialect completely different than any he had experienced before. Finally, one of them stepped forward and addressed him.

"Aye, I be willing. What will ye pay?" The man had a knife scar across his cheek and raised a threatening eyebrow.

"What do you need the most?" Patrick asked. That seemed to confuse the man, as he turned and talked to the others, apparently translating the message for them. An older man hobbled forward, shook his withered fist and grumbled a few words as the rest of the group quieted.

"We need fish. Our families be starving." The man with the scar said in a more humble demeanor.

"Well, let's go fishing." Patrick said with a wide smile. "What is your name, sir?"

"Byort," the man replied with a questioning look. "We have fished all day and only caught a few fish."

"Will you allow us to go fishing with you now?"

"Yes, maybe you strangers can teach us how to fish, or maybe we will use both of you for bait tomorrow," he said with an unsettling smirk, as he motioned the others toward the boats.

As the men began to ferry the currachs to the ocean, Bard whispered, "How are you going to find fish for them? I don't want to be bait tomorrow."

Patrick smiled, "I'm not, but God knows where they are. Do you recall what Jesus told the fishermen? **'And he said unto them, Cast the net on the right side of the ship, and ye shall find. They cast therefore, and now they were not able to draw it for the multitude of fishes.'** (77) Have faith, my friend."

Patrick and Bard waded out into the salty surf, and each were guided to a separate boat. Patrick climbed in and sat down in the stern, Byort rolled gracefully into the bow. He immediately grabbed the oars and started rowing away from the beach. Patrick smelled the bait bucket before he saw it, filled with entrails and unidentifiable rotten fish parts. Next to it was a long line of twine with hooks tied in.

Once they were beyond the breakers, Byort grabbed the hook at the very end of the line, reached into the bucket and speared a small piece of meat on it, then he dropped it over the side. He handed Patrick the next hook and began to row. Patrick understood and began to bait the hooks as he tried to carefully unwind the lengths of cord from a tangled pile. When the boat hit a large wave, the hooks would bite into his flesh, eliciting a loud laugh from the oarsman. Eventually, the line was paid out, and Patrick washed his stinging hands as well as he could in the sea spray as it hit the small hull. In a few moments the sailor's eyes widened, he pointed at the taut hook line, said something that Patrick couldn't understand, and began to turn the boat toward the beach again. As he rowed, Byort shouted at the other boats bobbing in the swells. Patrick noticed that Bard's currach was also headed toward the shore.

Patrick was ignored as the man rowed directly up to the beach and scrambled out, grabbed the line and began to pull. A fish appeared on the first hook, and he hurriedly motioned at Patrick to drop it into the boat. Almost every hook had a fish attached, and by the time they pulled the last hook out of the surf, the entire bottom of the craft was covered with flopping fish.

Bard ran up and peered at the catch. "We caught just as many."

As the other boats beached, the fishermen showed that they only had a few fish between them. "How did you do this thing?" Byort asked.

"First, keep as many fish as you need to feed your families and release the others back into the ocean. When everyone has eaten their fill, I will be glad to relate how and why this happened." Patrick said, as he raised his hands and showed the man that he had no cuts or punctures on them from the hooks. The man's eyebrows raised as his mouth fell open, then he turned and hurried over to give the instructions to the other fishermen.

The meal on the beach was a festive occasion for the inhabitants of the shoreside huts. The only other food besides the fish was some beans and a tasteless flat bread, but to the starving families, it was a feast. After everyone had eaten their fill, Patrick stood up and began to preach. When he finally finished, many of the residents were sound asleep. "I hope they understood my words," he said to Byort who was seated nearby on a piece of driftwood.

"Not all of them I'm sure, but enough. I know they will ask me questions." He shifted his weight to face Patrick. "When do you want to leave for Valentia?"

"If the weather is fair in the morning, let's leave then."

Patrick awoke to a pale blue sky with a light wind

blowing. *Perfect weather for boating.* He gathered up his belongings, yelled at Bard, and walked down to the water's edge. *Thank you, God, for letting me share your Word with these people. Bless them from now on.*

"Bishop, are you ready?" Byort called behind him.

Patrick turned and watched the man drag a currach across the beach. He placed the bow in the water and began to load Patrick's possessions into the bow. "Where will Bard sit?"

"My friend will take him," he said, motioning at another man and Bard walking toward the beach and carrying a boat between them.

# Chapter 31
## A Sister Found

Patrick relaxed in the stern as he watched the morning sun dance on the waves. Byort never seemed to tire as he rhythmically pulled on the oars, defying the unseen currents running around the island. "Do you visit Valentia often."

"Maybe twice a month. Will you be needing a return trip?"

"I don't know when yet. We may spend some time on the island, maybe even years."

"Years?" the man said surprised. "I don't think I could spend years with my sister."

"I never know how much need people have where I go. So, I don't know how long my trips will take."

The man nodded with understanding. "You sure brought us much needed blessings. I hope you find your sister well and have a wonderful visit. Stoke a fire the evening before you decide to leave, at the spot where I drop you off. I'll look for it every night and try to pick you up the next morning."

"Thank you, Byort, that is very kind of you."

"Not near the consideration you gave us. Thanks for the fish and the words of wisdom you spoke last night. They were a comfort to us all."

"I hope they will continue to give all of you the fortitude and grace to face any challenges in the future. When I return to one of my monasteries, I will be sure to send others to visit and minister to you." Patrick said as he felt the bow grind onto the rough sandy shore.

Patrick and Bard waved at the small boats as the fishermen departed. Then they turned and began walking up the sloping hill into a rising headwind.

"That will help them get back quicker," Bard said, leaning forward into a strong gust. "Where does your sister live here?" Bard asked.

"I have no idea, but when has that ever stopped me?"

At the top of the hill there were the crumbling remains of a very small village that seemed to be deserted.

"Hello, is anyone here?" Patrick shouted against the wind. "Hello, we are seeking my sister. We mean you no harm." They walked through a clutter of dilapidated structures of wood and stone until a weathered wooden door blew open ahead of them. A withered arm reached out in a vain effort to close it, but the wind was too strong. "Wait." Patrick cried. "We'll close that for you." The arm retreated into the darkness of what looked like a root cellar, as Patrick and Bard rushed forward. They stumbled down worn stone steps into a small room as Bard struggled to close the door behind them. The flickering light of a candle burned upon a tall rock placed in the center of the room, barely illuminating the dank space.

"What do you want?" A weak voice crackled from a pile of filthy rags behind it.

"Only to find my sister Darerca. I have heard that she lives on this island."

Boney fingers rose up slowly and clutched at the rags, separating them until a shrunken face appeared, wrinkled white skin with blue veins running across the forehead. When the thin-lipped mouth opened, they saw blackened stubs of teeth as the voice sputtered again, "I know no one by that name. I alone am left in this village. The others have gone."

Patrick smiled warmly at the watery green eyes of the horrific figure. "Madame, can we offer you some food?"

For nearly an hour she picked at the morsels of dried meat and bread that Bard placed before her. Each time she took a swig of wine, she cackled with glee. Finally, she rocked back and sat against the wall. "You are too kind to an old woman. What do you want from me?"

"I am looking for my sister. If you don't know her, we will inquire elsewhere." Patrick bowed.

"Wait, what kind of a man are you? I've never known a man to act like you do. What compels you to offer compassion for a poor, useless woman?" she spat.

"I am a humble servant of the one true God. I have compassion and love for all, including those who believe they are my enemies."

"He destroys wizards and brings the dead back to life." Bard interjected as Patrick shot him a glance to be quiet.

The old woman gave him a side-eye look. "That I cannot believe."

Patrick sighed, "I don't think she would be interested in eternal life either Bard." He noticed her bite her lower lip in concentration.

"Wait, what is your God? Is he different from the gods of my ancestors?"

"Night and day different, dear lady. Let me tell you a story."

Later, as they walked in the clear twilight, Bard said lyrically, "Another day, another soul baptized and saved, and she really appreciated your gift of a blanket."

Patrick was happy they had found the lady. *That poor struggling woman now has hope and some understanding of Divine Love to support her.* "What is that?" he said, suddenly stopping and pointing in the distance. "Is that a tower with a lighted room?"

Bard stared at the dark horizon and said, "Yes, I see it."

"Our guide to another destination," Patrick said as he

trotted down the pathway. When they drew closer, a large cluster of stones came into view below the tower.

"Wow, that would make a beautiful monastery." Bard whistled.

"Shush, there may be sentries. Maybe this wasn't a good idea," Patrick whispered.

"Maybe not, but you're here now. Why not visit?" The gruff voice came from behind them, and others joined in a loud laugh.

Patrick turned graciously and bowed. "Why certainly, we will be honored to be your guests."

Surprised at Patrick's nonchalant demeanor, the man holding the spear peered stupidly at him. "Come on, move you two." One of the others said as they were marched down the hill and entered the stone edifice. "Sire, we have apprehended two interlopers," the guard announced.

A very large man shuffled into the room and sat down on a wooden bench that creaked and popped loudly in its efforts to hold him up. "Who are you, and what are you doing in my kingdom?"

"My liege, my name is Bishop Patrick, and this is my attendant, Bard. We are here to visit my sister. I know she was supposed to live on this island, but I do not know where. Her name is Darerca, and I believe she has married." Patrick bowed in deference.

"Darerca, you say," as he tapped a finger on his lip. "She might be the girl that married Conis, one of my captains. Was she a captured slave?"

"Yes, sire, as was I."

"A slave, you were a slave?" The king squinted his eyes in disbelief. "I have never seen a slave dressed in robes such as yours."

"Well, I am no longer a slave. I am a crusader for Christ and have traveled across much of this country. Can you direct us to my sister?"

The king's brow furrowed. "Who was your master? Did

he release you? How did you become free?" he roared.

"A man named Milcho purchased me after I was kidnapped from Briton by Hibernian raiders. I served him six years before the Lord allowed me to escape to Briton. After my religious training, I returned to help the people of this island know the one true God."

"You came back?" the man was astonished. "I have never heard of a slave that escaped our land, let alone one that returned to bless his captors."

"I am unique," Patrick replied, holding a serious countenance.

"Darerca, you say. Conis lives not far from here. I will accompany you to their village on the morrow, stranger. I want to listen to this reunion if it is the same girl. Guards, show my guests to a room." He sat, pondering the conversation. Patrick watched him as he and Bard were led to a nearby sleeping area.

In the morning, they began the short journey to Glanleam. The king struggled to walk and was supported by a guard on each side helping to hold him upright. The trip was a short one, but they stopped so many times to let the king rest that it was nearly noon by the time they finally entered the village. "That hovel ahead there." The king pointed a stubby finger forward.

Patrick took a deep breath outside the doorway. "Hello, is this the home of Conis and Darerca?"

A rugged man suddenly appeared in the doorway, and seeing the king, immediately knelt. "Sire, what is it?"

Patrick continued, "Could I please meet your wife?"

The man looked confused, but stood up and called, "Darerca, we have visitors, the king, his guards, and two strangers."

A woman came to the door holding a small boy on her hip. "We are honored that you…" The words died in her mouth as she recognized something in the stranger's eyes. "Maewyn?" she uttered slowly. He smiled, as she quickly thrust the child into her husband's arms and turned to wrap her arms around Patrick.

He saw her tears flowing, just before his own eyes clouded over. "Darerca, I told father and mother that I would find you." He sobbed. He felt foolish crying in front of strangers, but when he finally pulled away, he noticed the king wiping away a stray tear also. "I have found my sister at last. Thank you, sire."

"A touching reunion," said the king with a pleasant smile. "How long have you two been separated?"

Patrick thought about it, "I was sixteen when we were captured, six years a slave, then sixteen years before becoming a bishop, and eighteen years in my ministry here. My goodness, it has been forty years. Darerca, I cannot believe that you recognized me."

"Your eyes have not changed my brother. Maybe they are less mischievous, but they still shine with love. Who is your handsome young helper?"

"My name is Bard, ma'am," he suddenly spurted.

"I think there might be a few young girls in our village who might like to meet you."

"My dear sister, please don't put any such ideas into his head. I need him to concentrate on his duties for me for now. His assistance is vital to my ministry here. I have enough problems keeping him focused as it is," Patrick said with a wane smile. "Who is this little rascal?" As he pointed at the child squirming to get out of his father's arms.

"That is our youngest grandson. His name is Cillian, and he is a handful. Come inside and meet your other great nephews. They are Cathal and Coner."

"I hope they will join me someday. Maybe they will become bishops too. How many children do you have?"

"We have three sons. Our son Moch and his wife will be by to take these ruffians home tomorrow."

Darerca suddenly stopped and turned in the doorway. "How in the world did you become a bishop? All these years

I thought you probably died in hard labor as a slave. I could never have imagined that you would become a man of the cloth."

"Some days I still wonder how I succeeded in that myself."

"Come in and sit down. I want to hear all about it, big brother."

"I want to know how a mere slave became whatever a bishop is," the king announced in a questioning voice.

As they entered the dwelling, Bard whispered, "Here we go again, another all-night sermon."

# Chapter 32
## A King Healed

*Bard was right, it took nearly until daylight.* Patrick admitted to himself as he sank down onto a bench and finished the story of Saint Paul's adventures. The king, his guards, and Bard had been snoring for nearly two hours, but Darerca and Conis still listened intently as they sat on the floor before him.

"I can't believe you did all those wonderful miracles for people. Are you sure you are my brother?" she laughed.

"I am proud and happy to be your brother and finally meet your family." He nodded to Conis.

"Able to perform miracles, but still so humble." She sighed as she grasped her husband's hand.

"Stop right there." He held up a finger. "I have never performed any miracles or healings or resurrections. It is God who does everything, I only strive to be a humble servant to his children, and to express His harmony in their lives. Then healing happens."

Seeing the perplexed looks on their faces he finally said, "Sleep on it, I hope it all makes more sense to you tomorrow, or I mean later today."

Patrick awoke to the chatter of young boys and the low tones of adults talking. "He's awake," the king announced. "I'm sorry I missed the end of your stories."

Patrick rubbed his eyes and tried to focus as he sat up.

Bard handed him a bowl of warm gruel and he tipped it to his mouth for a long drink. Wiping his mouth he said, "You know, sire, I never run out of stories, just the strength to tell them."

"You have the kindest heart of any man I have known. How have you survived in this world of savages?" the king asked.

"By living my life in God's kingdom. I look away from what you see every day, toward the harmony and Love that you don't see. Jesus said it best, **'And in them is fulfilled the prophecy of Esaias, which saith, By hearing ye shall hear, and shall not understand; and seeing ye shall see, and shall not perceive: For this people's heart is waxed gross, and *their* ears are dull of hearing, and their eyes they have closed; lest at any time they should see with *their* eyes, and hear with *their* ears, and should understand with *their* heart, and should be converted, and I should heal them.'** (78) At some point, the power of Truth will dispel the darkness covering your eyes and be visible to people across this world. I am just a small candle bringing light to as many souls as I can through my ministry."

"Can anyone join your church?" the king asked.

"Any who are ready to enter His kingdom and love their neighbors as themselves."

The boys ran outside to play, as the adults waited for the king to respond. "I have never been particularly good or kind, I have been selfish and taken that which did not belong to me, but only out of ignorance of your God," he added. "Can I be forgiven, redeemed, and be baptized as a Christian?"

"Yes."

"Can you do it now? And for my guards too?

"Only if they have free will to accept it themselves, but yes."

"Us too?" Darerca asked.

"I would invite everyone to join our movement, but they need to want to experience something beyond the life they are living, and be willing, humble and compassionate for others."

"I can't just make a decree that my subjects join your church?"

"No, sire. They need to decide for themselves. You can be an element of change though. Show them what a true, compassionate, Christian king is."

"I give you my oath that I will try, but only if you stay here to advise and instruct me with your knowledge of this God of yours."

"As you wish, sire. Valentia will become fruitful and bless all of its inhabitants with a glimpse of the true Kingdom. By the way, there is a ruined village on the east coast of your island. Could one of your guards provide some supplies and blankets to an old lady we discovered living there?"

"I will see to it as soon as I return to my castle. Can you help me up? I have trouble walking anymore," the king said with a wince as he struggled to rise.

Patrick laid his hand on the king's shoulder. "Sire, before you go, let me tell you another story about a beggar who couldn't walk. Two of Jesus's disciples were entering a temple when he asked them for a handout. **'Then Peter said, Silver and gold have I none; but such as I have give I thee: In the name of Jesus Christ of Nazareth rise up and walk. And he took him by the right hand, and lifted *him* up: and immediately his feet and ankle bones received strength.'** (79) Your subjects need you now more than ever my liege." Patrick grabbed both of the man's hands and pulled him upright. Walk with the Lord."

The man's eyes widened in amazement as he took a few steady steps forward. His mouth fell open as he side-stepped and spun in a circle. "I can walk," he said with gratitude filling his wide smile. "Maybe I can dance?" As he started to hop from side to side. His guards rushed toward him, but the king waved them off. "Thank you, Bishop Patrick, I never thought this…" emotion caused the words to catch in his throat.

"My son, you are experiencing the perfection that God knows is you. Don't thank me, thank only Him."

Tears streamed down the king's face as his guards followed him outside with quizzical looks at each other. Darerca ran over and hugged her brother. "Thank you Maew…, I mean Bishop Patrick. You've made him so happy."

Patrick started to admonish her but closed his mouth and embraced her in a hug instead.

# Chapter 33
A Resurrected Giant

"I believe it is time for us to leave you, my sister. It has been almost two years since I showed up on your doorstep." Patrick said quietly one morning at breakfast. "Bard, gather up our things when you finish eating." The boy responded with vigorous nods of his head.

"But everything is going so well, building the church and monastery has brought the whole island together. The children are learning so much from your acolytes and the priests you sent for. Thank you for sending them to help us. Our king has become a wonderful and healthier ruler. Why not stay and enjoy the fruits of your labor for just a while longer?"

"It is not easy for me to go, but there are many other poor souls that continue to suffer across Hibernia. As our master said. **'Then saith he unto his disciples, The harvest truly *is* plenteous, but the labourers *are* few;'** (80) I yearn to stay, but I must leave to feed his sheep dear sister. I will return to you if and when I can."

"I don't like it, but I understand." She squared her shoulders and looked him full in the face. "You have brought hope and healing into our lives. I can't possibly express what you mean to me. I love you, Maewyn Succat," she laughed as she wrapped her arms around him.

"Not more than I love you and yours, Darerca."

"So, where do we go now?" Bard asked as they slowly walked away from the village.

"Well, first we go back to the mainland, and from there, wherever the good Lord leads us."

"Same plan as always. The Father's plan." Bard grinned and began to whistle.

Patrick said, **"Trust in the LORD with all thine heart; and lean not unto thine own understanding."** (81) He felt the cold sea breeze caress his neck, and he pulled his hood up. *The only plan we need.*

They spent a chilly night huddled on the narrow point of land where they had first arrived on the island. After building a fire that could be seen on the other shore, they laid down and watched the stars. "Hey, did you see that?" Bard asked excitedly.

"Yes, a beautiful arc of fire."

"What makes that happen?"

"I don't know, but it was beautiful, like specks of lightning."

"The wrath of God?" the young man asked.

"The wrath of man." Patrick yawned. "Jesus calmed the storm. **'And there arose a great storm of wind, and the waves beat into the ship, so that it was now full. And he arose, and rebuked the wind, and said unto the sea, Peace, be still. And the wind ceased, and there was a great calm.'** (82) Men could too if they understood the law of harmony."

Patrick heard, "I can't imagine how…" as he drifted off to sleep.

In the morning, they awoke in a brisk breeze and tried to keep warm as they watched two small boats row toward them.

"Morning, Bishop. I thought you might never light a fire. I almost stopped looking after a year, but I gave you, my word. Other than fog and rain, I've looked every night that I could see the island. What all did you do since we saw you last?"

"I'll tell you all about it on our way back to the mainland." Patrick kept trying to wrap his robes tighter around himself to ward off the ocean breeze that seemed to cut right through him.

"Tis a bit chilly today." Byort smiled. "I should have let you row, I'm building up quite a sweat myself."

"I'll survive." Patrick said as he tried to huddle lower in the currach. "How is your little community doing now?"

"Much better than before you visited. We have been able to eat regularly now, thank you." He winked. "We told some of the priests that you sent to Valentia that we would like to build a church someday."

"A longing is a prayer. I'm sure you will have your church before long, my friend."

Once they reached the beach, Patrick and Bard waved goodbye to the fishermen and climbed the narrow trail to the top of the bluff. While they rested after the climb, they watched the morning sunshine hit the waves like dancing gems on the ocean far below.

"Beautiful, isn't it?" Bard asked as the chilly wind blew in his face.

"Remember, things in this world are poor substitutes for glimpsed perceptions of the real world, but sometimes they are breathtaking."

"Yes, I know, you've seen the way I look at girls." Bard's face reddened.

"They can be quite beautiful at times, I agree. Let's get going, wherever we are going. You decide this time."

"We are close to the southern edge of the island; we should head north." Bard announced.

"I'll follow you. Lead on young man, I shall follow."

They wound their way through a maze of shrubs and rocks on rough hillsides for several hours until Bard suddenly stopped. "What is that?" He pointed at a particularly long and wide sepulcher standing atop a hill in the distance. "Do you think that's only for one man? If it is he must have been huge."

"Could be for a family?" Patrick offered. "I see a town in that valley to the left. Let's see if they know anything about it."

As they entered the shabby village, a group of men and women quickly swarmed in front of them. "We don't allow strangers here," an older man with wild eyes shouted as the others raised menacing farm implements.

"We may be unknown to you, but we are friends of yours," Patrick said.

"We have no friends other than ourselves."

"That is untrue. If you allow me to speak, you will find that you have much in common with other inhabitants of this island. For instance, who lies in the grave at the peak of that hill over there?"

"Glarcus was his name. He was the champion of our village until Flynnan Mac Con ambushed him after he turned one hundred years old. No telling how long he would have lived if he hadn't been murdered. His killer didn't enjoy his victory for long though." He and the others snickered among themselves.

"The death of any man is a tragedy for someone," Patrick said quietly, and the people finally became quiet. Turning to Bard he said, "I told you that crypt was for only one man," and winked out of sight of the others.

"I don't believe it. They must be lying to us; no man could be that big." Bard shouted.

"I swear to you, young man, it is the truth," the old man spoke again.

Patrick turned to the group with his arms wide open. "You people must understand, youngsters are sometimes hard to convince. I only know of one way to convince him that you tell the truth. Let us all go up there and ask Glarcus himself."

"He is dead, did you not understand?" The old man said

again as a loud murmur spread through the group.

"Let me ask him if he is dead. If he does not answer, we will know – and we will leave your village at once, ashamed of our insolence. Do you all agree?"

A short discussion followed between the villagers. The old man spoke up, "You must be mad, but we agree to watch your folly, and jeer as you leave us in shame." A cluster of nodding and laughing heads affirmed the decision.

"Let us go then," Patrick said as he raised his staff and began walking up the hillside.

As they approached the sepulcher, the villagers formed a semi-circle around a short wooden doorway, as Patrick and Bard knelt in prayer for a few long moments. "In the words of Jesus, the son of God, **'Father, I thank thee that thou hast heard me. And I knew that thou hearest me always: but because of the people which stand by I said** *it,* **that they may believe that thou hast sent me.'** (83) Glarcus, come forth."

Nothing happened immediately. The villagers began to be edgy and started to whisper among themselves as a few more minutes passed. Patrick looked at Bard's wide eyes filled with doubt and placed a steady hand on the young man's shoulder before he stood up and said, "Don't be shy, my friend. Come forth now, into the glorious sunshine."

A scraping sound came from the doorway as some dust fell from the sill. The door suddenly quivered as a large thump was heard. Again, the sound came as some of the rocks shifted. Another blow, and the door fell forward in a shower of rocks, dust, and debris. The villagers scattered and hid behind nearby boulders as a massive hand emerged from the crypt. Patrick noticed that only the old man stood rooted and staring at the spectacle with wide eyes. *Probably too frightened to move.*

"Look," Bard gasped.

Patrick found himself staring at the creature slowly emerging from the grave. His shoulders were so wide that they scraped the sides of the doorway as he crawled through.

"Glarcus," the old man moaned as he fell to his knees, before passing out.

## Chapter 34
### Baptized in Spirit

A hoarse voice roared from the creature, "Who hath awakened me from my torments?" It continued to crawl out and groaned loudly as it began to pull itself upright.

Patrick felt the hair on his neck stand up, and noticed that Bard had risen to a crouch, ready to run. He realized he needed to force himself to see only God's creation. Suddenly the thought came, *"I have raised him up in righteousness, and I will direct all his ways:"* (84) and Patrick relaxed a bit. "I have Glarcus. I am Bishop Patrick, and I have called you back from your agonies in death. Come forward and learn of the one true God."

A hideous face raised and looked at him with watery eyes. "Bless you, sir. You have delivered me from the horrid afflictions of hell. I am your most humble servant," he said in a great, deep voice that seemed to shake the ground, as he knelt down on one knee.

Patrick stood up and realized Glarcus was still a head taller than him even though he was kneeling. Looking around he saw that the old man had fainted, and two of the villagers were trying their best to revive him. "Dear Glarcus, I apologize, but I have called you back to witness to these people the salvation that is possible in this life and beyond. **'If I ascend up into heaven, thou *art* there: if I make my bed in hell, behold, thou *art there*.'** (85) Do you now know and believe in the God of Jesus and have forsaken all other idols?" he asked.

A great exhale accompanied the giant's answer, "Yes, I see he is all in this world and beyond. He is everywhere. He was with me in hell, but I couldn't see him. You have shown him to me!" Two great arms wrapped around Patrick and drew him tight against the massive chest. "I am delivered from the lies of evil that have bound me to punishment in death. Thank you for saving me."

"Please don't squeeze your benefactor so hard, he's turning purple." Bard jumped up and shouted.

"Oh, sorry," the giant said as he released Patrick and stood up. "I will be glad to follow you on your ministry and help spread your message throughout this land."

Patrick coughed and drew a few deep breaths as he considered the man's offer, *he was so fearsome looking that the faithful might just turn and run away, instead of being drawn to his sermons*. He took another glance back at the villagers who were starting to slowly draw closer again with concern still etched on their faces, before continuing to speak with a smile on his face. "Glarcus, believe me, I love your exuberance." Turning, he said to all those listening, **"Know ye not, that to whom ye yield yourselves servants to obey, his servants ye are to whom ye obey; whether of sin unto death, or of obedience unto righteousness?"** (86)

The giant grumbled, "I was raised in ignorance of your God. I want to be with him. I didn't know of him before. I only knew the creations in this world, but you have given me a glimpse of the real world of God that your Jesus spoke of. I do want to follow him." The man suddenly clasped his enormous hands together in prayer, eliciting a small cloud of dust.

"Then, dear Glarcus, I bless you in the name of the Father, the Son, and the Holy Ghost. Return to your rest, enter into the kingdom of the almighty and be tormented no more by images of anything other than Love for you and all mankind."

A look of bliss softened the features of the man's terrible visage, and a smile emerged on his dusty lips. For a moment he swayed back and forth, then he laid down, stretched out, and breathed no more.

"Is he…" Bard asked.

"Yes, he is again asleep, but peaceful now." As he still silently prayed for the man's salvation and protection in the world beyond.

"You didn't sprinkle holy water on him."

"What?" Patrick asked as he focused. "Oh, yes I know."

"Is he baptized then?"

"If God is a spiritual and infinite, he is everywhere. Glarcus is baptized in Spirit. I still use water for most people, because it is tangible for them. Also, because John the Baptist used water. Glarcus didn't need water, he just needed the qualities of God revealed to him to quiet his agony. He is at peace now."

"Bishop Patrick, forgive our ignorance, our unbelief." The old man staggered forward and fell at his feet, along with a number of the other villagers. "Teach us of your God who restored our great giant."

"First, replace him in his resting place and repair the doorway. Then I will be glad to preach words of salvation to your people." He whispered to Bard, "Looks like we are building another church."

"Yay," came the reply, without much enthusiasm. As they sat and watched the people repair the crypt Bard asked Patrick, "So are all the dead who died not knowing God doomed to suffer forever?"

Patrick felt a wave of compassion as he gazed at Bard's distraught look. "No Bard, even those who dwell in darkness will at some point see the light, because it continues to shine forever, even though their eyes may be closed to it for some time."

"Like King Leogaire?"

"Yes, and all the others who passed before him. I pray that they all see the light someday."

"His tomb is sealed again," the old man interrupted. "Will you both accompany us back to the village? We want to hear about your God, and we will feed you."

"We will be honored to join you, won't we, Bard?" They followed the procession of villagers back to the town below. The older man walked alongside them.

"I still can't believe you called old Glarcus back from the shadows of death. You know he used to be a swineherd for King Leogaire himself. Have you met him yet? He's the Chief King of the island."

"Yes, he has built a church in Tara for the faithful to worship there."

"Really? That's hard for me to believe. He was a stalwart follower of our old gods and idols. I was in his temple once and saw all his idols."

"Now his wife is a believer, and I think deep down he wants to be, but his pride prevents him. Someday, I pray he will join us, but at least he isn't against us." Patrick smiled. "Who is the king in this region?"

"Would you believe that I am?" the old man said with a smile that stretched across his face.

"It would surprise me, sire."

"Well, I am. I dress like this because I fit in with my subjects. We don't have that many inhabitants in this kingdom, and we all live like an extended family. I try to be humble with them, and if we are ever attacked, who would think that I was the king, or even worth killing? That is my home before us. They should have a meal prepared soon."

"Do you have guards?" Bard asked perplexed.

"If I had guards, any attackers would know that I was the king."

"It makes sense, it's brilliant." Patrick said with a new admiration for the man. "I think you will really enjoy learning about Jesus and his disciples. He was their Lord and master, yet he bathed their feet, in humility. **'Jesus knowing that the Father had given all things into his hands, and that he was come from God, and went to God; He riseth from supper, and laid aside his garments; and took a towel, and girded himself. After that he poureth water into a basin, and began to wash the disciples' feet, and to wipe *them* with the towel wherewith he was girded.'** (87) He shunned the world's concepts of power and status, and just loved."

"Did he do it to escape harm?" the king asked confused.

"No, he did it to express love to his disciples, and the world. To show people the meaning of life and how to live it. He allowed himself to be put to death on a cross, so that he could show that death of the body was not the end of life. Life is eternal in God."

"That's how you brought Glarcus back. By knowing he never truly died but was trapped in a world created of his own sins," the king stated.

"My liege, you are the wisest king I have ever met. I can't wait to tell you more."

"I apologize for the way I welcomed you, my friend I'm so glad you refused to leave. I could never have imagined a day such as this."

"Apology accepted." Patrick said as he stepped into the king's home. "Let me now start from the beginning. **'In the beginning God created the heaven and the earth.'** (88)"

A year and a half later, Patrick and Bard finally said goodbye to the little community. They paused climbing the hillside and stared down at the flourishing new church that had sprouted in the middle of the village.

"That was a wonderful experience," Bard said, surprising Patrick. I think those villagers appreciated your gift more than all the others that we have visited."

"Not my gift, God's," Patrick corrected. "But I'll agree that the humility and love they express to each other, and now even to strangers, is heartwarming. I think the king's humble attitude made the difference. Jesus would have loved him."

"Jesus does love him." Bard laughed as he started walking up the hill again.

# Chapter 35
## A King Returns

"What is this region called?" Patrick asked as they wandered into the next small hamlet.

"You be in Humestia, strangers," a street vendor answered. "Are you looking for someone?"

"Who is in charge here?"

"Why the prince, of course. He resides across the valley in that hillfort." As he pointed to a rocky crest.

Patrick and Bard looked across a lush green meadow below and up toward the hilltop where walls of stones were visible. "I think we should visit him. What do you think, Bard?"

"Lead, I will follow."

When they finally approached the outer wall, several heads popped up from the other side. "What's your business here?"

"I am Bishop Patrick; I trust your prince has heard of me. I seek an audience with his highness to benefit him and his subjects."

"Wait." Came the only reply as one of the heads disappeared, while the others watched closely. Many minutes later the man reappeared. "Walk to the east side. I will meet you there."

Patrick and Bard walked around the pile of rocks until they came to a crude gateway. A heavily armed man stepped out and motioned them inside. Saying nothing he led them around a long round inner wall, past groups of armed men, and through another smaller gateway, where they saw another rounded wall.

"How many walls are in this fort?" Patrick asked.

"This is the last one," the man answered. "Keep following." As he led them around another wall and through an opening in the rocks.

They emerged into a large area filled with hovels and mounds of dirt which Patrick knew were passage tombs. Bard paused to look at them, but when the guard said, "Hurry up." Bard scurried forward. They followed him to a large hovel where he entered and kneeled before a seated young man. "These are the visitors your highness."

"Ah, finally, the great Patrick has come to grace us with his presence. You may leave us Gar."

The guard hesitated for a moment before standing and walking out the door.

"Welcome, Patrick, son of Calpurnius." Patrick's eyes widened in shock as the prince clapped his hands and continued, "See, I knew I could surprise you. I have asked many people a myriad of questions about you. I've been awaiting our meeting with much anticipation."

"Sire, I am greatly humbled by your interest in me. What prompted it?" Patrick asked with a bow.

"I studied you, because your religion fascinates me. How you have used it to persevere in your various adventures. I've heard you defeated Dichu the Savage, vanquished King Leogaire's wizards, healed illness, and built a multitude of churches and monasteries across this isle. I have even heard outlandish stories of you raising some of our dead souls to life again. At that point, I decided to wait patiently to meet you and find out which stories were true, and which were complete fabrications."

Bard suddenly spoke. "They are all true, they…"

Patrick quieted him with a motion of his hand.

"All true, you say. We shall see, but I do want to learn more about this religion of yours. It sounds marvelous. Please, come and dine with me and tell me the stories of your heroes and villains."

Patrick laughed. "I hope you won't be disappointed because we have many heroes, but only one real villain."

"I can't wait to hear all about it," the prince said as he ushered them toward a table filled with food. The fare was common, but filling. Patrick began with accounts from Genesis and spoke for hours, retelling his favorite stories and parables. "Jesus visited a city called Nain and, **'Now when he came nigh to the gate of the city, behold, there was a dead man carried out, the only son of his mother, and she was a widow: and much people of the city was with her. And when the Lord saw her, he had compassion on her, and said unto her, Weep not.And he came and touched the bier: and they that bare *him* stood still. And he said, Young man, I say unto thee, Arise. And he that was dead sat up, and began to speak. And he delivered him to his mother.'** (89) And all the people glorified God..."

Suddenly, the prince stopped him. "I love your stories, but I cannot imagine the dead being returned to life. Reanimating a soulless shell has to be impossible."

"Sire, you are concentrating on nothingness if you look to the body for life. We, as individuals, are eternal expressions of God. As I told you before, **'So God created man in his *own* image, in the image of God created he him; male and female created he them.'** (90) We are spiritual creatures, eternal with God. We don't reanimate the dead, we see the impossibility of them to ever stop expressing God, Life. That's what Jesus did..."

"Stop. I tell you I will never believe this thing unless I could witness it with my own eyes. It is beyond comprehension," the prince blurted.

Patrick sighed, "It is the Truth."

The prince gave a derisive laugh. "Next, you'll be

telling me that my grandfather could rise again. He who has lain cold in the grave many days now."

"Can you take me to his tomb?" Patrick asked.

The prince's brow furrowed deeply, "Yes, if you want to see it, follow me," the prince said as he stood and strode out the door.

They followed him to one of the larger burial mounds within the smaller ring of rocks. "This is it," the prince said. "He died and was interred nearly a month ago."

"Please have your men open it."

"This is ridiculous, why the smell alone…"

"Please." Patrick repeated as he knelt on the ground with Bard next to him.

With a disgusted look, the prince called several of his guards over and had them start removing the stones that blocked the entrance. "There, it is opened, now what?"

Patrick ignored him as he prayed to know Life is eternal.

Guards and others began to gather around the prince and their talk and jeers grew louder for a few minutes, until those sounds abruptly stopped, replaced by a collective gasp.

At that point Patrick opened his eyes and stood up. "Greetings, great king."

The crowd moved back in shock as a man shuffled forward out of the tomb. He was extremely tall and with a horrid visage, although Patrick noticed that he wasn't nearly as imposing as Glarcus had been.

"Grandfather?" a shaky voice squeaked. And the man looked over and smiled at his grandson. Patrick was glad the prince didn't faint.

Turning to face Patrick the hideous mask of the man's face wheezed, "Did you call me forth from my terrors in death?"

"I did my king, to quell your suffering and to offer you both Life and eternal peace."

The old king's body stepped closer and bent to look into Patrick's eyes. "Pray tell me what I need to do to escape the pains and thoughts that plagued me in death's darkness."

"Accept the Christ, receive Spirit and forsake your concepts of mortal existence with its false gods, pains, pleasures, and terrors," he added.

The man drew back and stiffened, even as his head rolled from one side to the other. "I want this Christ; I want relief from the tortures I've endured. I accept this Christ, your God, and the son?" He shook his head back and forth. "I hear a name, Jesus." He whimpered as he fell to his dusty knees with his head bowed.

"You are correct, my liege. You are perceiving Truth. It is my pleasure to welcome you into God's eternal kingdom. I bless you. Now you can return to your peaceful sleep and awake in His kingdom of Love, without any of the pains you endured before."

The man's shoulders shook for a few long moments as if he were crying, and then he stood up. "Thank you, sir, I feel different. I feel washed in Love now, and I am sleepy," he said as he turned and walked back, bent forward and entered the crypt without another word.

The prince fainted at that point. His guards rushed forward and carried him back to his palace. Bard and Patrick followed them in. The other onlookers rushed around the compound, as they shared the story of the old king's resurrection.

The prince awoke a short time later, surrounded by his guards. "Did you see him? My grandfather? He came back. He looked horrible, but it was him. Where is Patrick? I want Patrick," he screamed.

"Here I am your excellency." Patrick stepped out from behind one of the guards.

"Patrick, I apologize, I didn't…, Can you baptize me now? Right now?"

"Calm yourself, sire. Rest while I continue telling you the history of Christ. I want you to understand everything. I promise I will christen you into the church. Now, where was

I, oh yes, raising the dead boy for his mother." Patrick kept talking until the prince fell into a deep sleep. He motioned to Bard, and they both crept out of the room.

They found an unused corner of the palace and bedded down for the night. When they were settled, Bard asked, "I've asked before, but how do you do it?"

Patrick chuckled. "Do what?"

"Raise the dead. Especially the ones that have been dead for years." Bard said loudly and then slapped his hand over his mouth. "Sorry," he mouthed.

"The Lord has given me the power to work miracles among these Barbaric people such as have not been demonstrated since the time of Jesus and his apostles. Saint Martin raised the dead also, but God graced me with an abundance of His power to raise the dead. I guess, because he knows without works such as these, the people would continue to hold onto their idols and false gods."

"But how do you do it? I want to learn, so I can bring people back to life."

"Saint Martin provided the key in his scroll. Remember where he wrote, 'You are not mortals. You are spiritual creatures!' Before that I thought and saw everything as material and limited like everyone else. After reading that, I knew the material world was a false image, a poor substitute for the unlimited boundaries of Spirit. That is the key to my miracles in raising both the dead and the living on this island. First, you must understand that nothing ever dies. Nothing created by God can ever die. God is Life, and everything that he has created must express that Life forever, whether we can see those individuals who have passed or not. They are because God is," he added as he drifted off to sleep

Patrick awoke to raised, excited voices. "There he stirs," came a loud voice. The clamor of voices increased as a crowd quickly gathered around him.

Looking up, he focused on the face of the prince. "Stop talking," the man shouted, and the voices quickly quieted.

"I'm sorry Patrick, but the news about my grandfather's resurrection spread like fire in dried flax. I think all of my subjects are making their way here to learn about your God and be baptized."

"I understand, but show them out until I have time to wake up and take care of some things." He winked.

"Guards, move these people out into the compound. Bishop Patrick will see you all shortly. He will speak to you from the burial mound."

Patrick groaned as he stretched and rolled over to stand. "Are you awake, Bard."

"Maybe, not sure. I'll let you know in a little while."

Patrick yawned. "Come on, son. We have work to do."

They both staggered out into the early morning sun minutes later, and Bard steadied Patrick as he climbed up the slick, dew covered grass on the burial mound.

"Friends, I am Patrick." A loud cheer went up, and he waited for the crowd to become quiet again. "I am here to introduce you to the only God there is. The Father and Mother of us all."

A series of voices raised questions as soon as Patrick paused.

"Can you raise my husband?"

"What about my grandmother?"

"Can you bring back my son?"

Soon there were so many questions being asked that no one could understand them. Thankfully the prince clambered up the mound and took control. "Listen all of you. Patrick is not here to run around and resurrect your loved ones, as much as I'm sure he would like to. He has come to us and demonstrated the power of his God, soon to be our God. Allow him to speak so you can understand and join his ministry. Maybe then you will raise your own dead."

A quiet murmur spread through the crowd as Patrick began speaking again, "I will begin at the beginning of everything. The book is called Genesis."

Patrick was exhausted as he sat and slowly scooted off the mound after speaking for most of the day. He groaned as he looked at the growing crowd of people lined up and awaiting baptism. "Bard, I think I need you to take on the full duties of a priest. Find a tank of water, bless it and welcome those poor souls into the church. I need a nap."

Bard looked at Patrick with a satisfied grin. "I will not fail you or them, sir." As he ran off toward a wooden trough used for livestock.

Several guards assisted Patrick back to his sleeping area. Giving gratitude to the Lord for the day filled with blessings, he quickly fell fast asleep.

"Patrick, are you awake?" Bard asked.

"I am now, why did you wake me? What time is it?"

"The sun is just coming up, and I finally finished the task you gave me."

"The people?" Patrick tried to organize his thoughts. "You're just finished now?"

"Yes, I even had to refill the trough once, even though I just sprinkled them rather than immersing them. I don't know how many I blessed, but it had to be thousands. Groups of them kept coming from villages throughout the region."

I'm sorry I missed seeing that, but I really needed some rest. Thank you for your tenacity, tending to all the faithful. Help me up, will you? I feel stiff." Patrick raised his arms and Bard struggled to pull him upright.

"The prince has asked to see you right away."

Patrick bowed his head. "Thank you, God. Give me a few quiet minutes to pray, and I will be with him."

"He wants to start building a church and a monastery. Imagine that." Bard grinned. "Looks like our travels to Saul are paused once again."

## Chapter 36
Death from a Boar

"That is the most beautiful church and monastery we have built yet." Bard said proudly as he paused and looked at the imposing structure gleaming in the distance.

"I'm glad you appreciate the building, but it is the people who are the church. If they lose sight of the Truth, they will drift away, and the church will be no more."

"They are so excited now; it is hard for me to believe that they could ever forget that you raised their dead king."

"It doesn't take long for people to forget the Truth or to be lured away by false gods, Bard. Remember when Moses came down from Mount Sinai with the Ten Commandments? **'And when the people saw that Moses delayed to come down out of the mount, the people gathered themselves together unto Aaron, and said unto him, Up, make us gods, which shall go before us; for *as for* this Moses, the man that brought us up out of the land of Egypt, we wot not what is become of him.'** (91) Moses was gone only forty-seven days and forty-seven nights and what happened?"

"He came down, let me think a moment. **'And it came to pass, as soon as he came nigh unto the camp, that he saw the calf, and the dancing: and Moses' anger waxed hot, and he cast the tables out of his hands, and brake them beneath the mount.'** (92) He saw the golden calf that the people were worshipping, and he broke the tablets in his fury."

"Those people had seen the power of God hold back the Red Sea for their escape from the Egyptians. Those chosen people were led by a pillar of a cloud by day and a pillar of fire at night. They were even fed by manna from heaven. It took barely more than a month for them to forsake God and build an idol, a golden calf to worship. No, my son. Truth is a precious thing which needs to constantly be protected, practiced, and shared. Otherwise, in a short time it can be lost beneath the dust of history."

Bard was silent as they trudged onward through the hills, toward the next settlement.

"There it is." Patrick pointed at a fire on a ridge as the twilight closed around them. "Let's spend the night here and we can visit tomorrow."

"How will we cross that river?"

Patrick looked and saw a bit of reflected light glimmer as water flowed through a channel in the valley below. "I don't know, that might be the boundary line between two kingdoms. We will know tomorrow."

They reached the river late the next morning. A woman was wading and filling an oak bucket with water on the other side. "Hello good woman. Is there a bridge or shallow crossing nearby?" Patrick called out.

She sneered at him and turned. climbing the bank without an answer.

"I guess she doesn't know." Bard said. "Feel like a taking a dip?"

As they crawled out of the water and up the bank, Patrick's teeth chattered as he said,

"That must be spring-fed, I'm frozen."

"And deeper than I thought, it was up to my chest. I wish you'd teach me how to walk on it," Bard added.

"I'd like to know that myself." Patrick laughed as he tried to wring out his robes. "At least the sun is shining," he said as he started to strip.

"What do you two think you are doing?" a harsh voice demanded a few minutes later.

They looked up to see several large men peering at them from behind some bushes. "We have come to see your ruler." Patrick answered with as much dignity as he could, while naked and holding his dripping vestments.

"Are you going to see him nude?" the man laughed. "Put those back on and we'll take you to him." The armed men stepped out, and Patrick realized they were guards.

"But they're wet, can't we let them dry a bit?" Bard complained as Patrick gave a twist to his robe and a stream of water squirted from it.

"Fine, build a fire with dead branches from that tree over there. "We'll be back in a couple hours to escort you to the prince. Oisin, stay here and watch these two while we finish our rounds." Oisin nodded, walked a short distance away, and sat on a large rock in the sun.

Bard hurried to gather branches and start the fire, as Patrick finished wringing out their garments and stretched some heavy twine between two nearby trees. He hung their clothes up to dry, and walked over to warm himself at the small blaze as Bard kept adding larger pieces of wood to it until the heat finally drove them away.

"I see steam coming from your robes, it shouldn't be too long now."

"If we have to put them on soon, at least they will be a warm wet." Patrick chuckled.

The two kept checking the clothes until they felt dry for the most part. Patrick was just adjusting his cloak when the men returned.

"Are you dry now? The largest man said.

"Not exactly dry, but at least a more comfortable damp." Patrick said with a smile.

"Come along, the prince might enjoy meeting you."

They followed the men through winding pathways

across hills and valleys for nearly four hours until they entered another hilltop fort.

"Sire, we have apprehended two intruders next to the river. They've asked to have an audience with you."

"Who are they?

"The one is called Patrick; he says he is a bishop or something."

"What is a bishop? I have never heard of one."

"Tell him it is Patrick, who defeated Dichu," Bard said loudly.

Patrick rolled his eyes. *I shouldn't need to be introduced as a conqueror.*

"I have heard of that man; bring him to me."

Patrick and Bard were ushered forward into a darkened room. "Kneel before the prince," the guard announced.

"I kneel for no man, only for the one true God," Patrick announced defiantly.

The guard suddenly raised his staff to swing it at Patrick's head.

"Stop," the prince roared. "You interest me, sir. I have heard of your miracles. Tell me how you defeated the fearsome wizards of King Leogaire."

**"I can of mine own self do nothing: as I hear, I judge: and my judgment is just; because I seek not mine own will, but the will of the Father which hath sent me."** (93)

"What does that mean? Do you only speak in riddles?"

"I don't do anything myself; it is my God who works through me."

"Our gods don't work through us. Sometimes they work for us, but usually they work against us." The prince laid a finger beside his nose and appeared to be perplexed. Finally, he said, "Do you know who I am?"

"No, your highness. Rarely do I know who I will meet next, or who will listen to my preaching."

"I am Prince Elelius, ruler of this region. Entertain me with the tales you tell about your strange doctrine, please."

Patrick began speaking, and soon realized the prince wasn't receptive to his oration, the guards were listening though, so he continued talking until the prince interrupted.

"Stop, I'm getting a headache. Guards, give them decent accommodations. We will talk again later. I have a hog hunt today with my son, I may see you later at dinner." He stood up and walked outside.

When they were alone, Bard asked, "Was it my imagination, or did he not listen to a word you said?"

"No, he didn't. He ignored all that I said."

"Why?"

"I don't know. I think we arrived just in time to help him though. Let's be patient; an opportunity will arise, maybe soon."

Early in the evening they heard loud shouts from outside that quickly drew nearer and continued. The people coming ran around the concentric rings of the fort toward the center. "Bishop, please help my son," the prince rushed into the room and fell at Patrick's feet. "I swear I will believe in your God and obey his commandments. A boar killed my son! I beg you, please restore him," he collapsed in sobs on the floor.

Four solemn guards carried the boy's remains into a small room. Patrick looked away from the body of the youth as the guards carefully placed the remnants on the floor. Patrick couldn't help but noticed that there wasn't much of the boy that was still connected. The boar's razor-sharp tusks had ripped him to shreds. "Bard, you've been wanting to resurrect someone. Do you want to take this one? Remember the scroll," he said with a serious expression.

Bard stared wide-eyed at the body as his face turned white. "How, there's nothing left to resurrect. His bones are broken and missing, his entrails spilling out. Half his skin is gone! I'm sorry, I can't."  As he turned and threw up.

"Forget appearances, what is Spirit telling you?" Patrick asked, trying to make a point. There was no response from

Bard. "Leave me." Patrick commanded. "All of you, leave me." He noticed tears flowing from the prince, Bard, and even the guards as they hurried to leave.

Patrick threw a blanket over the body. Turning away from the devastated material image, he closed his eyes. *Father, this boy is made perfect in your image. He is only composed of your substance, Spirit, which cannot be hurt or destroyed. In your kingdom there is only harmony. You are omnipotent and omnipresent, everywhere. Spirit is always intact, perfect and untouched. This boy expresses Life because you are Life. He was never separated from you.*

———•●•———

"How long should I wait?" the prince demanded.

"Be patient. Wait for Bishop Patrick. If anyone can help your son, he can. I've seen him raise people that have been dead for centuries."

"He better raise him, or he'll wish he'd never been born," the prince hissed.

"Stop it." Bard commanded in a loud voice and the prince looked shocked. "You aren't helping your son with that attitude. Only Love can return your son now. Love for your son, for Patrick, for everything."

"Love? I do love my son," he shouted.

"Then act like it. Remove your pride, hate, and fear. Be humble before God and just Love. Feel Love. Be Love."

The prince didn't answer, but his expression quickly changed from righteous wrath to humility. Tears streamed down his face as he crumpled to the floor and clasped his hands.

———•●•———

Patrick didn't know how much time had passed, but he

was sweating profusely.  His vestments were soaked again. *Twice in one day. Immersed in a river first and immersed in God's Love always. Just like the boy and his father, immersed only in Spirit. Why did I think of the boy's father?*

"Who are you?" a groggy voice asked.

"Love," was Patrick's grateful reply.

"Why are my clothes torn to shreds?" the boy asked as he lifted the blanket and stared.

"I'll let your father explain that. Let me get him." Patrick stood up and smiled at the young man before he poked his head out of the doorway. "Your highness, can you come here?"

The penitent prince stirred from his prone position and blinked at Patrick with reddened eyes. "Is he?"

"Come and see."

Slowly the prince stood up and humble hope showed in his face as he walked toward the room, a changed man. Cries of joy erupted from him when he saw his son alive.

"I'm sorry," Bard said. "All I could see was devastation and…"

Patrick put a steady hand on Bard's shoulder. **"And Jesus said unto them, Because of your unbelief: for verily I say unto you, If ye have faith as a grain of mustard seed, ye shall say unto this mountain, Remove hence to yonder place; and it shall remove; and nothing shall be impossible unto you."** (94)

"I have faith, but it must be a lot smaller than a mustard seed."

"Keep working on it." Patrick smiled. "I need to take a bath now. Can you wash my sweaty robes? They're really starting to smell."

"Yes sir, I can't wait to write this day down in my journal."

## Chapter 37
A Wife Returned

"Are you happy to be leaving?" Patrick asked Bard as they waved at the crowd of new converts and walked away from the large church that Prince Elelius had built.

"Yes, that was your most traumatic resurrection yet."

"Traumatic? You can't let a lie about the real man affect you. You have to be able to see through it. I keep telling you. Look away from matter to Spirit."

"Are you trying to tell me that this material world doesn't even exist?"

"I am afraid so, my son, everything you see and everything you touch and feel are false mortal concepts of spirit. Reality is an omnipresent, harmonious God and his perfect ideas."

Bard grinned, "I think I'll stick to healing common colds and fevers, or maybe a strained muscle, rather than what you just did."

Patrick laughed. "You will see more of what God is until you fail to see what He isn't. At that point, you won't be able to avoid healing and raising others from their false beliefs and ills, whatever they may be."

"I hope so," was all Bard said.

"I know so, someone told me." Patrick laughed as he pointed upward.

"Why do you point up when you speak of God? Isn't he

here too?"

"Of course he is, but most people don't understand that. I guess I've made a habit of it to indicate a higher thought than what we see."

"Oh, no. Is that another river ahead?" Bard asked several days later as they topped the crest of a hill while following a well-worn cartpath.

"Yes, I think that must be Connactia on the other side. Prince Elelius told us to visit a man named Euchadius there."

"We have to ford another river?" Bard grimaced. "I hope it's shallow."

"I think it's shallow since this pathway tracks across it, but I just hope it's warm." Patrick chuckled as they began walking down to the water. when they drew closer, they saw a man sitting beside a bier on the other bank. A body laid on top of it. "Let's hurry." Patrick said as he lifted his robes and plunged forward into the water.

"Are you Patrick?" the man asked, offering his hand as Patrick neared the bank.

"Yes, and you must be Euchadius."

The man pulled Patrick up onto solid ground and with tears in his eyes said, "Yes, my wife lies beyond on the bier. I heard you performed the miracle of raising Prince Elelius's son from death and healed his extensive injuries. Please bring her back," he sobbed.

**"If thou canst believe, all things *are* possible to him that believeth."** (95) Patrick said as he walked past the man, over to the woman. He watched Bard crawl out of the river and kneel next to the man. Then he overheard him say, "Your wife will be returned to life. I've seen him do it numerous times before. Our God is good, and so is Patrick, he will not allow you or your wife to suffer in ignorance of the one God."

Patrick felt himself smile as he took hold of the woman's cold hand. He held it for a few minutes as he prayed silently. **"Maid, arise."** (96) Her eyelids fluttered.

"Who are you? Where am I?" she said, raising her head and looking around in shock.

"I am Bishop Patrick; your husband is coming." He nodded in the direction of the man and Bard hurrying over, as he helped her slide off the bier.

"Darling, I thought I lost you forever."

"I remember being sick, but then…"

"You were dead, but then I heard of this Bishop Patrick raising Prince Elelius's son after a wild pig killed him, and he came here, and you're back! He said throwing his arms around her.

"Never died," Patrick whispered to Bard.

Bard sighed, "I know, another church."

Euchadius insisted that they would stay at his home while he sent messages to all the nearby communities. As strangers and family poured into the village over the weeks that followed, Patrick preached all day and into the night, while Bard was kept busy baptizing everyone into the church.

Finally, the flow of people seemed to ebb, and construction started on a church, along with classes of instruction for the first acolytes. Patrick selected a priest for the community and sent a letter to his monastery describing the position and asking him to travel to there as soon as possible. When Father Cable arrived a few weeks later and began his duties, Patrick was finally able to get some rest. At the end of the year, the church was completed and once again, Patrick and Bard were ready to resume their adventure.

"Thank you for bringing my wife back to me and bringing the Christ to our community."

Euchadius announced in a celebration for them before they left. "Where will you travel next?"

"I think we will head eastward toward Dublina, and then up to see my friend Dichu." Patrick said as he smiled at the large crowd. He noticed several men dressed in dark clothes at the back of the group of villagers who weren't smiling, *Wizards? I wonder.*

# Chapter 38
A Trap

Patrick and Bard were walking on a narrow pathway through a dark and thickly wooded area late in the day. Patrick noticed a forest glade with huge oak trees scattered through it ahead. "This looks like it could be a grove for Druid worship. Keep your eyes open and pray." He said quietly.

"Look, a stream." Bard pointed and walked toward it to refill their waterskins. As he knelt at the edge, a woman jumped out from behind a tree and screamed at them. "There they are. They be the ones who stole my flax." Several armed men rushed from concealment and quickly surrounded them both.

"Robbers," one of the men exclaimed. "We kill robbers here." His smile revealed three teeth.

"I pronounce them guilty," another said. "How shall we execute them?"

"With great malice and bloodshed." Another yelled as they raised their weapons.

"Hello, gentlemen, I remember that all of you were in the crowd at our going away ceremony yesterday, except for you, young lady. Did these men coerce you into lying for them?" Patrick said with nonchalance.

"I, ah…," the woman shrank back.

"Don't answer the thief, we already pronounced them

both guilty of theft, and now let's carry out the sentence boys," three teeth announced as he raised his mace.

"Sir, I command you to come forward and confess who is lying. Who are the guilty parties here?" Patrick shouted at a jumble of stones set back from the water's edge.

"Who does he speak to?" another man implored nervously.

"What?" said Bard, eyes wide with fear and confusion.

"I compel thee. Come forward and share the truth in this matter with us, my friend." A random stone fell from the pile, and then several more, until a withered hand reached slowly toward the sky.

The woman fainted and the men shrank back as a squalid figure of a man rose from the dilapidated tomb. Rocks and dust fell from his body as he crawled out and stood upright. "Who calls and awakens me from my torments?" a crusty voice responded.

"Bishop Patrick, a humble servant of the Most High has called you from the darkness and your suffering. I adjure you, confess the truth about this accusation against us."

"These men are all servants of the devil, there is no light in them. Do you want me to take them back with me?"

"No, I want them to hear you and know the power of the Lord. You there, wake up that woman, I want her to hear also." As he pointed to one of the men who knelt and lightly slapped her face until her eyes finally opened. "Now, please continue."

"They conspired as servants of darkness to rid themselves of you because you are a threat to their gods and corrupt laws. They are liars and seduced the woman to bend to their will."

"Why did they accuse us of robbery?"

"They wanted to have a reason to kill you that others would see as justice, so they would not be punished. They are liars."

"What were we supposed to have stolen?"

"The woman washed flax in the stream. It is hidden in that hollow tree there," a boney finger indicated which one.

"Bard, would you do the honors?"

Bard went over to the decaying tree, reached deep inside, and strained to pull a large bundle of flax out.

"So, you have all conspired to murder us. What is the penalty? I should allow your accuser to drag to you all down into the fires of hell for that."

"No, please. We did not understand the power of your God," one man said as he fell to his knees weeping beside the woman.

The others quickly fell to the ground also and clasped their hands together. "Please have mercy on us, we who were brought up in ignorance," said another.

"Is ignorance an excuse for murder? Is hatred more powerful than kindness?" Patrick smiled as he looked at the confused faces. "No, go and practice deceit no more. Worship the God of Love, not hate. Learn to love others as you love yourselves and destroy those worthless, impotent idols that you worship. Go!" he yelled and watched as they scampered away like rodents.

"What of me your grace? Please don't return me to my terrors." The revived man pleaded.

"Thank you for your service to God and to us. Now I bless you and open your pathway to the kingdom of the Lord, fear and pain will no longer haunt you, you will live in harmony in His kingdom. I promise."

"Bless you, and thank you," the man said as he yawned and bent to stretch out on the ground, becoming still in a few moments.

"Bard, you can drop that bundle now, it's all over."

Bard dropped the flax and said with a shiver in his voice, "Let's get out of here."

"Not tonight, Bard. We need to rebuild our hero's resting place and place him in it. He deserves that, right? It's almost dark. I'll start a fire, so we can see to work."

"Yes sir," he said as he shuffled over to the pile of rocks and began moving loose stones from the floor of the crypt.

# Chapter 39
Youth Returned

"What village is that?" Bard pointed at a cluster of hovels and a hillfort, barely visible in the distance.

"I guess we'll know when we get there."

They reached the outskirts of the community that evening. "What village is this?" Patrick asked a man feeding swine.

"The Stronghold of Ros, if you value your life. I'd leave now," he grumbled.

"Ros, that wouldn't be the older brother of Dichu, would it?" Patrick inquired.

"You know Dichu?" The man's eyes widened. "You better leave, he and his brother don't get along at all."

"Ah, yes, all because of that rascal Patrick converted his brother to Christianity," Patrick said understandingly.

"Yes, how do you know?"

"I am Patrick," he announced as he walked past the man toward the hillfort.

As they approached the outer rock wall, a burly guard commanded, "Hold your place. What business have you here?"

"We would like to make a cordial call on Ros. Please tell him that Patrick has arrived and wishes to have an audience with him.

The guard's mouth fell open but quickly twisted into a

wicked smile. "Why shouldn't I kill you now? My master would like that," he growled.

"Your master would be furious. I would hate to think about what might happen to you. He wants the pleasure of deciding my form of death," said Patrick, defiantly staring at the guard.

The guard's vicious sneer faltered as he considered Patrick's words. "Wait here," he finally said as he turned and entered the stone barrier.

"Is this wise?" Bard stammered.

**"Trust in the LORD with all thine heart; and lean not unto thine own understanding."** (97) Patrick replied. "Man's wisdom is not God's wisdom.

The guard came back with a smile etched on his face. "King Ros will see you now. Follow," and he led them around the circular rock wall enclosures to a stone building in the center.

"Well, I have indeed waited a long time for this meeting," a voice growled. "I am glad you have finally paid me the honor of a visit after all these years."

Several other guards filled the doorway, cutting off the source of light, while Patrick waited for his eyes to adjust. "It is a bright day; in a few minutes I will be able to see you, King Ros."

"Don't worry, I'm not much to look at anymore. What is the purpose of your visit?" the terse voice asked.

"I bring the gifts of the Spirit which your brother Dichu and his subjects have been enjoying for decades now."

"I am not happy that you are destroying our gods, idols and history. You should never have come here, and you wouldn't have if you valued your life. Now it is forfeit; I just need to decide how to have you killed," a wicked laugh followed

Patrick could barely see a man rubbing his hands in glee sitting before him. "My life is not in your hands, my king. I know you don't understand, but you can't kill an image of

God."

"Image of God? You say you are an image of God? My word, he must be a very puny individual." The room reverberated with laughter.

Patrick waited until the sound quieted and said, "You are made in his image too, sire."

"Poppycock, do I present an image of a god to you?" and he groaned as he attempted to stand. A guard moved from the doorway and helped him upright. Daylight lit the small room and Patrick could see him now. "I'm alright." He shook off the guard. "I am going to die soon, but you have cursed this land with your presence and destroyed our gods, I will watch you die before I do," he spat.

"If your youth would return to you, would you reject your false ideas and worship the one true God?"

"If that were possible my wizards would have done it long ago. You mock me, Patrick. I do not like to be mocked."

Patrick straightened his back and stepped forward. "Your wizards are powerless because their gods are lies, oft repeated, but never true. I ask sincerely, do you want to see clearly, to speak clearly, to hear, and have your teeth, hair, and vitality back, or not?"

"Of course I do. What man wouldn't want that?"

Patrick saw the man's pale blue eyes begin to water. "Would you then worship only the one true God?"

The old king's voice faltered as he uttered, "Yes. If I could receive my youth back, I would believe and worship with my whole heart."

"Then send your guards away for a time and let me pray with you."

The king hesitated, but then waved the men outside. "Go, I will call when I need you," he said.

The king and Patrick sat down beside each other as Bard blocked the doorway. "Life is eternal with the Lord. **'God *is* a Spirit: and they that worship him must worship *him* in spirit and in truth.'** (98) Spirit has no age or decay, and you are made in the image of Spirit." As Patrick continued speaking, he noticed the man's countenance relaxing. Wrinkles faded and thin lips became full. The grim expression was replaced with a smile. In about an hour, Patrick asked, "Do you feel better now?"

"I do, but you said you would restore my youth, and you didn't." He reached up to scratch his bald head. His eyes sprang wide open as he felt hair. He leapt up and ran past Bard, out the doorway. "Look everyone, I have hair!"

The guards were aghast. The one that had confronted Patrick fell to the ground weeping. The others stood still, not knowing what to do.

"And teeth, I have my teeth back!" the king ran around with an open mouth, pulling it wide open with his fingers and showing his teeth to all of them.

Patrick stood smiling, watching Ros sprint and jump around like a young man. Bard asked, "How in the world did you do that?"

Patrick let a self-satisfied smile spread across his face. "If a man can be resurrected from death, his looks and vigor can return also."

The king breathlessly ran up and dropped to his knees before Patrick as he clasped his hands together, he stared at them. "Look at my hands, my skin has returned soft and supple. Forgive me, Patrick, my life I have lived in darkness. You have awakened me to eternal light and Life."

Patrick said, **"This then is the message which we have heard of him, and declare unto you, that God is light, and in him is no darkness at all."** (99)

"I need to find my wife's mirror. There it is." Patrick watched as the king ran over to a small shelf and grabbed a bronze mirror and took it outside to look at himself. "It's true, my face is clear of wrinkles, it's youthful," he shouted. Turning to Patrick, he asked, "Will you baptize me and my subjects?"

"Of course, my king. I will be honored to baptize you,

and any of your subjects who decide that they want to accept Christ in their lives. So now that you have glimpsed the kingdom, do you want a long life on this earth?"

"I could go to Life eternal now and be happy forever," the prince replied, "But I want to share your wonderous words and works with others who were as blind to the possibilities of life in Christ, as I was." He then rushed out the door to assemble any willing villagers for a mass baptism.

"Another good harvest for the Lord. I'll find a water trough." Bard sighed.

# Chapter 40
A Trick Gone Wrong

"How old are you now, Bard?" Patrick asked as they walked away from the village. The people were singing a hymn and waving as they walked away.

"Thirty-four, I think. Why?"

"Just wanting to ask God what our plans are. He will tell me." Patrick enjoyed the questioning expression painted on Bard's face. "So, you question that?"

Bard's gaze shifted down to the pathway they were following. "Nope, just glad to be traveling again. You lead, I follow. Which path are we going to take?" He pointed toward a fork in the trail.

"It will be a challenge, but let's take the right trail."

"A challenge? Have you been here before? What is it?"

"You'll see soon enough," Patrick said as he continued to stroll down the footpath. Eventually they came upon a group of solemn peasants.

"Look, here comes Bishop Patrick. He will help us," a voice raised.

"Your eminence, our friend Garbanus has expired on our journey, can you provide him the honor of funeral rites before we entomb him, or could you please raise him from the dead?"

Patrick looked and saw the body of a man covered with a blanket next to the trail. A feeling of unease crept up his spine, and he knew the man was lying. "It has been a long, tough journey, and I don't feel capable to resurrect anyone now. As for the funeral rites, sure, I'll do it right now, as he began to speak over the body. In a few minutes he paused. "That was the short version. We need to be on our way, but I hope the rest of your journey is blessed with good fortune. Bard, come on. We'll be late if we don't hurry." Patrick strode away as Bard hurried to catch up.

"What did you preach back there? Those prayers didn't make any sense." Bard stared accusingly at him.

Patrick smiled warmly and motioned for Bard to stop after walking a short distance, and quietly sat on the ground. Bard shrugged his shoulders and sank down next to him. They listened to the distant peals of laughter coming from the peasants they had just left. Bard raised a questioning eyebrow, but Patrick held a finger to his lips. "Wait," was all he said.

The laughter stopped abruptly, and anguished voices began increasing in volume. "Patrick, Bishop, where are you? We are sorry. Forgive us please." The voices were rushing toward them.

Footfalls were coming closer, but Patrick waited until the men ran past them. He said, "Here we are. What's all the excitement."

The men were out of breath but ran back and fell on the ground before him. One man lifted his head and spoke, "Bishop Patrick, please forgive our foolish prank. We didn't believe the stories told about you. We wanted to mock you and find some cause to insult you before the people. Please have us punished, but we pray that you will restore our friend Garbanus to life again."

"I told you I don't feel up to it right now, maybe in a week, or a year."

"But he is my sister's husband, she won't understand. Please restore him to us. We will do anything, please."

"Will you renounce all evil and hatred and become

children of God. Spreading the gospel to all that you meet?"

The men all lifted their heads and earnestly nodded in agreement.

"Garbanus, come forth and join this group of new converts that have been freed from Satan's lies." Patrick winked at the prostrated men. "It was a good joke on me, but a better one on all of you."

Bard looked extremely confused and agitated. Patrick laid a steady hand on his shoulder and whispered, "The man under the blanket wasn't dead, until they tried to make fools of us. However, when they lifted his covering, surprisingly, he had expired. That was why they ran after us. Probably afraid that I might kill them too."

In a few minutes a man lumbered into view and was quickly surrounded by his friends.

"Remember your promise to God." Patrick admonished the men. "Garbanus, are you going to join with them too?" The man looked stupidly at Patrick and nodded. "Good. Line up with them, and I will baptize you all here and now. Bard, the holy water please."

"How did you see through their ruse?" Bard asked later as they continued their trek.

"I didn't, but God sees all, and lets me know what I need to know, when I need to know it. The trick is to always listen to him. Like when the Pharisees talked among themselves and said Jesus was healing using the devil. '**Jesus knew their thoughts, and said unto them, Every kingdom divided against itself is brought to desolation; and every city or house divided against itself shall not stand: And if Satan cast out Satan, he is divided against himself; how shall then his kingdom stand? And if I by Beelzebub cast out devils, by whom do your children cast *them* out? therefore they shall be your judges. But if I cast out devils by the Spirit of God, then the kingdom of God is come unto you.'** (100) Once you get used to listening spiritually, you can know people's thoughts to help and heal them."

"And when he said, 'by whom do your children cast them out?' he meant we do it through listening to God too." Bard said smiling.

"Yes, the only true healing of any situation comes from understanding Him."

# Chapter 41
## The Scroll's Return

Patrick carefully pulled the worn leather cylinder from around his neck. He opened it and spread Martin's scroll out on the bench in his episcopium. Then he picked up a goose feather, carefully carved the tip into a point with a small slit and dipped it into a tiny container of iron gall ink. Taking a long breath, he lightly pressed it onto the old parchment.

*I Patrick, Bishop of Hibernia and privileged bearer of this manuscript penned by St. Martin, do hereby signify that his extraordinary observations on the human race are true as recorded. Especially the pure Love it expresses for humanity. Each time I read it, God's Love fills my thoughts for the world and all the souls in it. My ministry on this island would not have survived nor thrived without the spiritual insights it contains. The concepts recorded in Martin's scroll, coupled with my knowledge of the Bible, have given me victory over all the barriers I have encountered throughout my ministry. God has protected me from harm. I have touched and converted many lives with its eternal secrets. I pray that future generations glean the grains of God and reality from it and learn to ignore erroneous mortal concepts. Then God's kingdom can truly claim victory over the lies of man's separation from God, and Love will rule in continuing miracles throughout this world. Miracles always have, and will forever exist, in pure thoughts from the one and only source of Life.*

He scrawled his name and shook some pounce across his note to aid in soaking up the excess ink. Then he brushed the powder off. Smiling, he lay down in his bed, knowing that when he awoke, it would be dry enough to roll up again.

In the morning, he felt weak, and his joints ached, but he ignored the pain as he completed his task of rolling up the parchment and securing it in the cylinder. Then he replaced it around his neck and tottered down to the kitchen for breakfast. "What's on our agenda for today, Bard?"

"We are entertaining King Nalseous and his daughter to discuss arrangements for her wedding next month."

"Oh yes. A fine girl she is. You stared at her for a long time the other day. Did you have impure thoughts?

"I know that I can't hide them from you. Yes, I admit that I sinned, but only a little." Patrick watched his shy smile.

"Don't fret about it, Bard, just don't be overcome by them. Would you mind making the arrangements along with Brother Aghna for them today? I'm afraid that I'm a bit under the weather."

"Yes, we can do that. Is there anything else you need today, Father?"

"No, God will supply everything my boy." And he lifted a wooden spoon of hot gruel to his lips. After breakfast, he went straight back to bed. Chills and exhaustion ran through every portion of his body as he struggled for each breath. *This is ridiculous, I, who have revealed the power able to heal the masses, can't heal myself? No, this has to be a lie. God is my Life. God made me perfect. Am I going to transition now? Father/Mother God, I feel my work here is done, and I am ready to pass on to a higher adventure. I know that You made and maintain all of me perfect and untouched by age or mortality. I am never separated from You.*

Finally, he fell asleep.

*What is this place? It looks like an old palace. I feel*

*terrible, what kind of bed am I in? A guard's voice announced, "The prophet Isaiah to see the king." A man rounded a pillar and walked to his bedside. "King Hezekiah, I wish I could say live forever, but the Lord has told me that thou wilt die soon, I am sorry." Then the man turned his head and left the room. What is going on, I remember this, yes, I remember. This is when Hezekiah prayed to live.*

**Then he turned his face to the wall, and prayed unto the LORD, saying, I beseech thee, O LORD, remember now how I have walked before thee in truth and with a perfect heart, and have done that which is good in thy sight. And Hezekiah wept sore. And it came to pass, afore Isaiah was gone out into the middle court, that the word of the LORD came to him, saying, Turn again, and tell Hezekiah the captain of my people, Thus saith the LORD, the God of David thy father, I have heard thy prayer, I have seen thy tears: behold, I will heal thee: on the third day thou shalt go up unto the house of the LORD. And I will add unto thy days fifteen years; and I will deliver thee and this city out of the hand of the king of Assyria; and I will defend this city for mine own sake, and for my servant David's sake.** (101)

Patrick awoke, soaked in sweat. He sat up and reached over to ring a small bell at his bedside. The door opened almost immediately. "Yes Father, what do you need?"

"Bard, it is time for us to part ways. I now, reluctantly release you from my service."

"But I've been praying…"

"I know my son; I appreciate your prayers, and you have my assurance that I will not be dying anytime soon. While I slept, a message from the Lord came to me that my ministry here will continue on for years. I have recovered from this silly illness, but I have other challenges to meet and eventually that great horizon to cross. Nevertheless, I will always be with you. We live in an infinite God, and we can never be separated."

"But I need you to…"

Patrick raised his voice. "You need nothing, God supplies all and is all. I do have a final wish though, if you will accept the task."

"You know I am honored to do anything for you."

"I made a solemn promise to my friend Magnus years ago that I would return the Scroll of St. Martin at the point where I determined my quest on this island to be a success." Patrick fumbled as he pulled the coarse leather cord over his head with a worn leather pouch attached. Gently he spread the opening and carefully drew out the small scroll. "St. Martin's thoughts to heal the world, and all souls in it," he said reverently. "Guard it with your life until you can return it to the church in Kilpatrick. Make sure you cover it with thick wax in its protective cylinder and push it up inside the baptismal font." He fondled the items lovingly for a moment and then handed them to Bard.

"I remember the church. It wasn't far from our home."

"Yes, I pray the church has survived all these years, otherwise you must find a suitable, secure place for it to reside."

"I will, Father," said Bard as he carefully slipped the roll into the pouch and adjusted the cord around his own neck.

"One other small request I have of you, my son."

"What is it?"

"I believe you are about to turn thirty-five years old, correct?"

"Correct, Father."

"Please see to it that you find a woman, hopefully in the lineage of Cynde and marry her. She was such a beautiful woman. I'm sure her offspring are just as comely. Maybe Bertrona is still available." He grinned as he suddenly saw a red tint rush onto the man's face.

Bard was quiet for several long moments, and Patrick watched with pleasure as the man struggled not to smile. Finally, the man uttered, "I will do my best, Excellency."

"I know you will son, now hurry on your way. You're not as young as you used to be either. Brother Aghna will serve me well, until my next journey begins. Be safe and happy, Bard, my boy."

Patrick held back tears as he watched the man bow and kiss his hand, before leaving. Walking through the door without pausing, Bard said, "I will never stop praying for you."

"Nor I for you dear one. Remember, this is not goodbye." Patrick said loudly, and waved his hand as a ragged sob quietly escaped his lips.

# Chapter 42
Bard's trip

Bard stepped lightly onto the well-worn deck of the boat. "Are you in charge?" he asked a man coiling a heavy rope. The man didn't reply but nodded over his shoulder at a figure watching from the stern.

"You must be our passenger from the abbey. Welcome aboard. Stow your duffle where it suits you, we'll shove off soon," the man yelled.

Bard let his bag slide off his shoulder close to the bow and sat on it, leaning back against the gunwale. *I leave on a new adventure, but alone for the first time.* He swallowed hard and forced himself to focus on the ocean views until the ship shuddered under him. The sailors were using long poles to back the boat into deeper water. In a few minutes they raised the sail and as the land retreated, he fell asleep.

He tumbled to the deck and awoke in a haze. The wind was blowing hard now as sea swells rose and dark clouds rolled in. Sailors rushed to shorten the sail. *Where had this gale come from? What did Jesus do on the sea of Galilee?* **"And he arose, and rebuked the wind, and said unto the sea, Peace, be still. And the wind ceased, and there was a great calm."** (102) *Lord, I was sent on this holy mission to preserve and to bless generations to come. Please protect this ship and all the souls on it with safe passage, thank you.* The sea still raged, but his fear had retreated somewhat as he clung to his prayers. In another hour the wind lightened, and the ship was under full sail again.

On the third day they sighted land and beached the boat close to a small town. As the procession of villagers approached the ship to see what goods they had brought, Bard was able to get vague directions to Kilpatrick. Shouldering his bag, he continued walking northward, grateful for the feeling of solid ground beneath his feet.

He was surprised at the number of small churches that had sprouted in almost every village. As he walked through the towns, he made a point of locating a priest or acolyte and recited a brief history of Patrick's healing ministry to them. Most of the holy men scoffed at the unbelievable tales of healings and trials endured by the bishop, but a few of the younger men were interested and asked a multitude of questions.

After ten days he crossed a grassy ridge and could see the long brush-covered earthen embankment that was the Antonine Wall. He reached up and touched the precious cylinder hanging from his neck. *Hopefully it will be safe soon.*

He crawled through the brush entwining the aging fortification and stood up on the other side. A city was visible a few miles to the east. *That has to be Kilpatrick. I wonder how much it has changed in twenty-seven years.*

He worked his way around the outskirts of the town, until he saw the hillside where Calpurnius and Conchessa's domicile should be. Houses and barns filled the hillside all the way to the crest of the hill. *It sure has grown; I hope I can still recognize their home.*

He walked up cart paths until he reached the halfway point on the hillside. Looking toward the valley, he could see the church spire that towered over the village. *Thank goodness that survived. The house should be over to the left a bit.* Then he saw it a short distance away. He trotted up the road until he was knocking at the front door. He heard a board being removed from inside, as the door opened slightly. "Yes?" an older man asked.

Bard looked at the kind blue eyes that still sparkled with life. "Magnus? Is that you?"

The man's face clouded over for a moment, and then a wide smile broke through. "Bard, you have grown." Bard nodded as Magnus yelled, "Cynde come here, we have a visitor."

Magnus opened the door wide and embraced the man as he pulled him inside. "How is Patrick? Is he alright?"

"Yes, but he has released me from his personal service so that I can return this." He fumbled with his clothing and finally pulled the cylinder up far enough for Magnus to see it.

"I knew it would return. Patrick promised."

"He misses you, but his ministry covers the whole island of Hibernia. Christians are being added to the church daily, and he feels he cannot leave, even to visit his dearest friends."

"I understand." A lady with long white hair walked up behind Magnus. "Darling, do you remember master Bard? He used to be this tall," he said as he held his hand at his waist.

Her eyes flew open as she rushed forward and enveloped him in a hug. Stepping back, she looked him over, "My, but you have grown taller than I would have imagined. You were such a tiny little guy."

"I have grown in the Spirit too," Bard proudly remarked.

"Come sit down and tell us about your adventures with Patrick. We've had a few letters from him over the years, but he is so busy. It's a wonder that we received any.

"Are any of your children here?" Bard shifted his gaze as Magnus's face lit up."

"Bertrona was recently widowed, and I know she would love to see you once again. Come over to the door." Magnus pointed at a small, well-kept house three huts away. "There, that one with the pig standing outside, go and visit. We'll be here later." He smiled as he gave Bard a slight shove and closed the door.

*I've been thrown to the wolves.* Bard realized as he slowly walked up the street toward Bertrona's house. He paused for a long prayer before eventually building up the courage to knock. "Who is there," a lilting voice asked.

"I uh, I mean you…" The door opened before he could make any sense out of his words.

The door opened, revealing a beautiful blonde woman, as he felt his face flush beet red. "I uh…"

"You said that before, who sent you here?"

"Magnus." As he twisted a foot on the doorstep.

"For what purpose?" She revealed a beautiful smile, and his knees became weak. "Come in, I don't usually bite."

A strange sound forced itself from his throat as he stepped inside, adding to his embarrassment.

She seemed not to notice. "You look familiar, have I met you before?"

He nodded his head dumbly, as he stared at her. "Yes," squeaked out of his mouth, and he quickly cleared his throat, "Yes," in a deeper voice.

"Give me a hint." Her eyes danced like she was a cat playing with a mouse.

"Patrick, my name…"

"Bard," she suddenly exclaimed and threw her arms around him.

Heat swept through his whole body as he felt her press against him. *Thank you, God.* He wrapped his own arms around her, kissed her forehead, and she didn't pull away.

Finally, she relaxed her grip. "I have prayed for your safe return ever since you left. I feared for one so young and cute. Now you're big and handsome."

His mouth went dry. He worked his tongue back and forth to be able to speak. "Bishop Patrick released me from his service, so I could come back and see you." A single tear rolled down his cheek, and she wiped it away with a dainty finger.

"I'll thank Patrick in my prayers tonight," she said. "Did you tell my parents about your adventures yet?"

"No."

"Then let's go over to my parent's house, I'm sure they will want to hear about all your adventures in Hibernia, I know I do."

# Chapter 43
Ugly Removed

Patrick prayed for several days after Bard began his journey to Briton, and finally decided that it was time for him to resume his own travels. He, Brother Aghna, and Brother Roichus, left to visit Eugenius, a chief of Hibernia. Before they left, Patrick cautioned Aghna and Roichus that the man was deformed and ugly, and to be kind and respectful to him. After a week they finally spotted the man's hilltop fort and were invited in.

"Eugenius, it has been too long. How are you, my friend?"

"I'm here, still rich and miserable, friend Patrick," the man sneered.

"You have resisted the healing Spirit for a long time, but I know you have a good heart. Are you ready to be baptized?"

"Yes. I have heard about the miracles you have done. I want you to save my soul, but can you remove some of this grotesque face that plagues me also?"

"I can try, but I've never been asked to pray for a cosmetic solution." Patrick said graciously without a trace of a smile.

"Please, I am ashamed of this ugliness that grows on me."

Patrick could only see sincerity and suffering in the

man's eyes. "I will try, whom do you want to look like?"

"That man," he pointed a stubby, twisted finger. "Who is he?"

"His name is Roichus, my book bearer."

"The keeper of your books, Roichus. I would give anything to look like him."

Patrick looked at Eugenius and felt a wave of compassion for him as he wallowed in his grief. "I will do what I can, but it is God who has all power. Can you both lay down beside each other?"

Roichus immediately laid down on a nearby bed and stretched out. Eugenius waddled over and Patrick helped him climb up onto it. When they were both settled, he began to pray about what beauty is, **"As for me, I will behold thy face in righteousness: I shall be satisfied, when I awake, with thy likeness."** (103).

Patrick watched Eugenius wake up, and immediately touch his face. *He expects to feel a lumpy mis-shaped mass of flesh – but no, now he will feel smooth skin over high cheek bones.*

Wide-eyed the little man rolled out of the bed and tumbled to the floor. Scrambling up on his feet, he moved as fast as he could to a low bench and grabbed a copper mirror. "I'm changed," he shouted, "I'm not ugly anymore." He hopped around until he lost his balance and fell over laughing. "Patrick, I'm not ugly."

Patrick looked at him with tired eyes and smiled, "You never were," was all he said.

Eugenius decided to have a banquet that night to celebrate his new looks. His subjects were amazed at the transformation, and at first refused to believe it was him. "No, it really is me." He kept telling them. "Bishop Patrick healed my hideous face. You need to let him baptize you."

While the celebration was going on, Patrick overheard two women talking quietly in a recessed room. "Can you believe that his deformed head became so handsome? I need

Patrick to do some work on my face, maybe just these wrinkles." The other just said, "Handsome, but short and tiny, he should have made him taller too," and they both laughed.

"Patrick, my friend. I've been looking all over for you. It was a marvelous party. Many more people will be attending the church services now."

"I am gratified that you are happy with the results. Do you have any regrets? Or other needs?"

Eugenius was quiet for a few moments. "Well, to be honest, I wish I could be taller. I know I'm not respected by my subjects, and I feel trapped in this tiny body."

"So, how tall would you like to be?"

The man stood wobbling on his tiptoes and stretching the tips of his fingers up. "This tall," he said.

"Lay upon your bed again, let's see what happens." Patrick said as he helped the man climb onto the bed.

Eugenius awoke in the early morning light and saw Patrick asleep next to the wall. He slipped his legs over the side and stood up. "Ow," he cried.

Patrick bolted upright. "What's the matter?"

"This lamp was hanging too low, I hit my head…" as he stopped talking and stared at the floor. "It's so far away. You did it. I'm tall, and handsome," he said as his fingers glided over his face.

"You are perfect, because God is." Patrick grinned.

Eugenius suddenly looked troubled. "Will it last?"

Patrick emitted a loud laugh. "Will God last forever? It wasn't a wizard's spell that wears off in time. It was prayer to see the real you expressed. You now see yourself differently, so you are different. It is permanent, my friend. Enjoy your freedom."

# Chapter 44
First Kiss

"Father, I hear you sent this vagabond to my house," Bertrona said as she entered, pulling Bard behind her.

Magnus looked up and smiled. "I thought it might be a nice surprise for you."

"It was a wonderful surprise for all of us." Cynde said as she glided into the room. "I'll have some food ready soon. Come, sit down, and let's celebrate.

Bard started to recount twenty-seven years of travels, trials, healings, and spiritual warfare across the island, with every detail he could remember. He spoke throughout the dinner, and on into the night.

It was late when Magnus interrupted him. "I think we better continue this tomorrow. I'm beginning to nod off."

Cynde stifled a yawn, "Me too. Bard, let me show you to your room."

"That's alright, Mother, let me show him the room."

Her mother's eyebrow rose, but she nodded her head in agreement when Magnus offered her his hand. "I'll see you two in the morning, sleep well," she said as they left the room.

"Come on, let me take you to your room, then I need to get home for some beauty sleep."

"For someone special?" Bard heard himself say.

"No, but it must be obvious that I can use some sleep. I

look ugly with bags under my eyes."

"You could never be less than beautiful." *I don't want her to see me blush.*

"Thank you."

She was standing close to him with her face upturned. Without thinking, he bent and kissed her, and she pressed her lips to him.

"Wow," was all he could think to say when the parted.

"Was that your first kiss?"

Bard looked away. "How bad was it?"

He felt her fingers gently turn his head toward her. "It was wonderful," she said as she pulled him to her lips once again. Then she took him to his room. He unpacked his diary, small items, and clothes out of his sack as Bertrona stoked the fire until small flames shot high and illuminated the area, "Goodnight, I'll see you tomorrow."

"Wait. You can't walk home alone."

"I'll be fine, I do it all the time."

"I wasn't here before, I insist."

"Are you sure you don't just want another kiss?" she smiled.

"I just want you to be safe, but I probably won't turn down a kiss."

"Fine, come along then."

They walked up the dark street hand in hand. Until they arrived at her house. "I'd love to invite you in but…"

"I know, propriety. We don't want the neighbors talking."

"I'm a good person, Bard, I probably shouldn't have kissed you, but I couldn't resist."

"I'm glad you didn't resist." He opened the door to let her inside. "I'm looking forward to more of your kisses." He turned and headed down the road without looking back.

In the morning Bard joined the others for breakfast.

"Good morning, did you sleep well?" Cynde exclaimed as she turned her head and Bard kissed her cheek.

"The first decent sleep I've had in a week." Bard lied. "Is Bertrona here?"

"No, I sent her to the spring for some water. Funny, she was here early today, said she didn't sleep much."

Bard felt a grin crease his lips.

"Morning, son," Magnus said as he walked in carrying several fish. "Cynde, I brought lunch."

"Here's a pan, take them out and clean them first."

Bard followed Magnus out the door, sat on a nearby log, and watched him begin cleaning the fish. "Did you catch those this morning?"

"Yes, it was a good morning to fish."

Bard decided to fish a bit too. "Yesterday you said that Bertrona was widowed. What happened?"

"Well, it was a long time ago. Bertrona was seventeen years old and thought she was a spinster already. She fell for a young man in the village named Conal. His father was fairly wealthy, he owned a few trading ships and had a store and warehouse in town. He was a spoiled boy and full of himself, but she was captivated by him. So, against my better judgement, I allowed her to marry him. He built the house that she lives in, but he soon grew bored with domestic life ashore and talked his father into letting him sail on one of his ships. He would be gone for weeks or months at a time, and I'm sure he was cheating on her. When he'd return from a voyage, he'd lavish her with gifts the first night and spend the rest of his nights in portside ale houses. Then he'd leave again."

Bard suddenly realized that his fists were clenched, and he forced himself to calm.

"They remained married for twelve years but had no children. Then one day, Conal left for a voyage. The next day a huge storm struck the village. The lower streets were flooded. Conal never returned and Bertrona has lived alone ever since.

"Thank you for telling me. I needed to know." Bard

dropped his head.

"Why?" Magnus smiled knowingly.

"I need you to bless our marriage." Bard blurted.

## Chapter 45
Wood Cutters

Patrick traveled with Brother Aghna and Brother Roichus through a forest bordering a large lake in Midernia, on their way back to Ardmachia. They heard the sound of chopping wood that grew louder as they approached a large group of slaves. Patrick watched the men strike at the trunks of the trees. Only a few flecks of wood or bark flew each time. Curious, Patrick wandered over and looked at the axes they were using. "Can I see your axe?" he asked one of the workers. They were dull and rounded with no edge on them. "Why don't you sharpen these axes? That would make your work much easier."

"The master won't let us, he makes us work like this, our hands bleed and flesh falls from them. He doesn't care. He just laughs at us."

Anger flared in Patrick for a few moments until compassion for the men's miseries flooded his thoughts. As he passed through the group of men, touching and blessing each one in turn, their hands were healed, and their tools became sharp, and their strength returned to them. He had just finished with the last slave when he heard a threatening voice behind him.

"Who be you?"

"Who are these men working for?" Patrick turned and addressed a guard caressing a leather whip.

"They be the property of Tremeus. You best move along before I give you an axe to use too." Just to prove his point the man flicked the whip at one of the slaves. The tip of the whip licked the man's back between his shoulder blades, and he cried out in pain.

Unimpressed Patrick asked, "Who is Tremeus?"

"Do ye see that tarp hanging over there." The man pointed at a patchwork of animal skins tied between some trees to provide shade. "He be over there."

"Thank you. I will pay my respects on our way by." He motioned for the two priests to follow him.

Two armed men blocked their way as they drew closer. "What's your business, strangers?" the man under the tarp called out.

"My name is Bishop Patrick, we are here to save souls, maybe yours."

The man had been swallowing red wine when he suddenly laughed, and it spurted out his nose. Coughing violently, he gasped, "That will cost you. That burns." As he vigorously rubbed his face.

"So will you if you don't listen to our words."

"Come and enlighten me then. I have heard of the great and mystical Patrick and his adventures across this island." He motioned to the guards who led the group forward, still holding their weapons.

Patrick stepped into the shade and said, "I'm not mystical, and I'm definitely not great. I am a humble servant of the one true God. I implore you to free these men."

"Ha, I will never do that. They entertain me with their cries of anguish, with their axe handles so slippery with blood that they slide out from one man's hands and strike another. Stay and watch. It's hilarious." The man rocked back on the stump that he sat on and laughed.

"Have you no compassion? No feelings?"

"I have a great deal of compassion for myself. I like to make myself happy. I just bought these slaves to amuse me.

Look, look that little one stumbled and rolled into the ditch. Ha, ha."

"Suffering amuses you?"

"If it's not mine, it does."

"Have you ever considered loving another, as you love yourself."

"No, that has never occurred to me. Now you are beginning to bore me. Leave me so I can watch these fools work their hearts out. Or maybe, I will have you killed. That might be entertaining." His eyes gleamed with malice.

"We will go, but I'll be back to see you soon." Patrick said as he motioned to the others and walked over to the pathway that continued through the forest.

"What will we do, Master?" Roichus asked when they were beyond earshot.

"Pray for the guidance to lead those poor souls to the freedom which is their God-given right." They found a place next to a small stream to set up a camp. After an early meal, everyone sat and prayed far into the night.

In the morning, Patrick told his companions to stay and keep praying. "I am going to return and talk to Tremeus by myself."

"Is that wise, your holiness?" brother Aghna queried.

"Perhaps not from a human standpoint, but I think it's important to let him know that we will be persistent." Patrick turned and walked away.

Patrick walked straight up to the small shelter and hailed Tremus.

"You're back. I thought I made it clear that I didn't want to see you again, and I'm not going to set these slaves free, and that's final."

"Yes, but I thought…"

"Or have you come back to thrill me with some of you magic tricks? I'll tell you what, I'm kind of hungry, turn that stone into bread, and I'll listen to you," he said pointing at a large flat rock. The two guards moved out of the way to allow the bishop to approach.

As he hastily strode forward, Patrick was fighting to keep his emotions under control, but a small amount of angst slipped from him as he spat on the rock. Suddenly, it split into three pieces.

"Hey, that's not bad. How did you do it?"

"I am not here to entertain you. **'And the devil said unto him, If thou be the Son of God, command this stone that it be made bread. And Jesus answered him, saying, It is written, That man shall not live by bread alone, but by every word of God.'** (104) I am here to ask you for their freedom." Patrick indicated with a nod of his head. "I also want to save your soul from the terrors of death."

"You're boring me again. Don't preach at me. I'm not afraid of anything, especially the supposed terrors of death. I will do with those men as I will. Their lives belong to me, I own them. I saw that somehow you sharpened their axes yesterday. Look what they swing today. Not axes, just heavy pieces of wood. They swing them at the trees. It hurts their arms and the wood bounces and hits them, but it makes me laugh."

*He's mad, but he won't allow me to help him.* Patrick's shoulder's sagged in defeat. *Father, tell me what to do.* **"And the unclean spirits went out, and entered into the swine: and the herd ran violently down a steep place into the sea, (they were about two thousand;) and were choked in the sea."** (105) *How curious that citation came to me, maybe there is a chance.*

Tremeus was amused at Patrick's expression. "Cheer up, you can't expect to free everyone from pain and suffering. I am hungry now. Since you didn't turn that stone into bread, excuse me while I leave to grab a delicious meal. "You guards, keep the slaves working double time. I want to see their tongues hanging out when I get back, give them only a half ration of gruel tonight." he said laughing, as climbed up onto his chariot and slapped the reins across the horses' backs.

Patrick winced as he heard whips crack, accompanied by more cries of pain, but there was another loud cry.

"No, stop you stupid horses. Stop!" A  scream pierced the air for a long moment and was cut off by a large splash.

The guards ran to the cliff beside the lake and stood, looking down. Patrick wandered over and peered at the large ripples spreading outward in the dark water below, "The slaves are finally free now, and you boys are free too."

# Chapter 46
Surprise Proposal

"Does Bertrona know that she is getting married?" Magnus asked.

"Not yet," Bard admitted. "I didn't want to scare her off."

"Sounds like you haven't ever talked with my oldest daughter. Nothing scares her. Didn't you realize that when you walked her home?"

"Yes, sir."

"And you want to marry her after only talking to her a few hours?"

"Yes, sir."

"You are either impetuous, brave, or stupid, but you certainly have my blessing. I've wanted to see her happy for a long time. You know that you love her already?" Magnus asked as he began to fillet a fish.

"I do, and I hope she feels the same way about me."

"Hard to tell with a woman sometimes, but she does seem somewhat taken by you." He slapped the fillet into the pan. "Wait until you taste her fried fish, you'll want to marry her even more. How do you think I gained this much weight?" As he rubbed a hand over his protruding belly.

"What are you two talking about?" Bertrona's voice cut in."

"Maybe the weather. It's a nice day." Magnus said, not

even trying to hide a wide smile as he selected another fish to clean.

She turned to Bard, "Why is he smiling like that?"

"Can I tell you later?"

"No, what is the secret? Tell me now."

Bard reached out and held one of her hands as he slid off the log onto one knee. "I've asked for your father's consent to marry you."

"You what?" she stood stunned.

Not the response Bard was prepared for. "I want to marry you."

Tears began to flow as she suddenly shook his hand loose, turned and ran into the house.

"Like I said, hard to tell about women. Did I ever tell you about the time that Cynde punched me in the jaw?"

Bard was too shocked to answer.

"She was walking down a trail in the woods, and I jumped out from behind a tree. She laid me right out on the ground. Watch out, Bertrona might have inherited her mother's mean right cross." Magnus laughed.

Bard couldn't laugh. *Have I made a mistake?* "I think I'll take a walk down to the church."

"Good idea, get your mind back on your assignment. See what it will take to conceal Martin's scroll in the baptismal fount again."

"You're right." Bard said as he stood up and walked down the hillside. *God is in control, I will have everything that I need. I think I need Bertrona.* The sun was shining brightly, and a crisp breeze was blowing from the ocean as he trotted toward the church steeple. As he drew closer to town the streets became crowded with vendors and customers milling around. Occasionally a rider would pass by, and the pedestrians would barely scramble out of the way. He was having trouble seeing the steeple now as he walked through a jumble of narrow streets with tall shops and houses on either side. When he turned a corner, sometimes he could see it poking up above the rooftops. Finally, he stood before it. Looking up the street he saw his old house. A woman was sweeping the stoop. *Maybe I'll stop there after visiting the church.*

He entered the large double door and walked inside. He couldn't remember if his parents had ever brought him here or not. He found the small alcove and ran his hands over the smooth stone fount as he noticed the small recess in its base. "Beautiful, isn't it?" He spun around and faced a priest.

"Yes, it is. I wonder how much it weighs?"

"I would guess twenty-eight or twenty-nine stone."

"No one is going to carry that off."

"I hope not." The priest said. "It survived the last raid, some twenty-seven years ago. Our alter and cross were destroyed though. Are you passing through?"

"I don't know yet, I had planned to stay, but maybe not."

"What is your name, what do you do?"

"Bard, I served Bishop Patrick in Hibernia for the last twenty-seven years. Now I'm drifting."

"My name is Father Cameron. Are you a priest?" the man asked.

"Not anymore, Patrick released me from his service so I could return..., I could return and visit my home."

The priest's eyes lit with understanding. "You left with Patrick for Hibernia after that terrible raid. Where did you live here?"

Bard pointed through the still opened door. "That first house."

"Oh my." The man sounded distressed. "I was an acolyte back then. I'm the one who found your parents. I am sorry for your loss. We searched for you for days and finally decided you must have been taken captive. This is wonderful, will you be able to speak at church? Our parishioners have heard marvelous stories about Bishop Patrick, but only hearsay. They would love to hear all your firsthand adventures."

"I'd be glad to be of any service, Father."

"Where are you staying?"

"With Magnus and Cynde."

"Oh, they are a delightful couple. Their children are all wonderful. They have a beautiful daughter named Bertrona that was widowed some years ago. So sad. Have you met her?"

"Yes, and before you ask, I am smitten. I asked her to marry me this morning."

"Did she say yes?"

"Not yet, but my prayers continue."

"I'll include you both in mine, I would love to join you two in matrimony." The priest clapped his hands in glee.

"Thank you, Father, I'll take all the help I can get."

# Chapter 47
Shining Light

Patrick returned to his monastery in Ardmachia with his aides. After a few weeks of monotonous meetings and paperwork, he felt the need to travel to Saul and had his chariot prepared for the trip. He decided to travel early in the morning, and the night before, sent his driver out to catch the horses and harness them to the chariot. Nearly an hour later, the driver appeared before him empty-handed. "I can't find them your worship, I walked all over the pasture, but the air is dense and dark. I can't find the horses anywhere."

Patrick walked out the door, into a blanket of darkness. No stray beams of light shone from any star. He bent his head for a few moments and extended his hand from his sleeve. **"And when Aaron and all the children of Israel saw Moses, behold, the skin of his face shone; and they were afraid to come nigh him."** (106) Raising it up, his fingers began to glow and emitted a bright light that illumined the countryside.

"How are you doing that?" the driver croaked in fear.

"I don't do anything but listen. Just go and find our horses."

The chariot driver was easily able to locate the horses in the light from the bishop's fingers, and soon led them back to the carriage house.

"Be ready to leave at first light." Patrick reminded him.

"I guess if you can hold your hand up for a few more hours, that would be now," the driver quipped.

In the morning Patrick climbed aboard, and the driver slapped the reins. They rolled through the countryside at a brisk pace for several hours when Patrick laid a hand on the driver's arm. You see that man under that tree? Pull up by him and rest the horses in the shade.

The driver slowed the team to a walk and stopped them beneath the tree. Patrick jumped off the chariot and walked over to the man sitting with his back against the trunk. "Would you like to hear the word of God while our horses cool down?"

The man shifted without much interest. "I guess it will pass the time. Go ahead."

As Patrick preached to him the man's eyes grew wide with an expression of wonder, and he stood up, grabbing at the tree trunk behind him to steady himself.

"Do you behold the kingdom of the Lord?" Patrick finished.

The man took a deep breath and swallowed, taking a few tentative steps away from the tree. "Who are you?" he asked, still wide-eyed.

"I am Bishop Patrick, are you alright?" he asked with concern.

"When you spoke to me, I saw flames erupt from your mouth, they enveloped me and filled my ears and mouth. They didn't burn though, but they warmed me throughout my soul. How?"

"Our God is the light that illumines the entrance to His world. I have come to spread his words as a fire to burn forever in the hearts of those who are faithful."

"I'm burning, I must be faithful."

"He told me that you would be." As he grinned and pointed upward. "Are you traveling?"

"Yes, to Saul. My parents live there, and I haven't seen them for years."

"Driver, please make some room in the carriage, we have another passenger."

A few hours later, they finally arrived in Saul. Patrick and the stranger dismounted the chariot to stretch and shake hands. The traveler thanked Patrick for the ride and began walking to his parents' house. "Be sure and visit the church." Patrick admonished.

"I will. I am reborn." The man smiled and waved before he rounded a building and was out of sight.

"Drop me off at Dichu's house," Patrick said as he climbed back into the chariot.

Word of Patrick's arrival spread quickly, and people crowded into the streets to wave and cheer as he rolled by. "God's blessings to all," he cried to the well-wishers. The driver pulled up on the reins, and Patrick leapt to the ground to embrace Dichu. "I have missed you, my friend."

"Why didn't you tell me of your visit?" Dichu asked. "I would have arranged a great celebration."

"I know, that's why I didn't tell you. I am still a simple man. I am not what people seem to think I am. I don't need any acclamation or celebrations in my life, I just need to see my good friends once in a while." He smiled. "How are you? Is everything going well?"

"I don't think it could be any better, we have plenty of food and peace between our neighbors. Ever since your reckless visit to King Leogaire, life has been wonderful."

"How is he doing? I should visit him too."

"He is older, but still holding onto the throne. I had to visit Tara for a coronation of a lower king last month. I made a point of visiting your mother's beadwork in the church there. It is still as beautiful as it was when they first hung it up. His kingdom is doing much better since your visit too, everyone seemed happy," Dichu added with a smile, and then questioned, "Where is Bard?"

"I released him from my service and sent him back to Briton. It was time for him to find a wife and a life."

"He couldn't ever have a more fulfilling life than the one you gave him. You and he transformed the faith and trajectory of this whole island. No amount of gratitude would suffice to thank you enough." Dichu's eyes began to water.

"Thank you for the compliments my friend. I will say that Bard is still performing a necessary service for me though."

# Chapter 48
True Task

Bard decided it was pointless to visit his old house and tried to shake away the vision of his murdered parents that had sprung into his thoughts as he walked through Kilpatrick after visiting the church. Eventually he walked past several warehouses near the waterfront and idly wondered which one belonged to Bertrona's former father-in-law. He trod carefully out on a creaky wooden wharf and gazed at the few ships tied to the docks. *Maybe I should be a sailor. I could just apply myself to mind numbing work for the rest of my life. Watching the waves and storms and drinking myself into oblivion when I finally reach portside.*

*You're being like Jonah, running away from a Holy directive.* The thought was so clear that he stepped backward on a loose board and almost fell off the dock. He remembered the story of how God sent Jonah to Nineveh, but he disobeyed and boarded a ship going to Tarshish. During the voyage a great storm overtook the ship, and the sailors cast lots amongst themselves to find out who brought the storm upon them and the lot fell to Jonah, and they threw him into the sea. **"Now the LORD had prepared a great fish to swallow up Jonah. And Jonah was in the belly of the fish three days and three nights. 1 Then Jonah prayed unto the LORD his God out of the fish's belly, And the LORD spake unto the fish, and it vomited out**

**Jonah upon the dry *land*. And the word of the LORD came unto Jonah the second time, saying, Arise, go unto Nineveh, that great city, and preach unto it the preaching that I bid thee. So Jonah arose, and went unto Nineveh, according to the word of the LORD.”** (107)

"I understand, God. I can't run away from you I cannot ignore the path you have chosen for me, but what should I do? She doesn't love me." No answer came, so he walked ashore, and turned down a street that followed the river. He bent over to grab a flat rock to skim it across the water, and the leather tube fell out of his shirt and hung from his neck. *Oh yeah, my task.*

Forgetting the rock, he stood and tucked the scroll safely away as he began jogging through town, back to Magnus.

"Hey Bard, did you meet the good father?" Magnus asked as he entered the house.

"Yes, he thinks very highly of your family."

"Including Bertrona?"

"Yes, but I need to put those thoughts aside for now. I became so taken by her that I forgot my true purpose in coming here."

"The scroll."

"Yes, do you think I should make a copy before we hide it again?"

"We? I don't think I can help you. I'd have trouble crawling through that tiny window now." Magnus laughed as he patted his belly. With a serious expression he continued, "I would really like to have another copy though. I can work on that tonight."

"Who can we trust to help me hide it?"

"I can think of only one person, maybe we'll ask her at dinner tonight." Magnus smiled while Bard's heart sank. "Let's go out and feed the horses now. Trust God to overcome any obstacle son."

"When did Calpurnius and Conchessa pass away?"

Bard asked as they placed rope halters over the horse's heads to lead them to water.

"A number of years ago. Calpurnius passed first, and Conchessa a few years later, but they both were able to meet their grandchildren and spend happy times with them before their transitions."

"How many kids do you have?"

"Two boys and three girls." Magnus said with evident pride. "They all live nearby, but Bertrona is the closest."

"I imagine holidays are fun."

"The house does fill up quickly for family celebrations. We have seven grandchildren already." Magnus beamed. "Soon I'll need to add another wing. Especially if you two get married."

Magnus noticed that Bard didn't reply. "As soon as these boys drink their fill and we put them away, it should be time for dinner. Are you hungry?" Magnus coaxed.

Bard felt his shoulders respond with a half-hearted shrug.

They entered the house, and Bard stole a glance at Bertrona as she carried food to the table. Her eyes were reddened and her cheeks flushed. *I didn't want to make her cry.*

"Bard, give me Martin's scroll. I'll start copying it after dinner." Magnus said as he gathered up some parchment and ink from a wooden box.

He reached up and pulled the leather thong over his head as the cylinder dangled in front of him. "Here sir."

"Hang it on that peg over the fireplace."

"No, sir. I don't want it anywhere near a fire," Bard refused.

"You're right, come to think of it, I better copy it tomorrow in the daylight. Keep it on your neck for tonight, son. I'll start on it in the morning. Now, let's eat."

"I'm not very hungry," Bard said. His stomach rumbled as he glanced at Bertrona and took a step toward the doorway.

"You are our guest. It's an offense if you refuse dinner. Sit." Cynde demanded.

"Uhm, all right." Bard settled himself on a bench beside the table, as Magnus and Cynde sat opposite him. Bertrona carried in several dishes of food and finally a platter of grilled fish. She didn't look at him as she seated herself next to him.

"Now you get a treat. Bertrona's fish is excellent," Magnus said and reached for a big helping.

Cynde grabbed his arm and stopped him. "Wait for our guest, have you no manners?"

"In this house he needs to learn to be quick." Magnus laughed but waited as Bard filled his plate.

*I think I was too quick about some other things.* Bard sighed and lifted a piece of fish and bit into it. The taste and texture were perfect. "Magnus, you weren't lying. This is the best fish I've ever tasted."

"I would never lie about food, or anything else. Cynde won't let me," he added.

"That's right Magnus of Rau."

"So Cynde, how is your father and Dwig? Patrick told me about them and Hastell Cenllys."

"After you left with Patrick, we visited them several times. A few years ago, my father passed. Dwig and his wife are running the inn now and have five children."

"That's wonderful. I still have hopes that Patrick might be able to visit here, before he passes."

"How old is he?" Bertrona asked.

"I think he's seventy-four now."

"That's pretty old, I doubt if he could make the trip," Bertrona sneered.

"Bertrona, that's not nice." Cynde said.

"I've learned it's best to never underestimate the power of Spirit." Bard said as he risked a glance at the woman beside him.

"I'm sorry, but that is old."

"Your only as old as you feel, and I can't imagine Patrick acting his age," Magnus replied with a grin.

They finished eating. Then Bertrona said, "I guess, I'd better get home. I have some cleaning to do."

"I'll walk you to your door." Bard said.

"You don't need to." Bertrona kept her eyes averted.

"I know, but I want to. Don't worry, I promise to just walk you to your door and leave."

"That sounds nice, you two go ahead, I'll have young master Magnus help me clean up if he isn't feeling too old." Cynde laughed. "We'll leave the door unblocked."

Bard followed Bertrona out into the cool night air. "I apologize for whatever I said to offend you," he said as soon as the door closed.

She drew a long breath, "You didn't offend me," she walked few more steps up the street before stopping. "I'm afraid."

"You don't need to be afraid of me."

"I'm sorry, I'm not afraid of you. I'm afraid of being trapped."

"Trapped?"

"Years ago, I thought I was in love; I didn't listen to my parents' persistent and wise warnings. I married a man that I thought I knew would make me happy, and paid for it with twelve years of pain, distress, and shame. I'm afraid," she repeated as tears fell.

"Look at me. Look at me, please," he said as she wiped at her eyes and tried to focus.

"I don't know what you suffered through, I just know that you didn't deserve to be treated that way. I'm not a youngster, filled with thoughts only about my own pleasures and desires. I'm a man that thinks you're beautiful. I want to protect you, care for you, and share your life. If you want me to go away, tell me now."

She shook her head, "No, just give me time to know you

better, to quell my stupid fears."

"All the time you need," he said as he opened the door for her. "Sleep well, I'll see you at breakfast." He turned quickly and began to stride away.

"Hey. No kiss goodnight?"

He stopped as his mind went blank. *Am I weak? Yes, I guess I am,* as he quickly turned and embraced her.

# Chapter 49
Rome Trip

Patrick was sleeping soundly when an angel appeared unto him and urged him to travel to Rome. "The Pope will bestow many relics of the apostles unto you, to provide to the churches for their members to treasure."

He hadn't considered ever leaving the island, but he also needed more priests and bishops to lead his growing number of churches across the island. *Maybe the Pope will have souls to provide too.* He finally decided that it was God's design that he should make the journey and instructed his aides to make the necessary preparations.

He and Aghna stepped onto the deck of a large boat on a brisk spring day. "I pray this fair weather travels with us." Aghna said.

"He will see to it." Patrick pointed up and smiled.

In less than two weeks, they disembarked in Gaul and negotiated for land transportation. Arriving in Rome. Patrick sent Brother Aghna to the Vatican to request an audience with the Pope.

"You have an appointment in two days," Aghna announced breathlessly after jogging back from St. Peter's Basilica.

"Wonderful, that will give me time to pray for a harmonious and fruitful meeting and also have my vestments cleaned. Let's have something to eat first."

Two days later, Patrick was nervous as he walked toward the huge church, built over a century before. It was the center of the Catholic faith. *Nothing to be nervous about, he is only another child of God.*

He was ushered into the presence of Pope Leo the Great by several bishops. "Your excellency." Patrick kneeled and bowed his head immediately before the man.

"It is I who should bow to such a dedicated worker for Christ. My life is constantly refreshed and uplifted by the unbelievable reports of healing and resurections your ministry provides to the people of Hibernia."

"It isn't me, but He who works through me." Patrick winked as he clasped his hands together. "I thank God for giving me the honor of the title 'Bishop' so many years ago. I have tried to remain faithful, although I understand that I have created some large waves of dissent at times."

"Jealousy invites aggression," the pope said, shaking his head sadly. "I only wish those accusers had stayed true to the laws of the Lord, rather than the whims of man. If I had a hundred more soldiers of Christ like you, my friend. God's laws and demonstrations would have defeated all the pagan thoughts around the world by now."

"You are too kind excellency."

"Not at all, Bishop Patrick. Now tell me why you have made the long journey to bless this old man's final days."

"An angel voice visited me and told me to come here to beg some relics to display for the faithful in Hibernia. I would also like to have some additional priests to guide the faithful. I almost have more churches than priests," he added.

The old Pope's eyes sparkled as he replied, "If anyone else had said that I would wonder about their intentions, but I know you only tell me the truth."

"Thank you, your holiness."

"I will charge Bishop Marco to make a list of possible artifacts at once. I know we have some from Peter, Paul, and many others. Can you return tomorrow morning to take your pick?"

"Yes, your excellency."

"I would love to chat longer, but I have a delegation visiting from Jeruselem. Tomorrow, let's have lunch after you look over the relics." He turned and hurried away before Patrick replied.

In the morning Patrick returned with Aghna and asked to see Bishop Marco. They were led to an anteroom where Marco was waiting. "Bishop Patrick, I am honored by your presence, Pope Leo told me to gather some of our most precious relics for you to pick from. They are on this table over here."

Patrick slowly walked alongside the table and looked at the conglomeration of items. There were staffs, various collections of bones including several skulls, cups and containers, folded fabric, candle sticks and crosses. "Who do all of these belong to?"

"Many of the early church fathers and saints. For instance, this skull is from James, that staff belonged to Paul. Here, this is said to be the left hand of Stephen." As he cradled the bones and presented them in a napkin.

"Brother Aghna, please pick around twenty items and have them packed for transport. Don't pick anything breakable or too precious, but a good variety. Something interesting for our parishioners to venerate."

"Yes sir, it will be done."

"Thank you, I'll see you later at our lodgings. Thank you, Bishop Marco for your help and knowledge. I pray these items will bless many lives when they are displayed."

He passed out of the room and down the hall to inquire where the Pope would be dining. He was directed to a small building sandwiched between the church and a warehouse.

"Hello Patrick, I've been waiting for you." Pope Leo called out from a small table. "Did you pick out your divine artifacts?"

Patrick laughed. "No, I looked at them, but Brother

Aghna will decide for me," as he sat down.

**"He answered and said unto them, Because it is given unto you to know the mysteries of the kingdom of heaven, but to them it is not given."** (108) "You have acquired the knowledge of God and spread that light to the people. I hope those relics cause your flock to search for that knowledge and experience healing and regeneration for themselves."

"I pray for that your holiness."

"Patrick, I have also ordered that you be sent fifty priests in the spring. When will you travel back?" the Pope said as he put a slice of melon in his mouth.

"The day after tomorrow. God's work is done, but mine never is," he laughed.

## Chapter 50
Scroll's Return

"You're up early." Cynde said when she found Bard sitting in the kitchen, just after sunrise.

"I didn't sleep well."

"I know. I remember many sleepless nights after Magnus walked into my father's inn. One time he ran out when our patrons began throwing things and laughing at him. I was terrified because I thought he was a coward. I know I didn't sleep at all that night."

"But he wasn't?"

"No, I found out he was the farthest thing from a coward. He would give his life to save any innocent person. I thought he was scared because he wouldn't fight a drunkard that night, but he was only afraid of hurting a man that drank too much and couldn't control his mouth. The whole community could have thought ill of him, but he had enough courage not to care what they thought. Later, he saved our whole village from being murdered by raiders."

"Really? How?"

"He heard them one evening, a group of barbarians creeping through one of the valleys near our homes. He ran all the way to our village and could barely talk when he arrived exhausted. Because of him, we had time to evacuate before that horde attacked. We all ran up a nearby hill and sat in the darkness as we watched the spectacle unfold below us. I still remember how they fought amongst themselves and killed each other when they found the village empty. Such a pitiful waste of life," as she carried a bowl and some flour to the table.

"I'd like to hear more about Magnus."

"Just ask him, he can talk about himself for hours," she giggled as she poured water into the bowl and began mixing. "Bertrona is in love with you. She doesn't accept it yet, but she will. You'll be able to sleep soon."

Bard didn't know what to say, so he changed the subject. "Do you think Magnus will help me hide the scroll?"

"No, you already know who is going to be recruited to help you, don't you?" Cynde shot a hardened look at him.

"Yes, ma'am." Then she smiled, as Bard noticed his palms sweating.

"Where is Magnus?"

"He should be up anytime. He needs to bring me some firewood."

"I'll get it," Bard said, grateful for an excuse to leave.

"Don't bring big pieces yet, just small ones and some kindling."

"Alright." He hurriedly threw open the side door. It swung open and knocked Bertrona down in the grass. "Oh no. I'm sorry, so sorry," as he bent to help her up.

Her eyes were fierce and her face flushed red. "Never mind, I can get up myself," she fumed.

He recoiled as she scrambled to her feet and walked past him in a huff. *Wonderful, just wonderful. Now I'm a clumsy clod.* "Sorry again," he said as he slowly shuffled to the wood pile. He filled his arms with wood, until he couldn't carry any more. As he paused to reach for the handle to open the door, it suddenly swung open and knocked him over, into the grass. He laid there stunned, with the wood scattered about him. Bertrona stood over him laughing, "Now we're even," she managed to say as she smiled, bent forward and began to pick the firewood off his chest.

"I can't believe you did that to me," he said as he caught her wrist and pulled her down beside him. "You made a fool of me."

"It wasn't hard," she said as she rolled on top and kissed him.

Bard looked up at the two faces peering out the door with their mouths open. "I dropped my wood. She's helping me pick it up." He closed his eyes and smiled at the peals of laughter.

Later, as they sat and ate Bard asked Cynde, "I looked at the baptismal fount yesterday, how did you lift it?"

"Calpurnius had a wagon tongue and a sack of oak blocks. He put a big block on the floor by a recess in the stone base. Then he used the wagon tongue as a lever and lifted it up. I stacked smaller blocks on either side before he sat it back down, and that gave me enough room to get my arm up inside with the scroll," Cynde replied as her eyes sparkled. "When Patrick and Magnus retrieved it, they destroyed much of the church."

Magnus suddenly intervened, "It wasn't that bad, just the altar, lectern, the cross, and the effigy of Jesus."

"Much of the church," Cynde repeated with a sweet smile at her husband.

"Do you have any oak blocks and an old wagon tongue I can borrow?" Bard quickly asked Magnus.

"We can borrow," Bertrona corrected.

"I'm sure I can dig some up. First, I'm going to make a copy of the scroll." He stood and grabbed a few sheets of parchment off the shelf and sat back down at the table. Cynde handed him an inkwell and quill as Bard lifted the leather tube from around his neck and handed it to Magnus.

Carefully unrolling it, he asked Bard to read it slowly as he printed the words.

"I see Bishop Patrick added his own thoughts to it," Bard said as he finished.

"Read them so I can add them too." Magnus scribbled

them down. When he finished, he laid the copies out to dry. Bard carefully rolled the scroll back up and placed it in the tube, as Bertrona lit a candle and dripped wax all over the tube. Bard spread the hot wax around with a thin piece of wood until it was thickly covered. "There, that should protect it. When are we going to hide it?"

"Tonight's as good as any," Bertrona replied.

"How will we get in; the church will be locked." Bard asked.

Magnus spoke up, "I happen to have a key to the front door that our friend Sypher keeps, since he still does maintenance on the church. I'll have to return it to him tomorrow." Magnus held up a heavy brass key. "I guess I better find a wagon tongue. Bard, there are some pieces of oak in that woodpile. Here's my wood tools he said as he pulled a hide-bound bundle from the corner. Have fun."

Bard carried the bundle outside and untied the leather thongs. Inside were an axe, a draw knife, several large wooden wedges, some chisels and a wooden mallet. He searched around the property and found a loose stone in the rock fence. He pried it out with one of the long chisels and placed a large chunk of tree limb in the space. Then he took one of the wedges and drove it down beside the limb until it was secure. Next, he started pulling the draw knife across the face of the wood until he had a flat surface. Then he knocked the wedge loose, turned the chunk ninety degrees, secured it with a larger wedge, and began to shave it with the draw knife again. It took him until late afternoon to shape enough blocks, He replaced the rock in the wall and gathered up the slivers and curls of wood for starting fires. Then he wrapped the tools in the bundle and carried them back to the house.

He was sweating heavily and strolled to a nearby stream to splash water on himself and wash away the grime. The water wasn't too cold, so he took his clothes off, hung them over a bush, and waded in. After vigorously rubbing himself and dunking his head a few times he stepped up onto the bank, and found his clothes were missing.

He turned and jumped back into the water to cover himself. "Alright, who stole my clothes?"

"I didn't steal them, I was going to wash them, they stink. Since you're in the water, why don't you wash them yourself?" Bertrona flung the clothing into the stream.

"What did you see?" he demanded as he struggled to collect the pieces before they floated away.

"Enough," she said as she walked away smiling.

*This woman is maddening, I shouldn't love her. She is making a fool of me. I wish I didn't like it.* He smiled.

"Did you fall in a creek?" Magnus asked as Bard entered, still dripping.

"Nope, sudden rainstorm. It didn't rain here?"

Cynde glanced at Bertrona who turned to hide a grin. "I understand, go and put on some dry clothes. We'll eat, and then, in a few hours, it will be time for you two to leave on your errand," she said as she shook her head. "Children, they never grow up."

"Good thing." Magnus announced as he hugged his wife.

After dinner Bertrona and Bard crept down deserted streets in darkness. "No celebrations tonight?" Bard whispered.

"It is a pretty dull town other than holiday festivities."

"Are you sure we are going the right way?"

"Shush, just follow me," she said.

"Anywhere." He couldn't see her smile, but he felt her squeeze his hand as they picked their way down the rough Cobblestone streets. After a few more corners, the steeple came into view in the hazy night sky. "We should check if the priest is asleep first," Bertrona whispered. "I'll wait in the shadows at the front door for you."

Bard took the wagon tongue off his shoulder and slipped over the low stone wall next to the church. He walked quietly around to the small parsonage behind it and eased up against the shuttered window where he could hear the man's light snore. *Perfect.* He crawled back over the wall, and into the shadows of the church's portico. "He's asleep, try the key."

She turned it and was rewarded with a loud click. The heavy door swung open, and they darted inside and closed it quickly. "Feel around for the recess spot."

Bard dropped to his knees and crawled around the base feeling for the notch in the stone base. "Here," he whispered.

She hurried over and shoved the harness pole into the slot and handed the bag of blocks to him.

He felt around for the largest one and slid it under the pole. "Do you want the honor?" he whispered.

"You better do it. You carry a little more ballast than I do."

"I love your silver tongue; you make a man feel so good about himself?"

"I meant your muscles are so impressive, I could barely lift that heavy thing."

"Much better," Bard said as he strained to push the lever down.

The basin released from the floor and tipped up, as boards popped in protest.

Bertrona felt for the rim of the fount and placed blocks evenly on either side of the lever. "Release it."

"Are you clear."

"Yes. Thanks for asking."

He gradually released the pressure on the lever and heard the stack of blocks crack and pop under the weight of the rim.

"Alright, pull the pole out." As soon as he pulled it back, she slid forward on her back with her shoulder under the edge and shoved the wax-covered cylinder upward into the tapered hole in the center. She squirmed around until she got her feet under herself and stood up. Bard slid the pole back under the rim, pressed down and held it. "I've got the blocks out," she whispered as her lips lightly touched his ear.

*What a flirt.* He almost dropped the fount but forced himself to concentrate as he lowered it slowly until it ground itself into the floor. "You're a dangerous person to work with."

"But I'm fun."

"I can't argue that." They gathered the blocks and wagon tongue, locked the church doors and strolled through the quiet village.

They stopped at her doorway with Bard holding the bag and pole. "Goodnight, it's been a pleasure working with you."

"Are you hungry? Do you want to come in?"

He leaned forward and kissed her forehead. "Not tonight dearest, I'm still waiting for your final decision," as he abruptly turned and walked away.

# Chapter 51
The Bishop's Oxcart

"Are we taking the same route back?" Brother Aghna asked as the carriage neared the Oceanus Britannicus at the north coast of Gaul.

"No, since I'm this close, I want to visit Bard and my old friend Magnus in Briton. We can board a boat from Kilpatrick to Hibernia after my visit."

"Whatever you say, your excellency. I will make the arrangements. Where do you want to sail to first."

"Seaford Downs, I'd rather travel on dirt than waves if I can."

"Very good sir. I will arrange for our passage."

The next day Patrick boarded a ship for Briton. "Are the relic crates secure?"

"Yes sir, they are stacked in the center of the boat. Our guards will watch them day and night."

Patrick sat down with his back against the gunwale. "I'm going to take the same route that I took when I returned from my studies in Auxerre. I'm going to enjoy this, Aghna. I want to see how the country has changed."

"As you wish, sir. It will be an adventure. What is Seaford Downs like?"

"It was a beautiful little town with a safe harbor. Unfortunately, it once had a big church and monastery that were destroyed shortly before I traveled there."

The sailors cast off the lines and pulled on lines to raise the big square sail as they talked. It snapped taunt with a loud pop, as a strong westerly wind suddenly drove the craft forward.

"Who destroyed it? Picts or Hibernians?"

"Neither, the bishop was apparently a man of mammon, more than a man of God. He employed a group of Norsemen from the east as his personal enforcers. Eventually they turned on him and destroyed the whole complex."

The boat cleared the harbor and began to roll, rise and fall in large waves driven by the brisk wind.

"What happened to the monks?" Aghna asked as he grabbed at the rail to prevent falling over.

"Only a handful survived. One of them even spent the night hiding in a latrine. They robbed the church of any valuables they could find, stole a ship in the harbor, and escaped."

"And the bishop?"

"They found him laying on a table in his office, butchered."

"Butchered?" Aghna gasped.

"They said he was cut up in tiny pieces."

"Oh my." Aghna said as he turned and pulled himself up to throw up over the rail.

"Sorry, it is a gruesome story." Patrick grimaced."

A white-faced Aghna sank down against the gunwale and wiped his mouth. "Pray for me, your excellency, please."

"I will."

Eight hours later, a sailor caught sight of the white cliffs. "Land Ho."

Patrick felt the ship heel over as it changed course toward the harbor. "We're here Brother Aghna, you survived the trip."

"Just barely." He grinned weakly. "Are you sure you were praying for me?"

"I pray for everyone; did you pray for yourself?"

"Yes, except when I fed the fish."

Patrick shook his head and held a hand up as he fought to restrain a smile, "That's enough, let's get ready to disembark before you utter any more crude comments."

"I see the city there." Aghna pointed. "The church and some of the buildings are still standing."

"They repaired many of them since my visit. I wonder who the new bishop is? The monks who survived are probably still there, but there must be more of them now. Those people needed a place to worship."

"God will provide for them, I'm sure."

"Yes, he will, and you need to arrange for our transportation."

"As soon as my feet touch dry land. I've already asked the owner whom to contact, and he has promised to unload our relics first."

"Good man. I'll watch them while you find us a carriage or a wagon."

Aghna was the first passenger off the ship and headed toward two larger buildings along the waterfront. Patrick watched as the sailors carried the boxes off the boat and stacked them up on the pier. "Our thanks to all of you for a pleasant voyage." As he handed a few coins to each of the men with a few extra for the owner.

"Much obliged, sir," the owner said as he turned and followed his crewmen toward the nearest ale house.

Patrick settled himself on one of the crates and watched the activity on shore as he patiently waited for Aghna to return. A battered old ox cart rolled into view and to Patrick's surprise, he noticed Brother Aghna holding the reins. "That is neither a carriage nor a wagon," he yelled.

The man sheepishly looked at him after dismounting the cart, "They say all of the wagons are in use for the harvest the next few months. There were no carriages in the village. This is all they had, so I purchased it."

Patrick stared at the tired and boney animal hooked to the cart, "Does he have any teeth left? I doubt whether he can survive a trip to the next village, let alone Kilpatrick," he growled.

"Pray for him?" Aghna offered.

I will probably have to resurrect him multiple times. I've never raised an ox before," he laughed. "Let's load these crates and get started before he decides to die while waiting on us."

In a short time, the cart was full, and Patrick spread several robes and a blanket on top of a wide crate at the front of the cart for a cushion. "Forward Aghna, Let's spend the night with the brothers in the remains of the monastery and leave early tomorrow morning. I'd like to reach Hastell Cenllys by tomorrow night. Aghna urged the animal forward, and he plodded slowly up the hill toward the damaged complex.

A few monks appeared at the gate as the oxcart approached. Most of them held sharpened agriculture implements. "Your business?" one of the larger monks demanded.

"My name is Bishop Patrick, is Brother Sardis available?"

"Do you mean Bishop Sardis?" the group shared a laugh. "Follow us, we'll take you to him."

Patrick and Aghna were ushered into a small building adjacent to the church. "The bishop's palace," one of the monks announced.

"It's a little nicer than his root cellar, but not much." Patrick replied, eliciting a quizzical expression from the monk as he opened the door.

An elderly man rose from behind a desk, "Hello."

"Pardon my intrusion Brother Sardis, or should I say Bishop Sardis?" Patrick smiled.

"Do I know…"

"You put me on a ship to Gaul a few years ago."

The man's brow furrowed as he searched his memories, "Maewyn? Is that you?" as he tottered around the desk and offered his hand.

"Yes, but now most people call me Patrick."

"No," as realization focused the man's eyes. "Patrick? The Patrick of Hibernia? Oh, my goodness. I've heard stories, but I had no idea that it was you," as he clasped both of his hands around Patrick's and shook it vigorously. "How long has it been?"

"It doesn't matter, we live in infinity, right?"

"Oh, I can't believe that you returned. What brings you here?"

"I have been to Rome to gather some relics to distribute to the churches in Hibernia. I wanted to use this return trip to visit some friends and family that I haven't seen since my ministry started."

"I'm so glad that you stopped by. We have been blessed ever since you boarded that ship. Almost all of the buildings are rebuilt, and the monastery is filled with eager souls. Of course, it doesn't compare to the works you have wrought."

"Not me, your holiness; God gets all the credit."

"Of course, but it wouldn't have happened without your toil. I can't imagine what you've been through."

Patrick stifled a yawn. "Sorry, your eminence, but I'm tired, it has been a long day of sailing and travel. Can you have someone keep watch over our relics?"

"Of course, I understand," Sardis called to a monk. "See to it at once, two guards throughout the night," he told another monk. "Take Bishop Patrick and his friend to our guest rooms. Give them anything that they want."

"I wonder if they have an extra carriage?" Aghna whispered a little too loud as they followed the monk.

"What's that? Hold on, did you say carriage. How did you get here?" Sardis called out.

Patrick shot Aghna a withering glance, "We arrived in an oxcart, it was the only transportation available."

"An oxcart for a bishop's transportation?"

"Our master rode a donkey." Patrick winked.

"Take them to the guest rooms. I want to see this oxcart." Sardis said as he followed them out the door. "Sleep well, I hope you will grace us with some of your colorful resurrection stories at breakfast tomorrow, my friend."

"It will be my pleasure."

# Chapter 52
I Do


Bertrona walked into the kitchen before the sun was up. "Mother, I decided to accept Bard's proposal."

Cynde let the bowl and spatula slip from her hands and ran over to hug her daughter as her eyes filled with happy tears. "That's wonderful, I've been praying that you would. He's such a good man."

"I think so too. I'm going to let him know this morning. Do you think you and father could give us some privacy in the kitchen?"

"Anything that will help," she winked. "That reminds me, I've wanted to give you something to keep in the family for a long time. After you were widowed, I decided to hold on to it. Now, I think it is time." She left the room, and Bertrona followed her. Magnus was in the courtyard. "Go and eat something quickly, we are going to give the children some privacy this morning." He gave her a questioning look but shuffled off toward the kitchen.

"Your bedroom?" Bertrona asked.

"It used to be Calpurnius and Conchessa's bedroom. They left us a hiding place for valuables." She took an iron poker from the fireplace and shoved the end into a crack beside a flagstone. Prying down, she lifted it a few inches. "Now, help me tip it back to the wall." Together they wrestled the stone up. Beneath it were some weapons, including a bow and sword, along with a helmet and some armor. "This is Calpurnius's armor," she said proudly as she bent down and reached into a far corner. "And this is my gift to you, but also for the generations of our family to come," as she handed a small leather pouch to her daughter.

"What is it?" Bertrona asked as she fumbled with the knotted string.

"My very first needlepoint. Conchessa taught me how."

Her daughter finally opened the pouch and drew a small piece of multi-colored fabric out. She stared as she read the words sewn in it. "The greatest gift lies beneath the soul's shower. What does that mean?"

"You don't know? You were always the smart one." Cynde giggled. "It is a riddle for the greatest gift to our family. The scroll of Martin."

"The baptismal fount." Bertrona exclaimed.

"That's right. You protect that from now on and pass it on to your children." Cynde grinned.

———— • ● • ————

In the morning, Bard felt lazy, he was slow to get up. *What a night. I couldn't sleep thinking about her lips against my ear. She's tormenting me. My job is done for Patrick, I could leave now. That's it, I'll go back to Hibernia if she doesn't give me an answer today.* He was still yawning as he entered the kitchen and saw Bertrona dishing up a plate for him.

"Where are Cynde; and Magnus?"

"They already ate. I asked them to leave us alone." She put the plate on the table. "Sit down."

"Why?" he asked as he sat on the bench.

"Because I want to ask you something privately."

"What?" he stared at the plate, not knowing what to do.

"You say you want to marry me, but why? Do you just want a place to stay? I know you must not have any money since you were a man of the cloth, are you wanting me to support you, so you don't have to live in a cave like a hermit? Why do you want to marry me.?"

His head was spinning, suddenly he blurted, "Because I love you."

She put her hands on her hips, "Well, was that so hard?" as she leaned down and kissed him.

She pulled away a long moment later, "Close your mouth dear, and eat your breakfast. I need to gather some apples, but I'll be back later." She grabbed a basket off a wall peg and walked out the door as she flashed him a smile, "My answer is yes, I love you too."

He sprang to his feet and chased her out the door, catching her around the waist and spinning her around until his lips found hers.

"Um, you'd better do that inside. Don't want the neighbors to gossip." Magnus said a few moments later, as he grinned at them over an armload of firewood.

Bard felt himself blush, "We're going to gather apples."

"I've never heard it called that before," he said with a straight face as he carried the wood into the house, and Bertrona walked away laughing.

"Wait. Do you have another basket?"

"Everyone was smiling at the celebration that night. The whole community seemed to be gathered in the house. Bard got to see Sypher and meet his family, Magnus and Cynde's other children showed up along with many neighbor families.

"May I have your attention?" Magnus said as he climbed atop a bench and rang a small bell. The clamor of voices eventually stilled. "I'm sure you all know already, but I want to officially announce the engagement of my daughter Bertrona to Bard here. I will be proud to call him my son-in-law."

Cheers went up from the crowd as those with drinks raised their containers to toast the couple. Bard was shoved around until he came face-to-face with Bertrona. He instinctively took her in his arms and kissed her long and hard, eliciting a louder cheer from the onlookers.

"When is the wedding?" a woman yelled, as the people quieted.

Bertrona announced, "As soon as we can make the arrangements." Bard felt his lips smile widely as another ovation filled the room.

As the last visitors finished saying their goodbyes, Bard turned to his betrothed. "I'm the luckiest man in the world."

She snorted, "You only say that because you aren't married yet. Just wait, five or six months of marriage to me and you'll long for your freedom."

"That will never happen."

"I hope not," she said with a pensive look. "Will you walk me home?"

"I would be honored to," as he offered his arm to her.

As they walked up the cobblestone path in the moonlight, Bard asked. "Why were you so mean to me?"

"Mean?"

"Yes, mean. Pretending you were mad when I accidently knocked you down, stealing my clothes…"

"It worked, didn't it?" she winked.

He opened his mouth but couldn't think of anything to say.

"I'm sorry if you thought I was being mean, but I like to keep life interesting. I haven't let any man into my life since, well you know."

"You must have had a lot of suitors."

"Not that many," she grinned. "But I learned from my former experience. None of them possessed what I needed."

"Which is?"

"Strength, of course, but also things like empathy, caring, compassion, and of course, a sense of humor. I struggled with myself, whether to let you into my life or not, but you were tenacious and wouldn't go away. I just wanted to make sure that you could take a joke and still love me."

Bard swung in front of her. "Do your worst, madam. I love you with or without your teasing." He wrapped his arms around her waist and kissed her.

She pulled back and stared at him with eyes that glistened in the dim light of the moon. "I'm glad you passed my tests," she giggled and returned his kiss.

# Chapter 53
The Carriage

In the morning, Patrick and Aghna were ushered into the Bishop's Palace. A long table was filled with food and Bishop Sardis stood at the head of the end and spread his hands. "Good morning, gentlemen, be seated and enjoy some delicious fruits of our labor."

As they ate, Patrick recounted some of his adventures in healing across Hibernia. Sardis listened intently without interrupting. After an hour, Patrick took a long pause.

"Magnificent, you are truly following our master's instruction; **'Verily, verily, I say unto you, He that believeth on me, the works that I do shall he do also; and greater *works* than these shall he do; because I go unto my Father.'** (109) Your works have proved Jesus's words to be undeniable Truth."

"Unfortunately, there is great resistance to recognizing God's Kingdom on this earth. Your predecessor was an example of that. People are easily drawn to the riches and pleasures of this world, rather than eternal ones."

"And they even seem to enjoy the pains of this world." Sardis laughed. "I have trouble getting my monks to stop gossiping about their physical challenges, and to start praying about them."

"Because they are praying to the wrong god. They pray for health in a material body, rather than perceiving their spiritual identity. I couldn't raise the dead, if I believed that man ever dies."

Sardis looked thoughtful for a long moment, "I will try to impart that wisdom to my flock. Better yet, can you stay and address my community?"

"I would love to, but I need to finish my travels and return to Hibernia as soon as possible. I have new priests being sent to me soon from Rome. I know you are more than competent to convey the Divine message."

"I understand and thank you so much for gracing us with your presence, even for this short while."

"It was our pleasure, now we must mount our cart and be off with our swift ox." Patrick laughed as he and Aghna abruptly rose from the table, shook hands with Sardis and walked out the door.

"Where is our oxcart?" Patrick turned and asked.

"I believe it is coming now." Sardis said as he peered across the compound.

Two white horses were pulling something down the path. It was a white, four-wheeled carriage. "No, we can't accept that." Patrick said as the realization hit.

"My friend Patrick, I think that is an even trade. I fell in love with your ox, I named him Patrick, and we need another cart for our fieldwork." Sardis said with a straight face.

The carriage stopped in front of him, and Patrick noticed the boxes of relics had been stacked and covered with thick hides for transport. "Bishop Sardis, I thank you from the bottom of my heart."

"Oh, that reminds me." Sardis pulled a large cushion from behind the door and presented it with a flourish. "For your bottoms, on your journey."

Patrick and Aghna climbed aboard the carriage and carefully arranged the cushion before they sat down.

"Now, that is transportation befitting a bishop; safe travels to you both." Sardis said as he waved.

"Bless you and your flock Bishop Sardis." Patrick

yelled as Aghna drove the team forward.

As they passed through the gateway Aghna said with a smile, "God did provide. Now which way?"

"Follow the road to the east, we should make it to Hastell Cenllys by early afternoon in this rig. Do you feel that?"

"No what?" Aghna said.

"Exactly, no bumps and jars like that oxcart gave us. This cushion is marvelous."

They rolled into the dilapidated hill fort with its ring of decaying timbers around noon. People flooded into the spaces between the hovels, none of them had ever seen a carriage before. Aghna skillfully guided it in front of the old inn. "Ho," he said as the horses slowed to a stop.

"Bynelld, are you there?" Patrick yelled.

"Who calls my father's name?" A large man raged, until he stepped through the doorway and saw the carriage.

"Dwig, is that you?" Patrick said as he climbed down.

"You know me stranger?" Dwig said, still staring at the carriage.

"I stopped here on my way to Gaul a number of years ago, remember? I told you about your sister Cynde and Magnus."

"Yes, but what has happened? You dressed as a beggar before, you're dressed in fine robes now, and this..." he pointed at the carriage. "What is it?"

"Just a fancy wagon. How are you? Is your father still with us?"

"No, he passed some years ago, but I have married and have visited Cynde and Magnus a few times since I saw you last."

"Wonderful, we are on our way to see them next, but I wanted to stop by and see you too. Can I meet your wife?"

"Of course, come in, your driver too. Bethan, come meet..., I'm sorry, I don't remember your name."

"Call me Patrick"

"Come meet Patrick. A friend of Cynde and Magnus."

"Will our carriage be safe?" Aghna asked.

"Yes, I'll make sure of it." Dwig said as he poked his head out the door. "Bryn, make sure no one touches that wagon or its contents. They can look, but that's it." He turned back as a middle-aged woman entered. "This is my wife, Bethan; please, make yourselves comfortable. Are you hungry?

"Yes, and we would like to spend the night. Do you have some trustworthy friends who can guard our carriage tonight?

"I can find some. I'll have them take care of your horses too. Can you feed them, Bethan? I'll be back soon."

"Bethan, my name is Patrick, and this is my friend Aghna."

"Nice to meet you both. Have a seat, here are a couple mugs of ale. Elis, stay out of here, grandmother is working."

Patrick looked up to see a blonde-haired boy peeking through hanging deer hides. "He won't bother us. Let him come in."

"The man says you can come in but don't bother him." Bethan warned as she deposited a kettle of venison and two steaming bowls of beans to the table. "Let me know what else you want."

"Thank you, this will be fine," Patrick said as he bit some stringy venison off of a bone.

In a few minutes, Dwig returned. "Taken care of, they'll watch it all night, and yell if anything happens."

"I pray they don't yell." Aghna said with a mouthful of beans. Patrick just nodded.

"How long ago did you visit us?" Dwig asked.

Patrick sat back and smiled, "It must have been at least fifty years ago. I don't know where the time has gone."

"Are you going to visit Cynde and Magnus?"

"We hope to, and then we sail back to Hibernia. That is where I have been for most of the time since I met you."

"Are you a priest now?"

"Actually, I'm a bishop now. I am in charge of many churches."

"A bishop? Like the one that tried to kill Magnus?"

"I hope I'm not anything like that one. You have a good bishop in Seaford Downs now though. He's a friend of mine."

"I have not met him, but I haven't heard anything bad about him. Elis, stop that. Don't bother the man."

Patrick turned to see the boy pulling at his robe. "Come here son," he coaxed.

The boy looked at his father then back at Patrick before beginning to waddle over to his knee. **"But Jesus said, Suffer little children, and forbid them not, to come unto me: for of such is the kingdom of heaven."** (110) He said smiling as he lifted the child and sat him on his lap. "You have the same pretty blue eyes that your great aunt Cynde does."

"That he does. We hope to visit her again soon, if I can get my daughter and son-in-law to watch the inn."

"Why not come with us?" Patrick asked. "We have some room in the carriage, and we are going straight there. Free transportation, and I know Cynde and Magnus would love to see you."

"Bethan, do you think we could?"

# Chapter 54
Wedding Plans

"Father Cameron is looking forward to marrying us." Bertrona gushed to her mother.

"He's excited about any marriage." Cynde replied, "You're right though, he's wanted to see you married for years."

"Here is the fabric I bought for my dress, what do you think?" as Bertrona hurriedly unwrapped a tied bundle.

"I'm going to check on Magnus." Bard said.

"Oh, that's beautiful, did you get any lace? We need to make a veil and maybe some gloves too." Cynde said as she ran her hand over the bolt of cloth.

Bard sighed, turned, and headed out a side door. "Had to get away, didn't you?" Magnus grinned and drove an axe through a small log, splitting it.

"They didn't even acknowledge me." Bard said. "If I was a spider, they might have noticed me."

"Marriage plans have that effect on women. Everything else seems of small importance except for the ceremony when they get a ring on their finger. It was the same way when I married Cynde. She, Conchessa, and a gaggle of neighborhood girls fussed over every little thing for weeks. It was worth it though, after that she was all mine," he smiled.

"So, I just have to endure?"

"Nothing else you can do, except call off the wedding and run away."

"Never."

"Spoken like a true man with a ring already in his nose. Soon you'll join the club with the rest of us."

"Ring in my nose?" Bard asked.

"Yes, sir, like a pig. So, you don't root out under the fence." Magnus laughed. "I think you'll be a good hog and stay home. Not like her previous pig of a husband."

"I'll hang my hat where my wallow is." Bard grinned, but suddenly straightened and stared. "Who is that coming?"

"I don't know, but it's a mighty fine carriage." Magnus leaned on the axe.

The carriage slowed as it approached the house.

"Patrick and Brother Aghna." Bard cried out, and leaped over the rock wall to help the old man climb down. "I can't believe it's you."

"Surprise." Patrick coughed as he embraced Bard. "I had to make a trip to Rome, and I decided to route my return through Kilpatrick. How did you make out on your task?"

"The scroll is returned to its hiding place; Magnus made a copy for us to study."

"Not that," Patrick snapped. "What about Bertrona?"

Bard took a step back while trying to hide a smile, "Inside, Cynde and she are preparing for our wedding."

"Wonderful, I can't wait to see Cynde." He looked over at the wood pile. "Magnus my friend. Young as ever."

"I wouldn't say that, although I still swing a mean axe. Come in, I want to see Cynde's face when she recognizes you. Who are your other friends?"

"Don't you recognize Dwig?"

Magnus blinked, "Dwig? It is you and Bethan. It's been a long time. Welcome back to Kilpatrick."

"Is there someplace we can secure the carriage? I'm taking some church artifacts back to the churches in Hibernia. I want to keep them safe."

Bard spoke up. "I can move things around in the barn and make some more room by the chariot. I'll put the horses in the pasture."

"Thank you, son." Magnus responded. "Patrick, let me take you and your guests in to meet Cynde and Bertrona."

The four followed Magnus into the house as Bard climbed onto the carriage and drove it up the hill to the barn. *I wish I could stay and listen, but I had better get this carriage secured first.* He opened the barn's double doors and whistled. *This might be a bigger job than I thought.* As he looked at the collection of objects strewn around the floor. He tied the team to a post to prevent them running away and started dragging and stacking pieces of old furniture, leather harnesses, and various tools out of the way. Lifting the heavy tongue of the Chariot, he pulled it forward and then backed it closer to the side of the building. *That should be enough room.* He opened the other set of double doors on the back of the barn, mounted the carriage and drove the team forward. "Ho," he said as he pulled back on the reins, with the carriage inside, and the horses standing in the pasture. Then he dismounted, released the horses from their harness, removed the tongue and closed up the barn doors. He could hear loud sounds of conversations and laughter as he got closer to the house and stepped inside.

"My boy, you have found yourself quite a gem of a lady." Patrick said as he laid his hand on Bard's shoulder and whispered. "Sometimes even I have to admit that I wish I wasn't wedded to the church. I had a feeling it would work out between you two. When are you getting married?"

"Day after tomorrow. Will you stay for it?"

"Definitely, I took the liberty of stopping by the church in town on the way here and negotiating with the priest to allow me to officiate."

"You what?"

"I wanted to check on your progress. I am well pleased, my son. I told your betrothed that I would like to have a rehearsal for the wedding tomorrow afternoon."

"You always seem to know everything. Does God ever keep a secret from you?"

"Not if it's something I need to know." Patrick winked.

"There's Magnus; I wanted to ask him about something I found in the barn. I'll talk to you later." Bard said.

"Magnus, can you come outside with me?"

"I guess, why?"

"I want to ask you something." When they got outside, he continued. "I would like to give Patrick a gift for performing our wedding."

"Like what?"

"I was thinking about our copy of Martin's scroll. We have the original, so we can make another duplicate anytime we want to."

"Anytime we want to break into the church again."

"I can't think of anything he might treasure more."

"Me neither, the copy it is. When do you want to give it to him?"

"Let's wait until after the wedding, maybe right before he leaves."

"Sounds good to me." Magnus said, "Let's go back to the party."

The next day everyone gathered at the church for the wedding rehearsal. Patrick stood in the pulpit. "I do hope you will allow me some discretion to stray slightly from your conventional marriage rituals here in Briton. I have performed many weddings in Hibernia, and they have a custom that I find quite appealing. I won't tell you what it is, but I'd like to use it in the ceremony tomorrow. Is that agreeable?"

No one raised an exception. Bard watched as Father Cameron's eyebrows rose, but he remained silent.

"I'll take that as a yes." Parick said. "Now where is our little flower girl and ring bearer?"

Two small children were urged out of a pew and stepped

forward, followed by Bertrona's youngest sister, "Here they are your excellency, my two youngest."

"Marvelous," Patrick said, "Let's begin the rehearsal."

Bard rubbed his hands together. His palms were sweating.

# Chapter 55
The Wedding

The girls had taken over the parsonage and were busy getting the bride prepared. Bard, Magnus, and Patrick had moved the vestments and some dusty furniture around in the sacristy. Bard paced back and forth as the other two sat and watched. "Calm down Bard, you weren't this concerned when we were thrown into that muddy cell, practically naked," Patrick remarked.

"Who threw you in there?" Magnus wondered out loud.

"The king's guards, but they let us out in a couple weeks, even gave us our clothes and belongings back. Remember, Bard?"

Bard ignored the question. "I'm getting married to the most wonderful girl in the world. I don't have anything to offer her. I don't have any money. I don't have any real skills. How are we going to live?"

"You are absolutely wrong." Patrick thundered. Bard looked up at him and saw the fire in his eyes. "What do you think I taught you for twenty-seven years? You have been trained to heal, just as Jesus and his followers did. You healed that criminal's broken arm in that muddy cell. Stop feeling sorry for yourself and wondering what you should do. What does God want you to do?"

"You are right. You're always right."

"Don't let worry steal the joys of this day from you. You deserve to enjoy every moment with Bertrona."

"Thank you, I needed that." Bard smiled and hugged Patrick.

"We all do at different times, **'The light of the body is the eye: therefore when thine eye is single, thy whole body also is full of light; but when *thine eye* is evil, thy body also *is* full of darkness.'** (111) Keep looking at the concepts of God, and you can't help but see the light."

"I better go down and escort the bride," Magnus said as he left.

"Now, are you ready to get married?" Patrick queried.

Bard nodded, and the two of them walked out to the nave, and down the center aisle between the rows of pews filled with people. *I feel like a prize hog paraded at a fair.* He noticed his hands sweating again.

Bard stood at the altar while Patrick mounted the pulpit. "My name is Bishop Patrick, formerly Maewyn Succat, I'm sure many of you knew my parents, Calpurnius and Conchessa of this village," he waited for a loud murmur from the crowd to quiet. "I want to thank Father Cameron for the grace to allow me to perform this ceremony today. Thank you all for taking the time to attend this momentous occasion. You probably don't know the groom, but he has served as my faithful attendant in my decades of ministry to Hibernia. He has helped and supported me in bringing healings and the light of Christ to thousands and thousands of people across that island. I hope you all will welcome him into your community. Now, let us meet the bride," Patrick said as he exited the pulpit and walked down the steps to the altar.

Bard wiped his eyes before he turned and watched Magnus escorting his daughter down the aisle. He held her arm as she stepped up at the altar and next to him. Then Magnus turned and sat down next to Cynde in the front row.

"I'm sure you all know Bertrona, the daughter of

Magnus and Cynde. She has never looked more beautiful, am I right, Bard?"

Bard again had to wipe his eyes before gazing at her. He found that he couldn't reply, so he just swallowed and nodded his head, as she smiled knowingly and clasped his hand.

"Ring bearer and flower girl?"

Bard looked back to see Bertrona's sister pushing the two out into the aisle and pointing. "Slowly," they all heard her say. It was more of a trot than a walk, but the two arrived at the front and gave the rings and flowers away. Quickly, they were beckoned to sit down by their mother.

"I wish I still walked that fast." Patrick said to a chorus of quiet laughter. "Now, place the rings on each other's finger. These rings are a symbol of lifelong commitment. They seal the vows to love each other for the rest of your lives." Patrick paused and searched his vestments for an opening.

"Fine, shake hands now." Bertrona looked curious as she and Bard clasped their hands together. "Now I am going to add a bit of Hibernian culture to this ceremony," he said as he drew a colorful beaded sash from beneath his robes. "This is called 'handfasting', and it signifies a permanent relationship between these two." Patrick carefully wrapped the ribbon around their wrists and hands.

"Now Bard, repeat after me, I take thee to be my wedded wife, to have and to hold from this day forward, for better, for worse, for richer, for poorer, in sickness and in health, to love and to cherish, until death us do part, according to God's holy ordinance; thereto I plight thee my troth."

Bard and Bertrona repeated the words and turned toward each other. "By the power vested in me by the church, and by the strength of your own love, I now pronounce you, man and wife."

As they bent their heads toward each other Patrick stopped them. "Wait. Bard, I know the trials you have faced in life, they have all brought you to this moment. I released you from your service to me, and now I have bound you to this fine woman for the rest of your life. **'Who can find a virtuous woman? for her price *is* far above rubies.'** (112) You and this virtuous woman will live as one from now on. Before this congregation, I give you both my eternal blessings in your union. You may now kiss your bride, but please, do a good job of it. Long and hard," as the crowd erupted in applause.

As the people quieted, Magnus rose up. "You are now all invited to our house for a luncheon and maybe some songs and dancing after that."

People were leaving the church when Patrick finally said with a chuckle, "Good job Bard, but save some for later," as he reached in and untied their hands. "You'll want to hurry to Magnus's home and greet your guests."

"Yes, sir," Bard replied without enthusiasm. *I'm not looking forward to running up the hill to meet them, let them wait.* "Let's go, beautiful," he said, and walked her out the double doors where showers of rice began to fall on them, amid cheers.

"Look." Bertrona nodded. Patrick's carriage was parked at the curb with Sypher holding the reins, and Magnus and Cynde were seated there too.

"Your carriage awaits you," Magnus announced graciously as he offered his hand to Bertrona and lifted her in. Bard clambered in and wrapped an arm around her as they sat back and rolled through the narrow streets like royalty.

# Chapter 56
Goodbye

It was early morning and still dark when Bard felt something move beside him. Afraid that it was a wild animal, he suddenly sat up and rolled out of bed.

"What's the matter?" Bertrona's groggy voice muttered.

"It's going to take me awhile to get used to being married, but don't worry, I will," as he crawled back under the blankets and kissed her neck.

"You better," she uttered before snoring softly.

A few hours later he felt a nudge. "You better get up and get dressed. We have breakfast with everyone, remember?"

"I do now, tell them I decided to sleep in," as he pulled a pillow over his head.

"You don't want them to think I married a lazy man, do you?" she laughed as she pulled the blankets off the bed.

"You're lucky I'm newly married, or I might get cranky," as he smiled, jumped up and kissed her. "I'll be ready in a few minutes. Where did you put my traveling bag?"

"It's there in the cupboard, why do you need it?"

"It has my journal in it. I've written about all of my experiences with Patrick in it, and now, I want to write about my experiences last night with you," he grinned.

"You do, and I swear I'll burn it."

"I guess I need to start a new journal." He smiled and kissed her again.

They walked down the street to her parents' house. The carriage was parked in front of it with the artifact crates stacked in the passenger compartment. The horses' long reins were wrapped around a railing.

"What's the matter?" she asked.

"Patrick is ready to leave; I'm going to miss him." He took a deep breath.

"We all will. He's pretty extraordinary."

"Just like you my dear," he squeezed her arm. "Let's just enjoy our first breakfast together."

They entered the house and were welcomed by friends. Temporary tables had been set up, even in the courtyard. "Come, grab some food before these animals eat it all." Cynde smiled.

They made the rounds greeting the well-wishers as a couple, and finally approached Patrick, Magnus and Aghna in a far corner. "So, are you planning on leaving us so soon?"

"We must, my son. I have been away from my flock for an extended time now. Who knows how many of my sheep have jumped the fence. I need to return and round them up again," Patrick said with a sad smile. "Besides, my work here is done, and I am so grateful to have been part of it."

Bertrona leaned forward and kissed him on the cheek. "Thank you for your gift of Bard," she said shyly.

"And thank you for taking him. He's a handful." Patrick laughed.

Bard wasn't laughing. "Will we ever see you again?"

"Always, what did I tell you in Hibernia? We live in an infinite God, and we can never be separated. I hope you two will ride down to the docks with us and see us off."

"We definitely will." Bertrona answered for Bard.

"What time does our boat leave?" Patrick asked Aghna.

"In about an hour." He smiled.

"Oh my, we had better get going. Sypher, are you going to drive us?"

"Yes sir, this way gentlemen, and lady."

Sypher sat in front with Magnus, while the other four squeezed around the crates and sat down. "Ready." Patrick cried, and the carriage began to move.

As they neared the dock, Patrick asked, "Bard, can you help us unload these crates and take them onto the ship? Some of them are pretty heavy."

"You know I would do anything to help you. What are you going to do with this carriage when it's unloaded?"

"I'm glad you asked that. You know that I am a poor man because everything I own belongs to God. But since I was given this fine wheeled device, I think it is only fitting that I give it to you both as a wedding present, and something to remember me by." The carriage slowed and stopped beside one of the larger ships.

Bard's mouth dropped open as the bishop continued. "I have only one stipulation. You need to take Dwig and Bethan home in it. We don't want them to walk back to their inn, do we? After that, it is yours to do with as you will and keep healing too," he reminded.

"I don't know what to say, except thank you for everything, and her." He smiled as he nodded in his wife's direction.

"Thank you, Father, if you visit us again, it will be here for you." Bertrona said as Bard vaulted down and began to lift the crates out. They finished loading them aboard as the sailors began to untie the dock lines. Patrick and Aghna quickly stepped aboard before the gang plank was stowed.

Bard called to Patrick, "We have one more gift for you. Magnus would you do the honors?" Magnus pulled a large leather tube from behind his back and threw it underhand to Patrick.

"What's this?"

"I think you know. It's printed in large letters so you

can read it easier." Magnus yelled as the boat drifted away from the dock.

"Thank you so much. I didn't expect this," as he hugged the cylinder to his chest and wiped at his eyes.

"We had to do something to surprise you." Bard answered.

"Goodbye, safe travels," Bertrona yelled. The four waved from the dock, as the sail snapped taunt in the breeze.

Patrick replied with a tirade of his favorite quotes as he and Aghna floated away, **"The Spirit of the Lord *is* upon me, because he hath anointed me to preach the gospel to the poor; he hath sent me to heal the brokenhearted, to preach deliverance to the captives, and recovering of sight to the blind, to set at liberty them that are bruised,"** (113) **"And he said unto them, Go ye into all the world, and preach the gospel to every creature. And these signs shall follow them that believe; In my name shall they cast out devils; they shall speak with new tongues; They shall take up serpents; and if they drink any deadly thing, it shall not hurt them; they shall lay hands on the sick, and they shall recover."** (114)

Eventually, they couldn't hear him over the sounds of the wind and water lapping against the shore. "Are you ready to take a carriage ride again?" Sypher asked.

The others turned and walked away, but Bard hesitated. *Thank you, Patrick, for blessing us, Hibernia, and this whole world.* ***"Blessed be the God and Father of our Lord Jesus Christ, who hath blessed us with all spiritual blessings in heavenly places in Christ:"*** (115)

"Are you coming?" Bertrona stared at him with concern in her eyes.

"Yes, I was just saying goodbye," as he wiped away a tear.

# Chapter 57
Married

The next morning, Bard woke up alone in bed. The sun was high in the sky, and he hurriedly dressed and ran down to Magnus's house. Throwing the door open, he was met with the sound of everyone clapping.

"He made it." Magnus smiled.

"I knew he would eventually," Bertrona said as she rushed forward to him. "But he tossed and turned all night long before he finally fell asleep. Why couldn't you sleep, darling? I was worried."

"Did I keep you up? I'm sorry." Looking around he said quietly, "I struggled all night with thoughts about Patrick and you, my love. I've never been responsible for someone else. Patrick always directed me on what, when and how to do things."

"You don't have to worry about that Bard, you're married now, and my little girl will tell you what you need to do. Ow," he cried as Cynde elbowed him in the ribs. "Well, it's true."

Cynde stepped forward and looked Bard straight in the eyes wearing an understanding smile. "Bard, ignore him. We have all been plagued by the same thoughts you struggled through. You need to release them. They are about mortality. Give them to God, and don't worry, everything will unfold in your life."

"She's right, she always is." Magnus smiled.

"I've heard that they always are," Bard smiled. "Where are Dwig and Bethel? I also wondered when they wanted to go back."

"They went shopping down in the town. A couple more hours and they should be back. You can ask them then. Are you hungry Bard?" Cynde asked.

"Yes, a little."

"Come along husband. Let's go home and I'll feed you." Bertrona grinned as she grabbed his hand and pulled him out the door.

"I'm sorry I kept you awake," he stammered again.

"Stop it. I love you and to be honest, I promise you there will be some nights that I'll keep you up all night thinking about issues concerning me, but that's just a part of sharing someone's life. Didn't you ever keep Patrick awake?"

"Believe me I tried at times, but he just ignored me. He slept like a rock most of the time, even when we were imprisoned, naked, and sleeping in cold mud, crowded in with other prisoners."

"Wow, his faith must be great, to be comfortable enough to sleep in those conditions."

"After the first week, even I learned to sleep in the mud like he did."

"How?"

"Exhaustion works wonders for me," he grinned. "What are you going to make me for lunch?"

Bard spent the rest of the afternoon gathering and splitting firewood. *A never-ending job for survival.* He saw Dwig and Bethel return late in the day and stopped working to ask them when they wanted to travel back to their inn.

"I miss our kids and their babies." Bethel admitted. "We're ready to return when you have time to take us.

Dwig shrugged his shoulders, "You heard the boss."

"I'll talk to Bertrona about it, and let you know at supper," Bard said as he headed off to wash and change clothes.

"Bertrona?" he announced when he entered the house. "Dwig wants to return to Hastell Cenllys. Do you want to go with me?"

"Of course I do, I'm not going to let my new husband out of my sight for a month or however long it takes." She laughed.

He smiled, "I really don't deserve anyone as wonderful as you, but I'm glad you're mine."

They met the others at Magnus's house. "We can leave for your inn as soon as you are ready," Magnus said to Dwig.

"Whoa, Bard. You can't leave that soon. Patrick brought it all the way from the southern coast. You'd better do maintenance on it before taking it back down there," Magnus said.

"What do I need to do?"

"Oil the harness and reins, grease the axles, check it for any cracks or other issues before you take it out again. I can help you. Cynde, how much cooking grease have you saved?"

"I have that corked jug in the corner. It's almost full."

"Good, that might be enough. With any luck, you could leave the next day, but tomorrow we need to do maintenance first, and make sure you have enough tools to make any needed repairs on the journey. That means you need a good night's sleep tonight, Bard." Magnus chuckled.

"I understand, I'll do my best."

"We better eat now so I can take him home and put him to bed early." Bertrona announced as she began serving.

## Chapter 58
### The Carriage

Bard and Magnus worked most of the next day getting the carriage ready for the trip. Cynde and Bertrona gathered provisions and water jugs, along with extra blankets and a few hides to shed water in case of storms. By the end of the day it was washed, greased, and filled with necessities.

Cynde and Magnus's kids and neighbors gathered at their house for a goodbye celebration and potluck dinner late in the day.

Dwig stood up at the end of the dinner, "Thank you all for allowing us to stay here for the wedding. My thanks to Bishop Patrick, wherever he may be, for bringing us here in his carriage, and our thanks to Bard and Bertrona for offering to take us home tomorrow. We will miss all of you, and if you ever travel south, stop in and see us at Hastell Cenllys."

Everyone applauded, and the party broke up shortly after that with short goodbyes and well wishes.

As they walked home, Bard asked, "Have you ever traveled very far?"

Bertrona shook her head, "No, but I'm looking forward to it, with you."

In the morning, Bard headed to the barn early in the morning, opened the doors and attached the tongue to the carriage. Then he put harnesses on the horses and led them over and hooked them to the carriage. Finally, he drove it down the hill toward the house and tied the team to a post, before he went inside to eat.

"Is it ready for us?" Bertrona asked.

"We are ready to roll, as soon as my belly is full."

"Hey, Bard, can you give me a minute first." Magnus motioned him into an adjoining room.

"What's up?" Bard asked as Magnus lifted a thin wooden case.

"Last night, I decided to give you this for the trip." He lifted the lid. "It contains a couple sharp swords and daggers. I hope you don't need them, but traveling through the countryside can be dangerous at times. Keep it handy, will you?"

"Yes, does Bertrona know?"

"I told her this morning, and yes, she knows how to use them both. I taught her myself."

"I'll take them out now, and thank you," Bard said.

After breakfast, Dwig and Bethel climbed into the back of the carriage, while Bard and Bertrona mounted the front. Bard released the brake and shook the reins, while Cynde and Magnus waved goodbye. "Have a safe trip. Hurry back," they cried.

Bard drove the team at an easy trot through the countryside. "How long will it take for us to get home?" Bethel asked.

"If we can keep the team moving at this pace, only about a week I think," Bard answered.

"That's great," Dwig yelled, "It took us more than two weeks with Patrick."

"Well, he had this loaded down with his cartons of relics. We're a lot lighter on this trip, and that means a lot to our two horses. Did you stand watch at night on your trip with Patrick?"

"Sure did, he wanted to make sure his artifacts stayed safe."

"We'll do that too, to keep the women and the carriage

safe. I'll try to find out of the way places to camp, and we won't have a fire at night."

"So, we have to cuddle?" Bertrona interjected.

"Yep, that's my only reason." Bard laughed.

When they drove through the towns, people stopped and stared at the elegant vehicle as it rolled past them. Bard kept a close watch behind them and prayed that they wouldn't be pursued by unsavory characters. On the final night before they reached Hastell Cenllys, Bard was on watch and the horses were hobbled nearby, when he heard a twig snap in the opposite direction. It was the night of a new moon, and clouds obscured most of the stars. He bent down and shook Dwig's shoulder enough to wake him. "We may have visitors, wake the girls, stay low and watch for any movement," he whispered as he handed over a sword and the two daggers. Crawling toward the sound, he kept praying for a harmonious outcome. He heard a stifled sneeze and froze as several others cursed. **"Thus saith the LORD unto you, Be not afraid nor dismayed by reason of this great multitude; for the battle *is* not yours, but God's."** (116) "Alright God, our lives are in your hands, what do you want me to do?" He heard a horse snort behind him and could just dimly see the two white animals had wandered over near him. *Don't spook guys.* As he crawled over between them and began to saw at the rope hobbles with his sword. Just as he cut through the second horse's restraint. It reached down and nudged him with its nose. *Thank you boy, be ready to fight for the right.* He slowly stood up between them, scratching their hides next to their tails as the two horses leaned into him.

Bard saw a number of figures creep out of the bushes and thought he heard one whisper, "What's that? Ghosts?"

*Show time, boys.* He slapped his hands down on their rumps and the two horses erupted forward, straight at the interlopers. The group of men bolted in different directions while yelling loudly as the two horses frolicked among them, running back and forth. When the horses started to graze again Bard told the others, "We should be alright for now, but maybe we should start our travels as soon as I harness the horses." He walked off toward the animals.

"Good idea, I couldn't sleep again anyway." Dwig said as he and the girls started to gather up the bedding.

The rest of the trip to the inn was uneventful as they all chatted amicably on the final day of travel. They pulled up to the inn around noon. Dwig and Bethel jumped out as soon as the wheels stopped rolling and ran inside to surprise their kids.

"More primitive than Kilpatrick." Bertrona said as she looked dubious before dismounting.

"You should see some of the villages in Hibernia. Some of them make this village look like a palace."

"Oh my, I can't imagine. Are we going to spend the night here?"

"Yes, it will be safer for you, me, and the bedbugs need to eat too." He laughed as he saw her shiver. "I'm sure we'll be fine, and I want a good night's sleep before we head back. I think we should travel at night and rest the horses in the daytime. If we take turns watching for possible dangers, it should be easier to see them coming in the daylight. Let's go in and meet their family."

"All right, husband, lead on," she said as he helped her climb down.

They had a pleasant dinner and met many of Dwig and Bethel's relatives. At the end of dinner, they said goodnight to the others and Bethel fixed them a special sleeping area with a pile of new grass. "Sleep well, you two. I'll see you in the morning," she said happily as her face disappeared behind a woolen drape.

"It's crude I know, but I can tell you that it's better than sleeping in mud with smelly men."

"I'm sure of that, goodnight my love," as she smiled and curled up in her blanket.

In the morning, they had a breakfast of gruel and after saying goodbye to everyone, started their journey home. They attracted much less attention as they travelled in the nighttime. People tended to secure their doors at night to thwart any threats, so most didn't even bother to look outside as the hooves sounded through the streets. Bard used the north star as his guide for most of the trip and stopped alongside Hadrian's wall on the fourth day.

"I can't believe they built this all the way across Briton, amazing. Why didn't we see it on the way to the inn?"

"Navigating at night is a bit harder. I think we were west of here, where most of the wall was dismantled for building materials. Fewer people live here I guess."

"It still looks magnificent. Probably much like when Magnus and Cynde traveled to Kilpatrick to escape that bishop."

"I didn't know that."

"Yes, Papa was being chased by those mercenaries and he spent the night in one of the Milecastles in a terrible rainstorm. The next morning, he stomped around in a puddle of mud and ran westward until his feet dried. Then he retraced his steps and headed eastward. He thinks the mercenaries lost a whole day following his false trail and that saved him."

"Wow, I can't wait to get back and make him tell me more of his and Cynde's adventures."

"Better them than us, I want a boring life with you," she said as they mounted the carriage in the twilight, and she cuddled next to him.

He slapped the reins, and the horses started to trot. "We will be home tomorrow night, but I have a feeling. With you around, nothing will never be boring," as he kissed her.

# Chapter 59
God's Thoughts, Always Available

It was several weeks after Christmas and had been a long day of bitter cold with high winds. Patrick finally was able to return to his study after a full day of boring meetings about expansion plans with priests from several parishes. He was tired of organizing the building of parishes and monasteries. He longed to be healing people instead and felt a smile creep over his lips as he thought about some of his past adventures with Bard. A fire was blazing in the hearth, but the room still felt damp and cold as the north wind howled loudly.

Patrick groaned as he once again bent down and drew the worn leather tube out of its hiding place beneath his bed. He walked over and sat down at the desk as he carefully removed the rolled pages of parchment. He had studied Martin's words every night since Magnus had thrown the tube to him years ago. They always seemed to spark an inspired thought to fall asleep with.

Patrick was reading the last page of Martin's words, when he coughed and sneezed, he felt tired. *I'm going to go to bed, I'll put these away tomorrow morning.* He quickly shuffled the stack of papers into a loose pile on the very edge of his crowded desk, *Maybe, you should put them away now.* He ignored the thought as he crawled into his bed.

In the middle of the night there was a small knock on his door. "Yes, what is it?"

"It's a cold night, your excellency, do you want me to stoke your fire?"

"Yes, just be quiet please," as he rolled over and went back to sleep.

In the morning, he didn't feel like getting out of bed, but he forced himself upright. He was almost dressed when he noticed the empty spot on his desk. "Where are my papers?" he thundered as loud as he could.

The door burst open, "What's wrong Bishop Patrick?" Aghna asked.

"My papers, they are gone, stolen in the night. I had them sitting on my desk."

"What papers?"

"They were copies of a scroll that Bishop Martin of Tours penned. We have to find them." They searched the room but found nothing. "Who was on fire duty last night? I remember someone came into my room. Maybe he took them."

"Brother Fergus was, but he wouldn't steal anything."

"Wake him, I must find them." Patrick said, pacing back and forth as he waited.

In a few minutes his door opened. "Here he is, your excellency."

"Brother Fergus, when you kindled my fire last night, did you notice a stack of papers on my desk?"

"No, sir."

"You didn't see any papers."

"Just the ones you threw away sir."

"Threw away?"

"Yes, your holiness, they were scattered on the floor, so I gathered them up. There were only a few small red coals left in the fire, so I used them to re-light it. Did I do something wrong sir?"

Patrick felt ready to explode until he remembered the quiet thought he had ignored. *I ignored an urging from God.* "It was my fault," he blurted as the realization engulfed him that his precious pages were destroyed. "Leave me now." He spent the rest of the morning in prayer. Desperately trying to repent for ignoring the Divine urging. The citation popped into his thoughts. **"All go unto one place; all are of the dust, and all turn to dust again."** (117) *All materiality is of dust and returns to dust, but spiritual ideas are permanent and infinite.* "Martin's thoughts on those papers can't be lost, and they can't be ignored forever because they are still here and everywhere, because they are God's thoughts, always available to everyone," he said aloud, as he finally smiled. *At least the original remains safe, and the words of wisdom in that scroll will help bring a victory for Christ to the whole world. I wonder how Bard and Bertrona are getting along? How long has it been since I saw them? Ten years or more I bet.* He rose and left his office feeling relief.

He ignored the schedule that Brother Aghna had prepared for him and spent the day walking the frigid streets of the town, visiting, blessing and providing healings to many of the local residents in their homes. He returned to the abbey late in the day, and under the concerned eyes of Aghna, ate a hearty meal. Then he retired to his quarters feeling quite well and fell asleep quickly. He found himself in a vivid dream of a beautiful summer landscape, bathed in bright sunshine. As he waded through knee-high green grass while climbing a hillside, the vision grew brighter as golden rays of sunshine started to cascade around him like a gentle warm rain. Then he was caught up in swirls of the golden light that seemed to bathe his body in warm hugs. Friends called to him from beyond the veil of light, and Love welcomed him home.

———•●•———

"Is he?" Brother Fergus asked in the early morning

light.

"Yes, I'm afraid Bishop Partick has left us." Brother Aghna wiped away the tears filling his eyes.

"He looks like he is smiling."

"I'm sure he is." Aghna said as he choked back a sob, **"Mark the perfect *man*, and behold the upright: for the end of *that* man *is* peace."** (118)

To be continued...

# Epilogue

WWJD? Remember those letters that were popular years ago and stood for What Would Jesus Do? What did Jesus do (WDJD) that the rest of us don't do? He perceived ideas beyond the world of the body. He glimpsed the spiritual reality hidden behind the mortal dream. If you know nothing about the spiritual aspects of life – you're helpless against any and all material attacks.

Jesus taught how to heal, but many of us ignore or misinterpret his words. If men would study the laws of God instead of mortal laws, they would see that God's Kingdom is here, His power is here, as Jesus stated in the Lord's Prayer. God is Spirit. If Spirit is everywhere, what is your body? God made man in his own likeness. He hasn't changed, He is Spirit, but mankind refuses to stop believing in a life separate from God. A limited life, a limited existence that they think they can control.

Jesus didn't say wait until I return to start healing. His disciples and others (like Patrick) have healed throughout the centuries. The limited concepts of deity in men's minds, and arguments about minor theological issues destroy the understanding of spiritual healing. The concepts and laws of God are still here and operating today. Spiritual healing is not magical, it is Primal Christianity. Jesus, the prophets and others through history have healed and regenerated countless lives with their understanding of God's point of view (what

God knows is True about His creation).

If a fraction of the works of that Jocelyn of Furness recounted in his tales about the Saint are true, Patrick was certainly following his master's voice, **"He that believeth on me, the works that I do shall he do also; and greater works than these shall he do."** (109) The accounts of resurrections and healings are incredible. Just look at the sheer number of dead raised and length of time since some of the bodies had been interred.

Christians! Reclaim your heritage of healing and resurrection in Christ. It is your Divine right as children of the one true God. Just imagine how you can change this world! It can be His Kingdom on earth - as well as in Heaven.

Did you read *Quest for the Scroll*?

Bible citations:

| | |
|---|---|
| 1) | Matthew 14:25–27 |
| 2) | Mark 8:23-25 |
| 3) | II Sam 23:3 |
| 4) | 1Kings 19:13 |
| 5) | 1 Sam 3:4-10 |
| 6) | Mark 6:34 |
| 7) | Genesis 1:27 |
| 8) | Genesis 2:6 |
| 9) | Luke 2:49 |
| 10) | Luke 4:10,11 |
| 11) | Gen1:27 |
| 12) | John 4:24 |
| 13) | Genesis 32:26 |
| 14) | Romans 8:38 |
| 15) | John 8:44 |
| 16) | Matthew 12:28 |
| 17) | John 6:16-21 |
| 18) | Luke 1:76-79 |
| 19) | John 1:27 |
| 20) | 1 Sam 17:45 |
| 21) | 1 Sam 17:49-50 |
| 22) | II Corinthians 10:4 |
| 23) | Ephesians 6:13–17 |
| 24) | Mark 4:38–40 |
| 25) | Ezekiel 7:17 |
| 26) | II Corinthians 5:17 |
| 27) | Jocelyn of Furness |
| 28) | Joel 2:27 2nd 1, 28 |

29) Isaiah 40:30–41:0
30) II Kings 6:15–17
31) Psalms 8:2
32) Psalms 91:11, 12
33) Psalms 20:7
34) II Chronicles 20:15
35) Proverbs 10:25
36) Psalms 68:1
37) Psalms 18:14
38) I Corinthians 6:9
39) I Sam 25: 32
40) John 10:10
41) Exodus 10:22
42) John 8:44
43) Daniel 3:24, 25
44) John 8:58
45) Daniel 3:26, 27
46) Matthew 6:9–13
47) Ezekiel 14:6
48) II Corinthians 6:16
49) John 4:24
50) Luke 4:18
51) Matthew 7:15, 20
52) I Kings 5:4
53) Isaiah 41:10–13
54) John 11:25, 41
55) Ephesians 5:14
56) Genesis 1:27
57) II Kings 6:17
58) Proverbs 3:5
59) John 8:28
60) Romans 8:11
61) John 11:25
62) Mark 9:23 If
63) Luke 8:50 Fear
64) I Corinthians 15:57

65)        John 8:28
66)        Luke 8:50
67)        Isaiah 7:14
68)        Luke 24:51
69)        Genesis 1:27
70)        John 8:32
71)        Philippians 4:13
72)        Matthew 4:16
73)        Luke 2:49
74)        Mark 1:4
75)        Exodus 20:3
76)        John 13:34
77)        John 21:6
78)        Matthew 13:14, 15
79)        Acts 3:6, 7
80)        Matthew 9:37
81)        Proverbs 3:5
82)        Mark 4:37, 39
83)        John 11:41–42
84)        Isaiah 45:13)
85)        Psalms 139:8
86)        Romans 6:16
87)        John 13:3–5
88)        Genesis 1:1
89)        Luke 7:12–15
90)        Genesis 1:27
91)        Exodus 32:1
92)        Exodus 32:19
93)        John 5:30
94)        Matthew 17:20
95)        Mark 9:23
96)        Luke 8:54
97)        Proverbs 3:5
98)        John 4:24
99)        I John 1:5
100)       Matthew 12:25–28

101)     II Kings 20:2–6
102)     Mark 4:39
103)     Psalms 17:15
104)     Luke 4:3, 4
105)     Mark 5:13
106)     Exodus 34:30
107)     Jonah 1:17; 2:1, 10; 3:1–3 (to 1st .)
108)     Matthew 13:11
109)     John 14:12
110)     Matthew 19:14
111)     Luke 11:34
112)     Proverbs 31:10
113)     Luke 4:18
114)     Mark 16:15, 17, 18
115)     Ephesians 1:3
116)     II Chronicles 20:15
117)     Ecclesiastes 3:20
118)     Psalms 37:37

www.ingramcontent.com/pod-product-compliance
Lightning Source LLC
Chambersburg PA
CBHW070411310726
48977CB00003B/645